360 flip

Molly McGrann was born in the United States and lives in England. *360 flip* is her first novel.

360 flip

Molly McGrann

PICADOR

First published 2004 by Picador

First published in paperback in this revised edition 2005 by Picador
an imprint of Pan Macmillan Ltd
Pan Macmillan, 20 New Wharf Road, London N1 9RR
Basingstoke and Oxford
Associated companies throughout the world
www.panmacmillan.com

ISBN 0 330 41240 X

1 3 5 7 9 8 6 4 2

A CIP catalogue record for this book is available from
the British Library.

Typeset by Intypelibra London Ltd
Printed and bound in Great Britain by
Mackays of Chatham plc, Chatham, Kent

to Colin

In the United States there is more space
where nobody is than where anybody is.

Gertrude Stein

360 flip

Date Night

Above all, the sun beamed, naturally gregarious. The heat that May had been record-breaking, a taste of the summer to come, the *Post-Intelligencer* reported, and the paper was used to fan the trickling necks of those trapped in offices and teachers' lounges where the air-conditioning wouldn't be turned on until June. Cars lined up at the car wash for what felt like a splash of tropical rain, while teenagers sauntered in tank tops, plugged into their Walkmans—their lives—and new babies on parade in diapers and floppy sun hats waved soft, bride-white arms spotted with prickly heat rash. Just last month two inches of snow had sat all day on the ground. "Freak Snow on Easter Sunday" read the front-page headline, a short article of astonishment at this tangible, local sign of global warming. If people still relied on the *Farmers' Almanac*, they might have been inclined to brand the trusty book "a piece of crap" and set the damn thing alight in a backyard bonfire (along with other disappointments like the Homebrew Kit, a year's subscription to *Reader's Digest*, and some Trouble Dolls, each one stabbed through with a pin). If backyard bonfires hadn't been restricted, that is. If the weather wasn't so unpredictable, with trick winds whipping up from nowhere to set the normal backyard bonfire running like a bush blaze, the wind metamorphosing into an electrical storm, then giddy twin tornadoes, then sun, sun, sun like a toothpaste billboard looming over the Interstate.

With all of America streamlined on highways, the weather rode around the country like an outlaw, changing guises, switching lanes, the Weather Channel tracking every mile with minute-to-minute updates. No one was spared—not least yet another safe, neat, suburban pit stop in the throes of a glittering, unseasonable heat wave. Churchtown was a small community in a large county, its shops and services made to look, over the years, increasingly quaint, with country crafts on window display and knotted aluminum planks for siding. Surrounding the convenience stores, post office, bank, and fast-food Drive-Thrus were the housing developments of Honeybrook and Stonehenge, Briarpatch, Country Club Heights, and Weatherburn, a Milky Way of neighborhoods set behind imposing brick entrances. Had the stars of this constellation been connected, they might have formed a plow, symbolic of an area so recently rural. Now the real-estate developers were in charge of the pastoral scenery, and green lawns flowed where fields once ranged, intersected by willful rivers of asphalt poured dark in waves and curlicues. On these forged rivers, traffic surged or halted, given the time of day, but always there was traffic, more traffic every year, gobbling the taxpayers' dollars in repairs to the network required for their mail order, Fed-Ex, and mall hopping, their one-man carpools to work and biweekly orthodontist appointments.

As Jim and Eileen White drove off on their Friday-night date, they might have heard the rush and splash of traffic as it lapped the curbs, the gentle slap, slap of the cars' wheels clinging to the viscous tar, like waves beating the shingle. Had they not been sealed into the air-conditioned jumbo-comfort of their luxury car, the Whites might have heard this pantomime of the sounds of Mother Nature at work. Speeding to a just-opened Italian restaurant twenty miles away, they whizzed past the giant big-top mall, Park & Shop City—with its yellow tented dome lit up at night to bring in planes to the short airfield adjacent to its parking lot—and the motel, Relax Inn, that serviced airfield and mall. The Whites locked their car doors through Buckburg, where half-baked trucks were three to a yard, the truck beds displaying their wares: eight-track players, thick plastic beads looped on kite string and frilled with the scum of their molds, spangled diner stools, homemade prom dresses dribbled with stains, plentiful sets of carcinogenic Fiesta-ware in red-leaded glaze. In minutes, Jim and Eileen had emerged on the other side of Buckburg, by now a good distance from home where one son, Mitch, lay swathed to his eyes in bedsheets, asleep since noon, and the other, Babo, was eating a pair of Twix bars for his supper, washed down with Coke.

Jim and Eileen had been out on a date every Friday night for the last twenty-eight years. They weren't lovers of great food, but responsible to the romantic occasion, even if they never held hands under the table or kicked each other play-fully when the waiter mispronounced mascarpone. Eileen always ordered her own meal. She often wore her suit from work, and Jim did too. They might have appeared to be dining for business, not pleasure, for they often discussed work—but work was their shared passion, their pleasure, and they were academic about the law they pursued.

Tonight, however, they spoke of Italy, where they hoped to travel in mid-September when the crowds dipped and one could actually gain entrance to the Accademia to view Michelangelo's David. Or so they read. Already it was May, and Jim worried they had left their booking too late. Then there was the matter of passports . . .

"I called today," Eileen said. "Generally it takes four to six weeks, but in the summer they get busy. It could take twice as long. Or we could use their twenty-four-hour emergency service for three hundred dollars."

"Three hundred dollars each?"

"No, for both. And we'll need travel insurance."

"We should make the arrangements next week, first thing. I'll call the travel agent on Monday."

"I'll take care of passports," Eileen said.

Jim cut into his veal parmigiano, preparing a squadron of baby bites. He chewed thoroughly. "I suppose this trip will be the first of many. Sometimes I think we ought to retire early and begin to travel. What do you think? Say, in five years' time, we'll retire, both of us." His eyes brightened at the thought.

Eileen blinked and shifted her mouthful of ravioli from left to right. She, too, was methodical in her chewing, never too long on either side. She had had her teeth straightened late in life, in her forties, and the pain of wrenching her bite into place had been immense, almost worse than childbirth.

"What about college for Babo? He's only fourteen. You know how expensive Mitch's tuition was in the end—like buying a house."

"We'll budget," Jim said. "Like when we were first married."

"The boys need so many things."

"They *want* things."

"They're used to it. We all are."

"We'll downsize. We'll find a smaller house. We could move to a condo."

Eileen flared her nostrils, as if she had tasted something unexpected, bitter. "You said you never wanted to leave our house. You said you wanted to go out feet first. Where else would we live? Not another development. The houses they're building these days aren't so good."

"We could move to South Carolina, where it's mild. We could learn to play golf. We'll live in one of those condo developments they build around golf courses. A condo wouldn't be so much house to take care of, with plenty of time for learning golf."

Jim's eyes shone and Eileen wanted to let herself go with him. She knew that saying no would ruin their date—and deeply wound her husband, who was more sensitive than most people realized, afflicted with chronic insecurity. It was she who lay next to him as he tossed in bed at night, unable to sleep for worrying; who watched him eat, keeping the food apart on the plate, first vegetables, then meat, then starch, layering his stomach, for his digestion was often disturbed by the troubles on his mind. He dressed fastidiously, replacing clothes he had hardly worn for fear of looking somehow wrong, and kept his shoes shined. He always drove a new BMW. He showered the lawn with Green-Glo and Slay-Mor, kept abreast of game scores and player trades, and subscribed to the *Wall Street Journal*. If she stopped him now, he might not trust himself to make future plans for them, or indeed tell her of his dreams at all. Italy was his idea; she would have been content to stay at the house they always rented on the Jersey shore for two weeks, reading crime thrillers in the hot shade of her beach umbrella.

"Retirement sounds good to me," she said, smiling at Jim. "You're right. Italy is just the beginning."

He smiled back, radiant and relieved. "I thought you'd go for it," he said, swallowing the last of his meat and starting on a small mound of spaghetti.

After dinner and black decaf (never dessert, especially not tonight, as they had decided on an early night, citing long days at work), they drove back to Atomic View Estates and now they did hold hands over the gearbox, anticipating what came next. Jim White always drove too fast, but tonight Eileen didn't mind. She was ready for bed. Most Fridays the Whites made love after dinner, responsibly, tenderly, like adults. They brushed their teeth and gargled mouthwash, rinsed their bodies in the shower, then closed their bedroom door to let the boys know before folding into the most comfortable, reliable positions for gratification, moving fast or slow depending on need and how tired. Afterwards they slept peacefully, satisfied that this first chore of the weekend—that is sometimes how it felt—could be ticked off.

As the Whites pulled into Atomic View it was still light outside, yet small fireworks were going off in a neighbor's front yard. A handful of pre-teen boys aimed Roman candles at a charred soccer net. "Die, Dracula, die!" they screamed as the net sparked, its flaming strings a multitude of running fuses. Passing dog walkers shook their heads and their dogs cowered on their leashes, but no one told the boys to stop. If the parents didn't, well—they shook their heads, that's all. People didn't feel they could discipline children that didn't belong to them, not in the age of the lawsuit. Someday, some kid would lose a finger and whose fault would it be then? Who would pay for the surgery and therapy? Who would pay?

Ahead on Cosmos Drive, Jim and Eileen saw their younger son Babo on his skateboard, knees bent, head down, shoulders over his toes as he prepared to vault a dawdling toy poodle.

"Slow down, Jim," Eileen said, rolling down the window. "Babo. Babo!"

Babo stood up straight and stepped on the board's tail to stop, trick abandoned. The poodle skittered to safety in the dark tunnel formed by a row of Chinese firs planted between the Tans' rancher and the Masons' Spanish-style villa. Jim paused the BMW close enough that Babo could touch the car. "What?" he said, leaning on the hood with both hands, making sure to smudge that afternoon's wax job. Jim sighed deeply to show his disapproval of this.

"Are you going out tonight?" Eileen asked, making her voice pleasant.

"I guess. Yeah."

"What are your plans?"

"I don't know. Probably going over to Nate's."

"No other plans?"

"Why? Is there something wrong with Nate's place?" Babo tapped the car's hood with an overgrown fingernail lined with black—grease and tar and filth in general, driven hard into the skin like India ink. Like a manual laborer, Jim wanted to say, but he didn't. He sighed instead.

"I don't want to find out that you've been drinking again."

Babo flicked the BMW's hood impatiently. "Like I can buy beer."

"You'll scratch the car, Babo," Jim said over Eileen's shoulder. Babo snorted and put his hands in his pockets.

"Stay out of trouble. Home by midnight. I mean it," Eileen said. She looked like she did. She eagle-eyed her son as she rolled up her window.

"Whatever," Babo smirked. Dismissed, he skated off in the opposite direction, his shoulders shaking—he was laughing at them, Eileen thought.

"Well. That was positive," Jim said, driving on.

"It's his age. Be patient," Eileen replied, as she always did. "He'll pull through, just like Mitch."

"Has Mitch pulled through?"

Eileen chose to ignore her husband's question, which she found repetitive and unsupportive. "Look, Jim," she said, pointing to Deb Foster, who was seated out front of her house, squeezed onto a lawn chair whose legs bowed under her weight. Several other chairs were unfolded and set up and Deb looked cheerfully expectant. A pitcher and glasses were arranged on a card table, and she held a Japanese fan printed with sparring Sumo wrestlers, which she pumped vigorously back and forth. "She looks ready for a party, doesn't she? I wonder who she expects to come?"

"The pizza delivery boy," Jim said, and they both laughed.

Deb didn't wave at the Whites, although she had waved at the Christians and the Smiths and the Troys, as well as a handful of cars she didn't recognize (they might be prospective neighbors and she wanted to make a good impression). Deb didn't like the Whites. She had her reasons.

Jim turned onto Quasar Lane, where he and Eileen lived in a large colonial atop a silky green lawn. He noted that several stubborn dandelions had popped up. Tomorrow he would dig them out, before their butter-colored heads turned to seed, but for now the workweek was over. Lights were on all over the house, inviting them in. Upstairs, Mitch still slumbered behind his locked bedroom door—not that Jim or Eileen called "Anybody home?" when they set down their briefcases in the kitchen and shook off their suit coats.

As the Whites reached for each other, and Mitch dreamed of clamoring, faceless women, three doors down the Diamonds were coupling around Norm Diamond's basketball-sized belly, as were the elderly Wests muttering and adjusting. The Jollys on Cosmos Drive had just stepped out of the Jacuzzi where they had been drinking red wine, to make their way to the bedroom, while Mrs. Smith, the Powerwalker, straddled her husband enthusiastically in his den, her temperature just right, ready to be impregnated again. Directly across the street from the Whites, Dale Manley conjured up his wife, who had just hit the point of no return in her transatlantic flight; he ground a pillow between his legs and murmured her name, learning it before she arrived. All around Churchtown, countless teenagers in cars and basement rec rooms and movie theaters were doing it. Everyone was doing it, all the time.

The Road to the Mall
Dominates All

They bought the third house in Atomic View Estates, a pea-green, vinyl-sided rancher with a two-car garage and a red-brick fireplace, built in 1968. Deb and Don had been married two years then, living in a row house next door to her parents' house on what was Main Street, Churchtown (before the highway was finished and the mall went up), a rental property her parents owned and let to them for nothing. Deb's dad had started redecorating and never finished the job; no one but family could have lived in that house. The walls were unpainted plaster the color of orange soda pop, covered in scribbles from the last tenants' toddler, and the floor was scratched-up linoleum in a patchwork of remnants. The top of the toilet tank was missing, so you could see the scummy ball, brown with age, floating on its chain, while the tub's yellow enamel had worn away, as rough on the skin as fiberglass stadium seating. It was a shameful place to live, Deb thought, not worth the trouble of cleaning. What she wanted was a shiny new house, nothing that needed fixing up.

Atomic View was just an advertisement back then. It would be the first development in town, half a mile in from the new highway's exit to Churchtown, to be followed by Lazy Acres, Misty Meadows, and all the rest, poetically named according to the vision of their builders. Atomic View was built on the razed Shoemaker farm, with hillocks where hillocks never were before, the uniquely sloped lines of its streets poured from hauled dirt and concrete, giving vistas to what remained of Churchtown farmland, still with a thick fringe of haunted forest in its southernmost reach. It was a beautiful rural view, idyllic to the hilt, and soon to go: housing developments were the future and Deb knew it, sure as she had known that she would marry Don when she met him, aged twelve.

There were signs advertising Atomic View all over town, plus a billboard by the overpass, showing unearthly green lawns shaded by tall, swooping trees that sheltered colonial-style houses, a few mock-Tudors, and plenty of ranchers. Every day she stopped to study these signs, and at night she dreamed of living in one of the new split-levels, examining its knickknacks—she even dipped into a candy dish and thought it was the sweetest thing she ever tasted, after Don's kisses, that is. Deb had always lived in Churchtown, in an old-fashioned row house with a front porch where neighbors were entertained with gossip and root beer on unraveling wicker furniture. Her family parked their cars by the curb out front, but in Deb's house she would have an attached garage, heated in the winter and cool in summer. She and Don could have a garage sale if they wanted, instead of the usual yard jumble on a card table. Neighbors would drop by their built-in backyard barbecue pit, and they would have a basketball hoop at the side, and redwood furniture for their patio—no front porch here! It was a whole new way of life: modern, clean, close to the highway with all its conveniences. Deb told Don they just had to move to Atomic View.

He said, "But, hon, we cain't," in the Western twang he had lifted from the movies, a voice that always made her laugh. But that night Deb cried loudly, surprising Don, who said, "What? What?" and threw up his arms.

"I won't live my whole life next door to my parents! They walk in and out of this dump all hours—they don't even knock! We have to move, or I'll die," she sobbed.

"You won't die."

"I *dream* about Atomic View. You know what that means to me. My dreams are important. They *mean* something!"

Don looked ashamed. "There's nothing doing about it, Deb. We can't afford a house like that."

Deb sulked. She didn't want to, but she did, quiet for days, turning up the volume on the television so she wouldn't have to speak at the dinner table, rigid in bed. Don protested at first, then he, too, grew sulky—and like that they battled for three weeks, before he was promoted at the hi-fi shop and given a company car to drive: a blue Chevy Malibu with a sticky blue-vinyl interior. Deb rejoiced. With their old yellow VW Bug, they were now a two-car family, moving up in the world. Don went from in-store sales clerk to traveling salesman, still working on commission, but bigger jobs, fitting out corporate head-quarters and, once, a TV station. He worked like a backhoe to topple his competition. He left home at eight o'clock in the morning and returned at ten at night, when he would eat a sandwich and go straight to bed, where Deb rubbed his back and cooed encouragement. Don sold a record number of pieces of hi-fi equipment in two months, driving all over the county and then some, the Malibu's back seat piled high with speakers, the trunk full to the brim with turntables and receivers.

And he made sure, after he and Deb put their down payment on the new house on Cosmos Drive, they would have the very best hi-fi they could afford, with speakers in every room. Deb could listen to Joni Mitchell singing "California, California, I'm coming home," as she did her housework—even in the bathroom, Don boasted, and soon they would transform the basement into a rec room with a home entertainment system, pool table, and wall-to-wall shag-pile carpet to keep down the damp. With his promotion, he was full of dreams. Those there, he said, pointing to two square upstairs rooms on the floor plan, will be the kids' rooms, and Deb would need a room to call her own, a yellow-painted sun-catcher with trembling spider plants, sturdy cacti, and a plump aloe. She would have a desk for writing cards, a shelf for her favorite romance novels, and a La-Z-Boy recliner.

Only two other houses were built before theirs, and they weren't even finished, said Ted Jack, Atomic View's sales manager. Deb and Don would be among the first settlers. With Ted's help, they picked out their rancher, then drove around on the dirt roads that ran over the muddy mounds and planes that would become Atomic View. They picked their plot, with a view of Churchtown that was lit up and twinkling like Christmas each and every night, Jack promised. They staked their land with a red flag, and the bank approved their mortgage. Three months later the house was built, turf lawn laid, the driveway varnished with macadam, and Deb and Don moved in, celebrating with a keg and hamburgers under an orange harvest moon.

All that October it rained. Their front yard melted and the turf lawn sank. The basement flooded, then the power went; their water supply disappeared for three days during repairs to the main line that fed Atomic View. The phone went dead off and on through November while Don was away at a hi-fi convention in Pittsburgh, and Deb stayed with her parents until he came home again. Up there, alone, with no immediate neighbors to call out to, she felt like she was living in a horror movie, with the lights flickering and the house struck repeatedly by the wind and a steady drip-drip from the darkest corners of the basement.

That winter, Churchtown had a deep freeze. The muddy hills and troughs of Atomic View froze solid and Deb and Don's driveway buckled. When the sun came out, great chunks of blue tarmac were set adrift on a slushy, muddy sea—Deb attempted to pat them back into place with a stick, but too soon the puzzle had an unrecognizable face, refreezing that night into a disaster site, a brutish ruin. One morning when Don turned on the kitchen light, he got such a jolt that his eyes went bloodshot for three days; he called Ted Jack and yelled himself hoarse about value for money. Ted Jack promised him these things would sort themselves out in time, there were always going to be problems with a new house. The developers would repair any damages come spring, he reassured them. A big bunch of pink roses arrived for Deb that afternoon, plus a case of Rolling Rock for Don, and they sat and got drunk over TV dinners, warming themselves before the fire while their brand-new furnace shuddered and quit downstairs. They slept right there in the living room, still dressed in all their clothes, under piles of blankets and coats, just like the Old West settlers Ted had likened them to.

But Ted Jack was right. Come May, Atomic View was ticking regular as clockwork, with a new house finished almost every day and immediately occupied. Deb cooked up Cornflake Chicken and Broccoli Mayonnaise and Apple Dumpling for her incoming neighbors and took the food straight over, as soon as the moving vans rumbled off. She and Don went to barbecues, cocktail parties, and disco-dancing classes every weekend, and Deb babysat for extra money while Don sold plenty of hi-fis. They bought a cherry bedroom suite, a teakwood dining-room suite, and an oak kitchen table and four chairs—all real wood, finished to a high gloss, what you can't get these days. Their bed was four-poster, and the bedroom window curtains matched the daisy-print bedspread. It wasn't exactly masculine, but that didn't seem to bother Don; he was always downstairs anyway, fiddling with the hi-fi speakers, adding wires, changing records—CSNY, The Band, Curtis Mayfield, Jim Croce. "Put another one on, Don!" Deb would call. Already he wanted to install a state-of-the-art intercom system throughout the house, so they wouldn't have to yell.

In Atomic View, windows shone, American flags soared on their poles, and lawns glowed with health, sprouting oak, willow, and walnut trees—at least one tree in every front yard and two or three out back, between which a clothesline could be strung. Deb and Don had a young weeping willow propped up with stakes, and an ant-filled, bubble-gum-pink peony bush by the front door, plus yellow forsythia set to grow like a weed for next spring—four bushes in a row along their driveway. Deb planted marigolds around the lamppost and geraniums by the mailbox, and even as she kneeled to tend her buds, more families were moving in, filling their two-car garages with brand-new station wagons and soft-top American convertibles. She and Don didn't take a summer vacation that year. They didn't feel the need to get away; they had the good life right there in Atomic View and Deb didn't want to miss anything.

School days came, and then winter was back again. They settled in with a new furnace installed downstairs, an ambitious woodpile stacked out back, the driveway resurfaced, storm windows tacked on, and heaped sacks of salt in the garage. They had a twenty-inch color television to watch, and Don had bought Deb a sewing machine. She planned to make baby clothes, plus maternity clothes for herself—she and Don, after seven years together, three years married, one year in Atomic View, and all those years happy, high-school sweethearts, true love forever, were trying for a baby.

In November 1969, Don was killed in a car accident on an icy stretch of road. Deb was washing the breakfast dishes, looking out to the backyard where there was no motion in the bendy, knee-high trees, worrying that they would freeze to death if she didn't wrap them up in some kind of shelter, maybe give them a cup of hot water to drink, when the doorbell rang. The doorbell was always ringing at Deb and Don's, and she didn't think anything of it. The brims of the police officers' navy caps were hung with miniature icicles in a row—there was a glaze of sugary crust over everything, the guttering beaded with crystal, a fresh coat of silver paint on the mailbox that had shattered at her touch. Her sleeves, damp with dishwater, stiffened with the cold shock, winter pouring into the house as Deb stood there and tried to understand what had just been said to her.

Don had stepped out wearing his old football spikes, grinning as the ice broke up like cheap glass beneath his feet. He faked a running dive and caught an imaginary football, his footprints making clumsy angels, like stars around the edges. Deb told Don to be careful, driving in those. She should have told him to take them off—it was stupid that he had them on at all! But they were young, they didn't always think, and besides, he didn't have far to go, just to the hi-fi store's new mall outlet, with four sets of speakers piled up in the back seat, one on top of the other to the roof of the car, using his side mirrors to see. The radio station, Wink 101, was urging people to stay indoors, at least until the sun broke through the clouds and melted the ice. If the roads were empty, he would be done in half the time, Don said. Deb agreed, saying she would have a fire and hot cocoa waiting when he got home. That's what they always did when it snowed.

Stopped at a red light, the Malibu's radio blared from the additional two speakers installed on either side at the rear of the car, the motor idling and Don's foot clamped on the brake pedal's grooved metal surface. Moments later he was hit from behind when a tractor-trailer jack-knifed on black ice. Don never saw him coming—and even if he had, with the truck's eighteen-wheel, thirty-five-ton thrust, his cleat couldn't have held the brake. The Malibu shot into the intersection, but Don was already dead: one of the speakers had knocked a hole in the back of his head. Deb was a widow at twenty-one, while the truck driver walked away from the accident.

In the first days after Don died, she was swamped with relatives, neighbors, and friends, who piled in with meals or sat vigil while she wandered from room to room, just looking at the way things were instantly different. The house, the furniture and pictures on the wall, the friendly, concerned faces passing her in the hall looked strange, like nothing to do with her and Don. Deb picked up the music box that played the same old tune, "Bicycle Built for Two," and the music sounded full of wrong notes, like some phantom part had snapped. She took down their wedding pictures and examined them over and over again with a magnifying glass. Was that Don? Suddenly she couldn't remember his face. She panicked. She mustn't forget! After that she took the pictures with her to bed, rolling over them, sleepless, until the glass broke up like ice. She wanted to keep him close to her. She wouldn't wash the sheets for fear of losing the smell of him, and wouldn't wash his dirty underpants and socks, or the last coffee mug his lips had touched. Doctor Greaves came and gave her some sleeping pills, and Deb didn't know whether it was night or day after that, not that it mattered much; she slept through both, if she could.

Don's death was the first tragedy of Atomic View. Others followed—one child would drown in an abandoned septic tank, a relic of the old Shoemaker farm, while cancer, sudden heart attacks, and more car accidents took their toll. Butch Masters would commit suicide rather than face jail over embezzlement charges, while his wife Judy went into rehab for cocaine addiction, then ran off to Oregon with her counselor. But Don's death was the first. No one was safe, not even in Atomic View, like Deb had believed. Anyone, everywhere, was vulnerable, even the best. Especially the best.

Deb slept all that winter (she even slept through Christmas and the big parties of New Year's Eve, although she heard about them later), straight through to the end of February, when she woke to her mother pulling her hair, her face wet, the pillowcase soaked with the cold water that had just been thrown at her head.

"Get up," her mother said.

"I feel terrible," Deb said, rolling over to stuff herself into the crack between the wall and the bed.

"I bet you do," her mother said, her voice tough. "Now get up. Get!" She swatted Deb's backside through the bedspread.

"I'm dizzy. I'm cold." Deb buried her face in the dark quarry where she thought she could still smell Don, and sniffed: dust, only dust, enough to make her cough. She sat up and cleared out her lungs.

"That's because you've been in bed since November. I bet you're hungry, too."

Clutching her mother's arm, Deb tottered down the hall

on legs that cramped. They took the stairs slowly, one by one, resting in between, and Deb was panting by the time they made it down all twelve steps. Her bathrobe was covered in stains: coffee, tea, grape jelly, butter and egg, and what looked and smelled like vomit. The house was a mess, its surfaces crowded with coffee cups rampant with mold, beer bottles, pill bottles, plates glued with dried orange cheese and rancid tuna fish. There were greasy handprints all over the doors and walls, and a slime of mildew around the kitchen sink. When the last visitors had gone after Don's funeral, Deb hadn't bothered to clean up. Everything was out of place: kitchen chairs pulled into the living room where people sat for the wake, a card table set up in the hallway for the many flowers she had received, some still rotting in their plastic vases, encircled by wreaths of dropped petals and tarnished leaves. Confronted with this mess, she collapsed against her mother, nearly taking them both down, except that Deb was skin and bones and could have been carried in her mother's arms. "I can't make it," she wept.

"Just a few more steps." Her mother guided her to the sofa—*their* sofa, hers and Don's, the brown plaid one they picked at Ethan Allen. "Now let it all out. You'll feel better in a minute. Come on, let it go," her mother said, rocking Deb on her lap. "I never thought you'd be so young when you lost Don. You think your children will outlive you, and Don was always like a son to me. My only son."

"How am I going to go on? How am I, Ma? I can't live without him. I can't live in this house anymore."

"None of that, Deborah," her mother said firmly. "Stop

right there. I don't want to hear talk like that. You're giving yourself funny ideas, and it won't do you any good. You'll get yourself all worked up, then we'll have to call Doctor Greaves again."

"I can't stop," Deb sobbed. "I just can't. You don't know how I feel. I could kill myself."

"Don't you dare! Do you want to give me a stroke?" Her mother's voice softened. "Your pain won't last forever. You'll feel better one day soon, and when you do you'll marry again. I'm sure of it. There's plenty of men that would marry you. A pretty girl like you. You've made a beautiful home here—just a bit of spring-cleaning and you'll feel better about everything."

Deb shook her head in disbelief. "How can you say that? There's no other man for me. Don was my true love!"

"Be reasonable, Deb. You've got to get on with your life. Don would want you to," her mother replied.

Friends and neighbors agreed. "You're young. You'll have no trouble finding a new husband."

But Deb wanted Don or no one. She even said it once or twice, but people's eyes glazed over when she mentioned him. To them, he was gone already, gone and forgotten. No, people didn't like to talk about the dead; they preferred to talk about the living, about who had done what to whom and what happened last night in Brandi's Tavern, where everyone went to watch the game on a big-screen TV.

Deb had Don's life insurance, plus a payoff from the hi-fi store—and their house in Atomic View, of course—and when her parents died a few years later she had her inheritance. She was set for life. She didn't *have* to marry again.

Eventually she packed away Don's clothes and started to decorate the house with things that reminded her of her: a collection of clowns, and soft, cuddly toys for every occasion, scented candles, potpourri, finger-sized glass animals in unreal colors—violet, aquamarine, and sunbeam. Twenty years on, her house was painted sky blue, the willow tree grown taller than the roof and heavy with branches the neighborhood children liked to tear off for whips and tails. Times had changed—*Atomic View* had changed. People didn't talk so much to their neighbors. Both parents worked. Teenagers blatantly smoked cigarettes on the street, and last year there had been a drug bust on Jetstar Drive, when sixteen-year-old Bobby Troy was taken away in handcuffs. Deb tried to stay on top of who moved in and their children's names. She cooked them something nice and took it around hot, ready to eat. She tried to be neighborly, but sometimes they just wouldn't let her be.

She knew people said she had got too fat to get a man, but Deb didn't care. Her life was a full life. She filled every day.

Skater

He was down on the new, blue macadam of Cosmos Drive, on his hands and knees, those extremities electric with tiny shocks: pebbles of broken glass worn smooth by traffic, slivers of black rubber from a blown-out tire, the nubbly cotton of a shredded cigarette filter, ossified bubble gum. His flesh bubbled and dented where the rubble stuck. He had bitten down hard on his tongue, forking its tip, and blood ran in drips like candle wax from a broad, split bruise on his forehead where he walloped the tree branch—what sent his skateboard scuttling out from under his feet.

He crouched there, injured, catching his breath. He heard, over the noise of his harried breathing, the unmanned board clattering down the street, headed for the intersection where Atomic View joined the busy Mother Road. It had happened before: the board would be caught up like an animal in the wheels of a passing car, then spat out, its own smaller wheels mangled, the wooden deck splintered, trucks hanging loose from their bolts or torn clean off and thrown to the side of the road.

Babo pushed himself from the macadam and gave chase. His thick-soled DCs were good for skating, poor for running, plus he wore them loosely laced so as to slide in and out easily when he woke in the night wanting to skate, already halfway out of bed before he was out of the dream. He thudded along, flat-footed, his heels slipping. The skateboard disappeared beyond a swell in Cosmos Drive. Another fifty feet and this board—his newest board, one week old, a hundred bucks—would be dead meat. Babo crested the swell and saw the skateboard catch on a plastic-wrapped coupon circular in the road. The board catapulted and caught air, a full seven-twenty, then smacked down wrong side up, its spinning wheels exposed, and slid, grip tape hissing, in a skid until it banked in the McCarthys' driveway. *Safe*.

Babo swooped on the board, holding it aloft triumphantly, then flung it under-arm onto the McCarthys' lawn and threw himself down to inspect for loose bolts or a wheel that turned half-heartedly. When the board was deemed in good shape, he surveyed himself more quickly, with disappointment, even. His shorts were made of rough brown canvas, still intact; his sweatshirt was patched at each elbow, as it had come from the shop; his wallet, in his back pocket, still hung from its chain. Babo smacked his brush burns to make them sting. He reached into his pocket for Binaca Breath Spray and spritzed his injured tongue one, two, three, four times, drawing tears to his eyes, then sprayed his scraped-up knees until they flared and burned. The clotted cut above his left eye throbbed, which he knocked so that it surged again.

"Ruf," Babo grunted. He was tough, hard at the core, even if his skin was soft and tore easily on the road. Rising,

27

he stepped from the McCarthys' lawn and laid his board down nice and easy, his movements greased with repetition. He pushed off, kicking big in even strides. He dug into the macadam with the sole of his right DC, stroke and glide, stroke and glide. Babo was sailing.

He circled Atomic View on Cosmos Drive, its peripheral loop of road, double-checking the flow of his wheels before he ollied an abandoned Big Wheel in the middle of the street. Landing without a hitch (ollies were *easy*), Babo grabbed hold of a passing Jeep's bumper and hung on for the ride, noting his reflection in its glossy finish: mismatched argyle socks bunched at his ankles, one pastel-colored, the other maroon and gold; knees spattered with burst blood vessels like diaper rash; shorts flecked with tar on the seat ("Poopy pants," Nate called them); and a T-shirt striped with chocolate milk from his lunch. Old blood streaked his forehead in garish lumps amid leaks of new blood, and above, a baseball cap teetered (FUCT, it read). His glossy black hair was cut in a sloping bang covering one eye, behind which he could hide. Every inch of his exposed surface was beaded with scars, and overall, Babo was pleased with his appearance.

When the Jeep turned onto Quasar Lane, Babo bailed— and lost traction in a bed of road sediment. He landed on the street with a crack from his tailbone, the pain so intense that he reached into his shorts and felt for blood, just in case the prickly point of his coccyx had poked through. He wanted to cry out, just one yelp, wanted to splutter through the exhaust pipe of his mouth, "Oh hell!" But Babo was no baby, however small his frame. He locked his jaw up tight until the pain passed. He farted, just to see how it felt. It felt fine.

Today was not his day. Yesterday had been something else, when he and his best friend Nate went to Highland Corporate Park, with its plentiful railings to slide, chunky ledges to nose-pick and five-O, park benches to grind. Everyday things were Babo's playground. No hoops, no goal posts, and definitely no fucking coach. There wasn't a time limit to what he could do—no quarters, no halftime water break, no assists, nor last-ditch end-of-game volley and the sporting handshakes that followed. On a good day like yesterday, Babo scored tricks left and right: a switch frontside noseslide on Colt Trucking's employee picnic table; a kickflip frontside boardslide down the steel stairwell at Bucky's Ball Bearings; a switch backside nosegrind right in front of Highland's manned security cabin. He was unstoppable, skating like a pro—Nate had said so. Nate had wished out loud for his camera. Babo's high-octane footwork was as good as that of anyone featured in *Thrasher* or *Transworld*.

"Dude, you're a one-ring circus show," Nate said. "You rip for real."

But that was yesterday. Now, scudding along, feeling pissed off inside, each mailbox he passed he yanked open, leaving their aluminum jaws gaping in surprise. He carelessly ollied a basketball that was dribbling itself down the street, and his heart skipped a beat as he heard the muscular "Hey!" that roared after it. Babo didn't have to look to know whose voice it was: two houses away, the four aggressive Johnson boys and a few of their mountain-sized friends were playing ball. "Hey!" Rob Johnson hollered again, red-faced, hands on his hips, stripped to the waist, dressed only in baggy team shorts that displayed his fluffy, hairy legs—the freshly sprung hair of an active teenager, not yet worn away in patches on the calf where a businessman's socks held tight.

Babo thrust his middle finger in their direction and pumped it wildly, then pumped his leg to get away.

"What's that, Babo? What did you say? I can't hear you!" bellowed Danny Johnson, a squatter, beefier version of his brother.

Babo flicked them off again—and lost his balance, lurching from the skateboard to land, once more, on his hands and knees. The board skipped playfully, teasing his reaching fingers so that he had to crawl after it down the street. God, how he hated this skateboard, this day, the Johnsons and their kin, tall guys on steroids in pressed flannel shirts and fitted jeans, their ever-expanding shoulders blocking the light for the rest of mankind.

"Pick up the ball, baby boy," someone hectored him. The others brayed and snorted, kicking out their restless long legs.

"Come on, runt, throw the ball to daddy!"

"Bouncing baby boy!"

Babo ignored their raucous laughter. He heard footsteps thundering behind him, but Babo on a skateboard was faster than any Johnson, and he was already up and skating away. The basketball streaked past his head and he glanced back to see who had lobbed it (he kept a mental list of who did what to him; he would have his revenge one day, when he was big): Rob Johnson was bearing down, flared nostrils belching fumes, gleaming eyes focused on the kill. Rob Johnson looked hungry. Rob Johnson was going to use Babo as his ball, slam-dunk him until Babo was black and blue, blooming with blood.

Babo kicked off like an outboard motor mounts a high wake, turning from Quasar Lane (past his own house, but he would never hide *there* with a Johnson giving chase) onto Jetstar Drive. The steady metallic sound of his board's wheels grating over the macadam at top speed was reassuring, and the footsteps behind him finally tailed off. Then he was zipping up the driveway of Nate's house, where Nate was outside measuring a dusty square of foraged plywood for the quarter pipe he was building.

"Jesus, that was close," Babo said, slinging his skateboard into the bushes—where the useless slab of stick could stay, for all he cared.

"Good wound," Nate grunted. Babo touched his forehead and nodded. "Where you been, Babo?"

"Around. I had detention and took the late bus."

"What'd you do?"

"I threw an eraser at Mrs. Kennedy. She threw it at me first."

"Did you hit her?"

"Yeah," Babo laughed. "In the back."

"Dude, they expel kids for shit like that."

"Nah. I didn't hurt her. Detention was so easy—Mrs. Moss let us talk. But man, the late bus sucks, full of jock-straps with track practice. Those assholes never shut up, you know? I was trying to listen to music and they were making so much noise I couldn't hear, even with *my* head-phones, which get a good seal."

"Your Sennheisers rule. I wish I had some."

"Today sucks. Today reeks of ass. I don't get it. Yesterday was the best day. I was killing it. Yesterday I was the tech-dog. Today I can't skate for shit. I'm bailing every trick."

"You should've called me, Babo. I wanted to skate."

"I did call. It was busy. Nicole must have been on the phone or something. You should get your own line, dude. That girl is always on the phone." Babo went into the backyard and climbed onto Nate's trampoline. Nate turned up the boom box and Minor Threat sang about standing by friends—"You might need them in the end." Babo bounced, reaching for the treetops, looking out to see if any Johnsons were coming. The streets were clear and quiet, even after school—most kids stayed in with the TV, killing time until their parents got home. He saw the Powerwalker intent on her feet, swinging her arms like she was square dancing, and Mr. Diamond polishing his Corvette. Still no Johnsons in sight, who knew where to go if they really wanted to kill Babo. Nate's house was a favorite gathering place for skate punks.

Babo, bouncing, reached the height of the second-floor windows. Nate's twin Nicole was painting her toenails and talking on the phone in her room, a cigarette caught in the corner of her mouth. Babo thought Nicole was hot. She was tall, like her brother, and her hair was white blond, her mouth pink, breath sweet, eyes a clear, changeable gray, sometimes blue, sometimes green. Seeing Babo, Nicole gave him the finger. When he bounced up again, she snatched the curtains shut.

"You going to help or what? Or you just going to bounce around all day?" Nate wanted to know.

"Give me a cigarette." Babo bounced off, landing solidly, knees bent to cushion the blow. His knees were like elastic bands—his whole body was tightly sprung, flexible and compact, always ready to go.

"I quit," Nate said.

"Yeah, right," Babo grinned.

"I did, man. Last night."

"Then get one off Nicole."

"I'm busy, Babo. I'm *building*, can't you see?"

"Whatever, dude." Babo trotted across Nate's yard and slapped open the screen door, letting it slam behind him. He padded into the kitchen to the refrigerator, drank from a liter bottle of Coke, gasping and burping between gulps. Soda pop fizzed out his nostrils.

"Disgusting," Nicole hissed, suddenly behind him, drawing out the word. She reached for the Diet Coke and pointedly took a glass from the cupboard. "Who do you think you are?"

Babo was looking at her toes, painted mint green. "Cool," he said, pointing.

Nicole lit a cigarette and scowled at him. "You can't just drink out of the bottle like that, Babo. Not in our house."

"Oh yeah?" Babo drank some more.

"You're foul," Nicole exhaled.

"Hey, give me one, will you? Nate says he quit." Babo licked the Coke that had gushed from his nose to his lips.

"You are so gross!" Nicole squealed. Babo snatched her lit cigarette and dragged on it, then offered it back. "No way! No way will I touch that now," she said, tapping a new cigarette out of the pack. Babo grabbed it, licked it, and tucked it behind his right ear, smirking at her. But Nicole wouldn't smile back. She never smiled except at school or when she was with her bubblehead friends. Furious now, she tapped out another cigarette, and Babo seized that one as well, for his other ear, for later.

"Babo," Nicole wailed.

"Nicole," Babo echoed.

"Nate!" she called, but Nate was hammering away, the music turned up loud. Nicole stormed out the back door. "Your friend is such a loser! Why are all your friends losers?"

Nate ignored her, fitting another piece of wood, trying it this way, then that. Babo finished his first cigarette and lit the second from it, watching Nicole through the screen door. She stamped her foot and spun on her heel, flipping the hem of her red miniskirt, and Babo saw a slice of her high ass the color of a Creamsicle. When she ran inside and upstairs, he followed her, but she banged shut her bedroom door. Babo leaned against it, breathing hard. He groaned, twisting the doorknob. It was locked.

"Nicole."

"Go away, asshole!"

"Nico, please."

"Leave me alone, Babo. I mean it."

"I just wanted to say sorry," he whispered. It was always like this, Babo torn between wanting to torture Nicole and

34

wanting her. He kicked the door. She screamed. Her scream was shrill and piercing, the worst kind of scream, a little girl's scream. Why did she hate him so? What was it about him? Babo didn't know. He tried the doorknob again, twisting until the metal scalded his hand. Nicole screamed louder—she was hysterical. She sounded like someone was trying to kill her, her breath snagging in her throat when she pulled for more air. He left her screaming in her room, tearing at the yellow wallpaper.

Downstairs, he grabbed the bottle of Coke and charged outside. "Nate, your sister's a nut bar. She belongs in the psycho ward at General Hospital."

"Leave her alone, Babo. She's not into you. How many times do I have to tell you?"

"Don't you think it's weird I think your sister's the bomb? It's like saying I think *you're* the bomb, you two being twins and all."

Nate looked at Babo, his hammer poised above a nail. His arms were long and muscular, his large hands capable. His gray eyes were the color of a knife blade.

Babo offered Nate the bottle of Coke, but Nate only glared at him. Babo blinked first. "I'm kidding."

"Not about my sister."

"I'm not even into her."

"Yeah, right. You're full of shit, Babo," Nate sang. "Dude, just listen to her scream. That's all the proof you need."

"No way, man. I didn't do that to her."

"Then who did? Nobody else here, except the three of us."

"No way," Babo shook his head.

35

"*Way.*"

"I'm out of here, dude." Babo dropped the plastic Coke bottle and stomped it, twisting it out of shape.

"Yo, Babo, if you don't help me with this ramp, I'll never let you ride it."

"You will."

"I won't."

"I know you, man. I bet you this piece-of-shit skate-board," Babo said, picking it up and shaking it. "You'll let me ride whenever I damn well please. You better."

"That skateboard won't last another week, the way you ride. You ride like a crazy, fucked-up metal bastard."

Babo grinned, showing his straight white teeth. "Later, skater."

Connecticut College
1990–1994

Waking from his after-lunch nap, Mitch smelled Babo before he heard or saw anything. His brother was home, smoking his bong. Even though Babo stuffed towels around his bedroom door and exhaled into another tightly wadded towel spotted with brown rings, Mitch knew when Babo was smoking, and Babo was *always* smoking. Mitch figured that he smoked an average of four times a day in his room, bong hits before and after school, again after dinner (so that he dozed over his homework), and just before he fell asleep at night. Mitch was sure Babo smoked outside his room as well, at least once a day at school, just to get through. The kid was a big-time stoner.

It didn't take Mitch long to figure out Babo's smoking schedule, just a few days of close observation; Mitch didn't have much to do now that he was living at home again. Their housekeeper Luisa cleaned and shopped and washed the family's clothes, cooked their dinner, and made their beds. The lawn mowers mowed the encompassing green and trimmed the bristling privet hedge that fenced the property. A general handyman checked in once a month to change light bulbs, tighten screws, oil hinges, and touch up paint, while the thermostat was set to 64 degrees on a computer timer, to heat or cool in response to the slightest change in the weather.

Meanwhile, in New York, Mitch's friends were making important decisions: What kind of copy face? Who to put on the cover, the guest list? What shares to buy and what to sell for Client X? How fast to push the morphine? Where to eat tonight? Where to drink first? Was Gucci worth its price? (Yes, Mitch groaned, pounding his pillow with his fist. Yes! He dreamed of Gucci loafers, worn sockless, and for his girlfriend—an as-yet-unknown-to-him New York sophisticate—high-heeled Gucci sandals with glittering buckles and fly-away straps.)

There they were, stockbrokers-in-training, editorial assistants, first-year law and medical students, PR reps, and Internet entrepreneurs. Mitch longed to be among them, drinking a martini while listening to the Mingus Big Band at Fez, elbowing through the Saturday shopping crowd in SoHo, or simply sitting by his own apartment's living-room window with a view, watching and hearing the city ruckus below: the push-pull of sidewalk traffic, the caterwaul of a delivery truck's horn, its driver trapped in the limbo of gridlock. Mitch visited his friends in New York as often as he could, but he always returned to Atomic View. He had spent the last year of his life wandering his parents' house like a ghost, a whole year gone when nothing happened to him, nothing at all. He never ventured out into the neighborhood and rarely socialized with his family, choosing instead to recline in his old blue bedroom reading *Vanity Fair* and *New York Magazine* and *The New Yorker* (he had built a fortress of paper just inside his door). He listened for the phone's ring, half-afraid it would be a friend calling from the city, yet more afraid of being forgotten, for Mitch alone had moved back home after college.

"I'm just outside Philly," he tried to explain to Zack and Craig and Melissa and Ian. "Yeah, in the suburbs—no, further out than that. It's a *new* suburb of Philly, maybe an hour and a half away. Buddy, in Pennsylvania, two hours is *close*. Yeah. You know, I'm filming my documentary. The one I told you about. Anything you want to add, let me know and I'll film you. I'll make you look good, buddy."

Saying that would unleash a torrent of stories narrated in slang that had had its day. "You remember when I broke up with Sasha? And we sent that picture of her blowing me to her parents? And wrote on the back 'Having a mind-blowing time at college, Mom and Dad'? She had a killer cow, man! She went *off the hook* on me. If only you could film *that* . . . not!"

"Oh yeah," Mitch said—he always agreed one hundred percent with his friends—or, "That was the best night. *So* drunk. We'll have more nights like that when I move to the city. I'll bring my camcorder. We'll film *everything.*"

But as the months passed, his friends stopped asking when it was exactly that he would come. Since they stopped asking, he no longer had to lie and tell them, "Next month. I'll be there next month for sure." The longer Mitch stayed at home, the harder it was to believe that he would make it to Manhattan at all.

Still, he had his documentary, what he hoped would get him there in the end. Mitch could see his film in the viewfinder in his head, what he thought he would call *College Collage,* and he knew his idea was worth a fortune: to showcase the soft generation of prosperity whose tastes were formed during the Reagan binge, when credit meant everything. More kids than ever were enrolled in private liberal arts colleges like the one he attended, and Mitch wanted to show the world exactly who it was dealing with. The big trouble was getting the actual filming done, now that he was stuck in Atomic View. He had the camcorder he had received last Christmas (post-graduation, too late to film his college experience as it was happening), but he needed to be *with* his friends to get the job done. In fact, he really needed to go back to Connecticut College.

For Mitch, Conn College was the pinnacle of his existence. He missed the island arboretum of campus, mostly bereft of news of the world and further insulated by feet of snow in winter. At the expensive college, feeling both free and coddled, Mitch had begun to know the people he wanted to know, to live the life he wanted to live. His friends were the sons and daughters of TV executives, big-time lawyers and businessmen, stockbrokers, scions and heiresses. They drove Saabs and Jeeps and wielded credit cards with a direct, unchecked line to their parents' bountiful bank accounts. They refused to eat in the dining hall, preferring to order takeouts for their rooms or dine in downtown New London. As these young, suburban non-professionals ate their way up and down Bank Street, Mitch joined them, ordering his steak rare when he had always preferred it well done, eating salad after his main course. Soon he inherited a fake ID from a junior and could drink with his meal, then hit the bars. He developed a taste for gin martinis, downed with a handful of soft, salty cashews, and got fat on greasy-spoon breakfasts just after dawn. Mitch slept in every morning; afternoons were spent hanging out, drinking coffee, drifting late into classes, leaving early when he saw a game of Ultimate Frisbee picking up on the green. As a member of the social elite, it was more important that he hang out than study.

Over the years, Mitch visited the grand homes of his college friends, including four Park Avenue penthouse apartments with their teams of housekeepers and doormen in regal uniform. He spent one New Year's Eve in a Cincinnati house with ten bedrooms, a five-car garage, swimming pool, tennis courts, and golf course access through the backyard. In Chicago, he slept among Rodin sculpture and a collection of African boiled heads. In Boston, under beams from the *Mayflower*, he laid his head on airy goosedown pillows, tucked under a weightless, warm duvet, the ironed white sheets thick with laundry starch. How clean he felt, how soundly he slept in that guestroom's antique sleigh bed, its firm orthopedic mattress much better than his own at home.

This is what it's all about, he thought. This was the life he wanted.

Mitch had never worked hard at school—he didn't need to. He scored twelve hundred on his SATs without any preparation and with a startling hangover, his first, although he had been drinking for years. The five colleges he applied to unanimously accepted him; he chose the one where he had the best night out on his overnight visit, and when the time came to go he packed his bags without really knowing why or what he was doing. But at Conn College, he felt strongly—overwhelmingly—that for the first time, he had found his place. He was with his own people. He *identified* with his classmates' collective ease and sense of entitlement. At Conn College, Mitch began living a rich person's life. When he stood at a bar to order a drink, bills and coins poured from his fingers like wishes into a well. He offered rounds of drinks to his new crowd and soon had a running tab, payable at the end of the school year (and if he was often so drunk that strangers ordered drinks on his account, Mitch didn't care, for he had never been happier).

Returning home at Thanksgiving his freshman year, Mitch had the new perspective that exile affords. Viewed from behind Armani sunglasses, Atomic View looked shabby. The lawns were generally cramped, and double front doors were ludicrous on boxy houses, the hollow columns that flanked them unimposing. Fake brick fronts—who were they trying to fool? How had he never noticed the lawn statuary before, those red-capped mushrooms and silvery reflective balls and pastel Madonnas presiding over birdbaths like they were baptismal fonts? The only swimming pool in the neighborhood had a beer can painted on its bottom!

Mitch vowed he would never bring his college friends home, not even to the biggest house in Atomic View, built on two lots, freshly painted every third summer, with a flowing lawn and two BMWs in the garage. A long time ago—although he didn't remember—he had thought it was a glamorous place to live, the houses big and new, just like the cars parked in their garages. He didn't remember how proud he felt when the school bus turned into Atomic View after making its way through lesser neighborhoods like Fox Chase and Honey Brook. That Thanksgiving, Mitch only saw how *humble* his roots were.

As his college education progressed, Mitch began to feel more keenly that his parents hadn't given him enough. He had attended state schools! He had never traveled abroad! He didn't have a car of his own—not only that, he had to take Greyhound home, while his friends flew or kicked back in limousines. Worst of all, one summer he had worked in a *factory*, when everyone else he knew hung out in the mountains of Colorado, save the few hours one friend spent in his father's air-conditioned office, reading the sports pages and ordering lunch.

Now, post-graduation, Mitch was living at home again while his friends lived it up in New York. Having visited Career Services just once, the few interviews garnered by his half-hearted letter-writing failed to produce any job opportunities substantial enough to live on without parental subsidy. His friends didn't understand why he didn't just pack his bags and head for the city. They didn't understand that it was a question of capital, that Mitch didn't have any capital, that he had zero, zip, *fuck all* in the bank. That he had spent it all on college—and not even on college. His parents had paid his tuition and room and board, while Mitch spent fifteen thousand dollars in four years on booze, drugs, girls, and lavish spring-break vacations. Even if he had rich parents, or reasonably well-off parents, or comfortable parents who both worked long hours and so enjoyed the perks of housekeeper, interior decorator, lawn service, window-washer, and general handyman, they certainly weren't going to pay for Mitch to live in New York.

"You're done," they said when he confronted them one evening shortly after he moved back home. All day he had stewed in his bedroom: it wasn't fair that he should be so stuck! His parents wouldn't even give him bus fare to New York anymore—not unless he had an interview scheduled. What was their problem?

"You can live at home free of charge, but we're not paying for anything else," his father said.

"You've got plenty of money. What are you saving it for?" Mitch demanded.

"We've got Babo to think about," his mother replied.

"Babo's never going to go to *college*," Mitch stated, slitting an overstuffed cheese and onion pierogi and gutting it with his fork.

"Mitch, you'll ruin your appetite," said his mother. "We're eating in half an hour."

Mitch ignored her, gobbling the pierogi in huge bites, chewing with his mouth open, smacking his lips—the bad manners his mother despised.

"Babo might choose to go to art school," his father argued. "He's good at art. He might get into RISD. I know what the tuition is there. And," he added, sucking his teeth, "it's steep. As much as Connecticut College was." His father filled two tumblers with ice and poured bourbon brim-deep.

Conn College tuition, Mitch had always been pleased to

note, was almost thirty thousand dollars a year.

"I'm fifty years old," his father continued. "And so is your mother. We don't want to work forever just to pay for you."

Mitch looked at his mother, appealing for her sympathy—futilely, he knew. She was exacting in her arguments, her integrity absolute, commiserate with the truth of the situation rather than the emotional point of view. She was a *lawyer*, for Christ's sake. Still, he tried. "Mom, I just need one chance, one opportunity. Pay my rent for three months and I promise I'll land on my feet."

"Mitch, we told you all last year that you should be saving money if you wanted to move to New York. You might have lined up a job, but you didn't, so here you are," she said, tugging at the Tupperware container of spinach salad Luisa had prepared.

Mitch banged his plate with his fork. "All of my friends are in New York! I'm the only one not there!"

"Don't do that, Mitch," his mother said. "You'll break the plate."

"Is it my fault your friends are in New York and you're not? Is it *my* fault?" his father asked. It was a rhetorical question he had been asking the boys for years. "You shouldn't have been out partying. That's what I told you."

"New York is dangerous and expensive," his mother declared. "If you want to live in a city, try Philadelphia. It's much closer."

"No one I know lives in Philadelphia. Philadelphia is a *suburb* of New York."

"Well." His mother sipped her drink. "That sounds like

something your friends think."

Mitch ignored her. "I want to be a filmmaker," he insisted. "I need New York to make films. I need *experience.*"

"Since when do you want to direct movies?" his father asked.

"Since forever!" Mitch replied, not honestly.

His parents exchanged glances. "This is the first we've heard of it. You were an American Studies major—" his mother began.

"I took a filmmaking class," Mitch interrupted. "You gave me a camcorder for Christmas."

"That settles *that,* I guess," she said. "Now I've got to get dinner together or we'll never eat." She inserted a foil-wrapped wand of garlic bread into the oven, which she hadn't bothered to preheat.

"Get a job," his father said, taking over the argument. "We've given you a place to live and we can take it away. As long as you're living under this roof, you'll listen to us. Do you hear me? If you want to live in New York, then get a job that takes you there. It's that simple."

"And what *kind* of job do you suggest, since you want to run my life?" Mitch snapped.

His father placed his drink on the counter. Both parents ran their fingers through short, grey, exceedingly clean hair. His mother spoke first. "You had your choice of college and we never said a word about what it cost. You could go where you wanted, and we were happy to give you that. It's why we work, so that you and Babo have a good future. But now it's time to move on, Mitch. You're not a college boy. You're a grown up."

"No one ever told me *how* to grow up! No one showed me!" he wailed.

"That's the whole point, Mitch," his mother said.

"You're *done*," his father added, and his parents moved into the living room, ending the conversation.

Mitch watched his parents drinking bourbon from monogrammed tumblers, talking shop. They looked self-satisfied—and for all the bourbon they drank, they never looked drunk.

"I can't get a job!" he howled after them. "No one will hire me!"

Within a few weeks, Mitch had made secret arrangements by phone to occupy a small Manhattan studio apartment a friend told him about. He wrote a check and mailed it off, packed his bags and stowed them in his closet, ready for the first of the month. But the check bounced, and the agency, Finders Keepers, wouldn't return his calls. He contemplated insurance and credit-card fraud, dealing drugs, and selling the contents of his bedroom in a garage sale, before he decided that he would make a documentary. *That* would make him rich enough for New York. It was a great idea—and hadn't his teacher said filmmaking was all formula? Who you knew and who you could get to be your star, that's what was important. Mitch had already met the kind of people that appeared in the *New York Times* weddings and obituary pages; he would be the Bret Easton Ellis of film.

Yet here he was, nine months later, still in Atomic View, his college years clouding over, no longer the summer of his life, filled with lovers and jumpy golden retrievers named Budweiser and Miller. He had filmed nothing but his family unwrapping their Christmas presents, Babo strapped into a new snowboard, pretending the white carpet was fresh powder, his mother inspecting a flannel robe and slippers. He spent his days wandering the house, hating it more and more with each circuit. Who really played the piano? No one did. Mitch noted the reproduction prints of old-looking flowers framed in gold—they don't even buy real art, he thought. Wall-to-wall carpet was tacky. Didn't they know better? The dining table was too new, matched with eight chairs covered in gold velvet, and he doubted the table was real mahogany; he suspected a more ordinary wood stained dark, but it had yet to wear enough to tell the truth: his parents never entertained, and the family ate in the kitchen.

Mitch, car-less, broke, his hair reaching what should have been a stiff white shirt collar but instead was the frayed cowl of his bathrobe, gazed, as he often did, out of his bedroom window. Across the street, where the Loser lived, a woman was smoking out of *his* bedroom window. The Loser had scored again. The Loser himself appeared behind the woman, eagerly taking her in his arms even as she stubbed out her cigarette.

Mitch sighed. Even the Loser scored.

A New World

After the long flight (boarding delays at Heathrow while the plane was cleaned, then an hour and a half in the runway queue), hassle at immigration when she landed (what would she *do* in the States, they wondered?), lost bags (she had two hundred American dollars in her pocket, courtesy of British Airways, while her luggage would travel on the next flight and arrive to the new house sometime in the middle of the night), Dale met her with flowers. Cathy saw the red bouquet as soon as she passed through the swinging steel doors of International Arrivals, the moment before Dale thrust them aside with a foolish grin and opened his arms and she fell against him, nearly knocking him over.

He does love me, she thought, bowing to the perfect roses now crushed to her chest. She inhaled deeply. They didn't smell of anything. Were they real? She pinched a shining stem, thornless, leafless, and real, bruising at her touch. Cathy flushed. Her first roses! She stroked their petals, relishing this love offering—just as Dale pushed her to one side before she collided with a porter who was steaming past, tangled helplessly in dog leashes and

49

squealing miniature terriers, their red-lacquered claws clicking like a hailstorm of Tic-Tacs.

Dale laughed and Cathy laughed with him, a high-pitched, whinnying giggle that she quickly smothered with a hand clapped to her mouth. Like the roses, she couldn't quite believe Dale was real. Yet here was her husband, leading her by the hand to the New World he had promised. She was here. She really was here. She looked around at the other arrivals, who gripped trolleys heaped with hard and soft cases and Duty Free bags—not one of them held a bunch of roses like she did. She saw the cheerful yellow flag of the hotdog vendor whose straw hat was shedding its brim, and all the waiting, bored drivers with their hand-drawn posters, searching faces for a sign of recognition. She saw families and friends reunited to a fanfare of affection, and anxious foreign-exchange students leaving with strangers who clapped them heartily on the back. Cathy would remember this moment, every detail, when she finally arrived in America. She looked out through the sliding glass doors to the sunny afternoon with no sign of rain in the big sky above and she wanted to stick a rose in her hair and skip all the way to Churchtown, where she and Dale would live together the next fifty years.

In the car, Dale talked about his job. Smart Cups had given him this green Ford Taurus, a mark of their faith in his abilities. The sale sticker, showing the car's final cost, was pasted in the back window, and a pine-scented tree with the dealer's name—Jack Giambo Jr.—dangled from the rear-view mirror. Cathy lit a cigarette.

"Not in the car. I thought you quit," Dale said accusingly. "If you have to smoke, then at least roll down the window."

She shook her head, smiling meekly at him.

"People don't smoke here like they do in England. We're health conscious. We want to live long lives. I know everyone smokes over there, but not here. Here, you have to ask before you smoke. If you're not sure, you should go outside. Even outside you're polluting the air."

She rolled down the window a crack and pushed out her cigarette.

"Why you would want to smoke in the first place, I don't know. You must be crazy. Only crazy people smoke."

Cathy shrugged.

"Are you tired?" he asked. "You're quiet."

She nodded.

"How was your flight?"

Cathy had been thrilled to fly—her first time. She stayed awake the whole flight, rigid through her back, seat upright (too afraid to recline lest she upset the person seated behind her, whose knees she could feel digging in). She had sat very still in her window seat, watching as the plane climbed through the rain and poked its nose into the bright, steep sky beyond. There it remained, bumping the clouds from time to time—what resulted in an uneasy ride, when Cathy gripped the arms of her seat in terror until it was kindly explained to her that turbulence was standard on any flight.

Dale flew at least once a month as a salesman for Smart Cups. "Flying can be a pain in the you-know-what," he said.

Cathy nodded.

"Are you shy? There's no need to be shy. You're my wife now." Dale rested his hand on her knee, a sly look on his face, half-smiling. "You know, I have just the cure for shyness." He took her hand, the left hand (for he was seated on the left-hand side of the car, the door that Cathy had gone for, making him laugh, "You're in America now!"), and laid the cold hand with its shiny gold band on the bulging zipper of his trousers, ironed to a sheen. "Unzip me, baby," he pleaded.

She giggled nervously, watching her hand tremble, feeling what swelled beneath with a suddenness of power.

"Just touch him. It's been a long time," Dale begged, unzipping himself with a flick of his wrist. His erection leapt through the gap of his zip and she saw the fierce purple head with its slit eye, the scar of his circumcision, and then the snarled nest of red hair.

"Baby," Dale insisted. Cathy covered the eye with her hand and he came immediately, stamping the brake so that the car behind him honked and squealed into the next lane. Dale laughed, veering slightly, sending another car wailing into the road's shoulder. "See what you do to me? I'm reckless!"

Cathy smiled and found some tissue in her purse to mop her hand and blot his trousers.

"Are you hungry?" A sign advertised the Lizzie Borden Rest Stop in five miles, boasting Roy Rogers, Dunkin' Donuts, and Mrs. Fields' Cookies.

She shook her head resolutely. She hadn't eaten on the plane, nor that morning in England, more than twelve hours ago, beset with butterflies in her stomach and a dry throat. She couldn't even finish her last cup of tea on English soil.

"Always watching your figure. That's my girl," Dale said, patting her thigh. "It sure is good to see you, baby. I counted every minute until I would see you again. Did you miss me? I got things ready for you at home. I don't know what you like to eat, but we'll go to the supermarket and you can pick out anything you like. My baby will have anything she wants. Nothing's too good for my baby." He sounded like he was singing along to a pop song. "Hey, do my zip, will you? I got truck drivers looking in the window. Perverts!" Dale shouted, beeping his horn. Cathy reached over and zipped him up and he tugged her blonde ponytail playfully with his teeth, causing a Mobil Oil tractor-trailer to honk twice. "That guy knows I'm lucky," Dale said, and Cathy took his hand to clasp it in hers—but his hand quickly escaped, twitching on the steering wheel like a fish out of water. Then he fiddled with the radio.

They had married six weeks before in the registry office in Manchester, where Cathy had lived until that morning. After their wedding, Dale returned to Churchtown while she stayed behind to knot the odd-ends of her old life and sort out her visa. She had written Dale a few postcards, and he had posted the odd letter, but they hadn't seen or spoken to each other since their short honeymoon stay in a local hotel. Cathy didn't use the phone—she just didn't use the phone. Dale agreed with her, citing the cost of long-distance calls and the difficulty of interpreting time zones.

"Oh boy!" he said, bouncing one hand to her chest and grazing her scant breasts. He punched the tuner buttons, finding a hard rock station, then accelerated. "Mama, I'm coming home!"

Cathy followed the scenery of their route through the window, the steady bump-bump of the road seams an assault to her spine, her chin bobbing agreeably. The motorway adhered to the non-contour of the flat terrain. Fields and forest blurred past, monotonous greenery that didn't look much different to England, and soon she dozed, her head lolling in the hammock of her seatbelt. Her sleep was hard and fast—she shot straight into the deep sleep that her exhaustion required, a blank, gray sleep, like being underwater. Cathy slept until Dale's announcement over a crescendo of sawing guitars, "Time to wake up!" and she opened her eyes to Atomic View.

It was a wondrous scene, the sky serene and blue as the placid seas of postcards, the flowers of late spring blooming in hedges and trees. Hump upon hump of verdant lawn ranged, like a train of camel backs, and atop each hump stood a solitary house, set back from the road. All was quiet at this hour—seven o'clock, the news hour—and apparently peaceful, with the rare rambler or car about. The suburbs, she told herself. She was in the suburbs. *American families* lived behind those doors.

"This street is Cosmos Drive and it's got a great view of the area," Dale said, pausing between houses so she could see the valley below, where more houses crowded in clusters, each with its squat wad of green. "But let's not dilly-dally. You've got a new home to see," he said, driving on.

The houses in this neighborhood were huge, Cathy thought, and detached as well, every single one. She hadn't known she was going to live in a mansion!

"This is our street, baby," Dale crowed, turning onto Quasar Lane. "See if you can guess which house." He hadn't shown her any photos, and his descriptions were mundane: three bedrooms, two baths, living room, dining room, kitchen, and den, all of it standard American, but uncolored, unshaped—he wanted her to be surprised, he said.

To Cathy, the brick-fronted houses all looked the same. She blinked rapidly, clearing her eyes. She must be tired. Her head fizzed like an alkaline tablet. *Think,* she thought, closing her eyes. Dale had mentioned that the door was red. Cathy opened her eyes—but there were many red doors on Quasar Lane, all red *double* front doors, so far as she could see. But no, she was wrong; there was a house with just *one* red door—it was a trick question, she thought. She hoped she got the answer right, so that she pleased Dale. Cathy pointed.

"That's right, baby! Welcome home," he said, turning up the driveway. He pressed a button on the Taurus's visor and the garage door began to make its ascent, revealing an empty, swept garage as big as some English houses. He parked in the middle of the garage, saying, "We'll get you a car, something sporty, a convertible maybe. A red convertible with a white soft top."

To match the front door, Cathy thought happily.

She trailed Dale into the yellow kitchen. "Kitchen. Your territory." They followed the cream-colored hall to the brown den—his personal space, he said in a stern voice— then the blue living room and the red dining room, upstairs into the green master bedroom with its ensuite peach bath with brass taps.

"Our bed." Dale pointed to the four-poster bandaged with an eyelet canopy. He tested its spring with both hands. "A nice, firm mattress, so it don't wear out too fast!" Cathy touched the wood of one post, smooth as plastic and the color of Sindy-doll skin. It was all brand new, this house, the walls fresh with paint, the gold carpet throughout spongy, resilient to her tread. Dale had lived here only a year and it looked like he hadn't really settled in: no pictures on the walls, no ornaments to state the place was his. The house was too big for one person, he had told her when they met. He needed a wife to look after it.

"I have a surprise for you."

Cathy looked at him as if to say, "More than all this?" Her eyes were wet and wide with love, and she kissed him, her mouth gobbling his, before following him downstairs to the kitchen, then down another flight of wooden stairs, the dim emptiness stirred awake at the sound of their clattering feet: the basement.

Dale switched on the bright overhead light. "Tada!" he cried, turning to her with his big grin.

Cathy ran to the Stairmaster's side. She caressed the cool metal rails and sniffed the foam handgrips. No other's sweat had stained any bit of it yet, and none would do. This Stairmaster was hers alone. Cathy looked at Dale, who pinched her skimpy bottom. He really did love her. "Try it," he urged, looking pleased with himself.

She stepped onto the paddle-like pedals. Immediately the monitor, sensing her presence, leapt to life, flashing red with excitement. Who was she? What was her age? Her weight?

What was her level of exercise? Her expertise? Her endurance? Did she want to run a manual program, or let the Stairmaster choose a course for her? Did she want to race?

"What do you think? I got the best one. Tell me, what do you think?" Dale babbled.

Cathy nodded enthusiastically, her ponytail wagging as she took her first steps. The machine whirred and the sound was familiar, even in this unfamiliar house. Tears streaked her cheeks, beading like sweat on the Stairmaster.

Dale persevered. "What do you think? Do you love it?"

Cathy opened her mouth, her vocal cords loose with joy, and the sound ricocheted around the cavernous basement with its concrete-block walls, her voice carrying, repeating itself, shrill and nasal, cracking in places, hacked off at the end of her verbs. She had the worst voice most people had ever heard. "Thank you, I love you so much, I want to be with you forever!"

Forever echoed, sinking into the foundation of the house. Her husband took her in his arms. "Dale," she tried to say, but he blew into her mouth so that her empty belly ballooned with hot air and she could only inhale and hold his breath: stifled, overcome, gagging, *loved*.

Dog Days

Mitch emptied his desk drawers of yellowed Richie Rich and Bazooka Joe comics, a bag of multicolored balloons (for water bombs), crumbling rubber bands, No. 2 pencils with stony erasers, dull toothpicks (some with food bits attached to their ends), a cracked water pistol that leaked when filled, and a rock-hard, bug-ridden Rice Krispy Treat. He couldn't remember the last time he had eaten a Rice Krispy Treat. Eighth grade? He prodded the gray block. It was possibly ten years old. Disturbed, a flurry of jet-bead beetles hurried out of their homely tunnels and across his desk.

Don't eat in your room, his mother always said. We'll get bugs. We eat as a family in this house, at the table, never in front of the TV.

"Bullshit," Mitch said, flicking the Rice Krispy Treat under his bed. He had started eating in his room last month. It beat eating with his parents, who talked about work, and Babo, who only hunched over his plate and sucked up his food as fast as he could, then fled outside to skate, or upstairs, locking his door. His family ignored Mitch: he wasn't supposed to be there.

I should be in New York, Mitch thought.

He should be at work, his parents said.

One supper, just before his decision to eat in his room, Mitch had tried to talk to his parents about his documentary, as if to prove he was doing something more than sleeping, eating, and relieving his urges. He meant to make a film about his college years, he told them. It would be an ironic film, of course. Irony was important to his generation. Irony kept them laughing all the way to the bank.

"Ironic? What's ironic about college?" his father had wondered. "College serves a practical purpose. College is an airport runway. You board the plane, fasten your seatbelt, the plane gains momentum, and you take off for unknown parts of the world." He turned to the peas that remained on his plate, rolling them neatly onto his fork with his knife. Mitch thought he had read somewhere that his father's eating habits—food not touching, one food group at a time—meant something about his personality. Eating and shitting, they both meant something, but Mitch wasn't sure what. Something negative, he thought. Mitch hated his father, who was humorless and uptight. His mother he didn't mind so much; she was distant, but could occasionally be drawn to sympathize when cornered during the few minutes she had in the morning before work—that is, if Mitch bothered to wake that early. Both parents worked long days and always had done, his mother pausing briefly, twice, to bear her sons. At home they remained working, discussing clients and cases and the subtle aspects of law. His parents' relationship was long understood to be exclusive of relatives and friends, even their own children, although neither son dwelled on it much, thriving instead on the material benefits, the privacy and safety of the empty suburban home.

"Mitch, this documentary idea you have—is there a market for it?" his mother had asked.

"This isn't about *money*," Mitch intoned dramatically, although he secretly hoped Miramax would pick up the option and make his fortune. "Filmmaking is about my self-preservation. To live, I have to make films, and to make films I need a city to meditate on. You know, like Scorsese. That's why I need to move to New York."

"When I was your age, people couldn't be filmmakers," his father said. "We got married and had children. We worked whatever job we could find. We didn't go to thirty-thousand-dollar colleges. Thirty-thousand-dollar colleges didn't exist."

"Inflation, Dad," Mitch said cheerfully.

"I didn't expect my parents to support me after the age of sixteen. I worked my way through college and law school—"

"I know, I know, in your uncle's hardware store," Mitch interrupted.

His father glared at him. Mitch looked down at his plate and pointedly mixed his peas with long-grain rice and the last of his pork chop, before shoveling in the bite.

"Well, he should at least try, if that's what he says he wants to do. We've always encouraged our sons to pursue their interests," his mother said. "I remember you put on some wonderful plays, Mitch. Do you remember? You had a big imagination when you were a little boy. All your counselors at Camp Mohican said they couldn't wait to see what you did next."

Camp Mohican in the Pocono Mountains had been the summer home of Mitch and Babo from the age of seven until they were fourteen. Mitch remembered only that he had kissed Gloria Stone from New York City, his first kiss. Gloria had nougat-colored skin and the largest breasts he had ever seen on a girl of thirteen. He grabbed at them during a summer thunderstorm when the power blew out, surprised at how soft and flat they felt in his hands—not the wriggling puppies he had imagined, but dandelion fluff stuffed in a sack. He and Gloria groped briefly in the dark of the camp's dining hall, where the campers gathered to sing, and managed to French each other before the lights came back on. Mitch ignored her the rest of the summer, and was surprised to meet her again at Conn College. By then Gloria was ten pounds overweight, attending on Financial Aid. Mitch and his crowd as a rule steered clear of the Cafeteria Kids, as they called them, who served meals and washed dishes for tuition dollars—although he had nearly been one, or so his father threatened after his low first-year GPA, which earned him warnings of academic suspension.

Mitch truly hated the idea of work.

These days he woke at whatever time, ten o'clock, noon, sometimes one or two in the afternoon. Upon rising, he ate a bowl of Fruity Pebbles standing in front of the television, then padded back to his room with a big mug of coffee and a plate of Pepperidge Farm Milano cookies, where he sat down at his desk to figure out the script to his film. The laptop he had demanded for college was already blinking in front of him; it dozed and waked all day, active in spurts, like a dog. Mitch got comfortable in his chair—the tapestry-upholstered wing chair once of the living room and recently cast out by Kim of Elegante—and sipped his coffee, feeling how comfortable he was. If he wanted, he could lean back and rest his head while thinking, or even nap with his computer, as he had found a half-dream state conducive to his creative work (he would wake with a jerk and write down the idea that might change the world).

Mitch tried to focus and visualize his film. What he was going to say to his audience. How he was going to make his connection. What his vision was. He gulped his coffee, ate a Milano, and waited. Old Mr. West from two doors down roared out of his garage aboard an enormous John Deere riding mower and began to cut lanes into his front lawn. Mrs. Diamond drove past in her white Cadillac and beeped. Mr. West raised a quaking, arthritic arm and waved back, keeping his mowing lines steady.

"I'm off to my bridge group!" Mrs. Diamond called out to him.

Mr. West nodded. "Good luck!"

Now here came the Powerwalker with her baby strapped into a stroller, screaming and biting his hands. Around and around Atomic View she went, wearing a Walkman and wagging her bony behind, a beatific smile on her face, her skinny arms rigid against the stroller's weight. Mitch watched her disappear around the bend after Mrs. Diamond's Cadillac, knowing she would stride past another six times, at least. She was trying to stay fit past her sell-by date, he thought.

He dozed, waiting to be inspired. Nothing came. He pushed back his chair, tightened his robe's belt, and wandered downstairs, dragging his hand over the walls as if they might give him something, the wisp of an idea. But the Whites were the only family who had ever lived in the house, and they were an ordinary family.

In the kitchen, Mitch brewed another pot of coffee. Back upstairs he went, the coffee splashing out in drips on the carpet—but he didn't notice. That was Luisa's job.

He sat down at his desk. He drank coffee and read random pages from Bret Easton Ellis's novel *The Rules of Attraction,* a book he had been trying to finish for months. He went back downstairs to the kitchen and posted his grocery list for Luisa, so she would know what snacks to buy him: hand-cooked potato chips, French onion dip, cashew nuts, Fritos, Cheez-Whiz. He made a list of friends to call: Steve, Blake, Adam. He would make a trip to New York soon to see them. He hadn't been up since the New Year. Mitch counted on his fingers: January, February, March, April, May. Where had the time gone?

One day he had given himself a manicure. He even retrieved a bottle of his mother's nail polish, a humble, dusky pink color, from her bathroom cabinet. After struggling with the tiny brush, he began to chip at the glops studding his nails. He spent the whole afternoon picking, filling his keyboard with plastic divots so that when the May sun rose and glared through his window each day, the keys of his laptop stuck. He needed a new computer, anyway. Mitch thought he might get one for his birthday. On June 26—just a month away—he would be twenty-four.

The thought depressed him and he cleared it from his head immediately, turning back to the window instead.

Mr. West was still riding up and down his lawn, mowing careful stripes. The Powerwalker whizzed past, her baby finally fast asleep and nodding. Mitch heard Babo come in and slam doors—the back door, the refrigerator door, his bedroom door, his closet. Luisa was vacuuming downstairs. Mitch couldn't work with all the noise. Besides, he should call Steve to discuss visiting the city. What time was it? Mitch hunted around the room for his watch, which had been missing for months. He gave up and went downstairs to the kitchen clock. It was already four.

Where had the time gone?

Upstairs, he stood outside the door to his room. No, he just couldn't face the blank screen—Mitch ran downstairs (his bathrobe open to reveal a grubby pair of underpants), through the kitchen, into the garage where he grabbed an old soccer ball. What next? He had an impulse to exercise, to do something with his body. He had drunk too much coffee, he thought. Mitch bounced the ball. It sank, dying on the concrete floor with a hiss. He rummaged around, found the old bicycle foot pump, and filled the ball. Now it really had bounce—he walloped the ball against the wall. It whizzed back, nailing him on the crown of his head so that his eyes crossed with the pain. He was blind, goddammit! Mitch heard the ball settle in the floor drain as he felt his way back into the house and upstairs, where he lay down. He felt sick to his stomach. His head ached. Sleep was the cure for him, and it was automatic.

He woke to the bang that was his father's car running over the soccer ball, hard and proud with fresh air.

"Babo!"

In bed, Mitch smiled the crooked smile he had often smiled as a boy, watching Babo scurry to hide in the laundry chute, small enough to slip out of reach and hold himself there indefinitely while his brother confessed his crimes, lying if need be.

"Babo!" His father was in the kitchen and something weighty thumped the floor—his fine leather briefcase, no doubt, replaced each year at Christmas when the hinges, stretched by daily overstuffing, began to squeak, an astonishing feat of wear.

Across the hall from Mitch, there was a listening silence. Then Babo's closet door thudded shut on his bong, followed by the "shhh" of an aerosol air freshener. Mitch sat up and reached for his camcorder, eager for what happened next. He heard his father slowly, deliberately, climb the stairs, his belt whistling through its loops—Mitch could almost see his father's rage, his woolly eyebrows purled, mouth a knife slit. With the camcorder rolling, he eased his door open and began to film.

Potluck

Cathy jabbed a fork into the casserole's crackling lid of melted orange cheese and cornflakes, and lifted, so that it came away all in one piece. Underneath was a mess of gray chicken bits and rubbery mushroom slivers in a colloid of soupy cream. Cornflake Chicken, the fat woman had called it, and here was a second Tupperware container of Broccoli Mayonnaise, and a third of Apple Dumpling.

Cathy took all three to the toilet and flushed them away, pushing at the toilet's handle impatiently while the tank refilled. She panicked as swollen cornflakes and knuckle-sized broccoli stalks drifted in the bowl, refusing to disappear. Dale would be home soon. She prodded a lump of dumpling dough, coaxing it down the hole. She didn't want him to think there was something wrong with her for not wanting this food.

Deb had appeared at the front door that afternoon, ringing the bell merrily. "Welcome to Atomic View!" she cried, her cheeks exuberantly rouged, nose slick with grease, chin a pincushion of dark, thick hairs.

Cathy was in the kitchen making her lunch of boiled green peas topped with ketchup, to be followed by three teaspoons of strawberry jam for pudding. She wore the purple Lycra bra top and matching sweat-stained shorts from her morning workout. "Oh!" she squeaked when she answered the door. She tried to cover herself with her hands, as if she were naked.

"Hi there!"

"I wasn't expecting anyone," Cathy explained. "I should change. I'm not properly dressed."

"I'm just dropping these off." Deb offered the Tupperware she clutched with twin pig oven gloves. "Some supper for you and your husband. I know how busy life can be at times like this. Cooking is the last thing on your mind, I bet."

"Erm," Cathy stammered. Do the right thing, she ordered her brain. Make friends. Start today. But the woman was obese! So disgustingly fat she filled the doorway! Short as a stump, as wide as she was tall, her neck coiled in rings of flesh, her back humped with blubber. Even her earlobes were oversized, like pendulous Christmas tree baubles. "I'm—I'm Cathy. Won't you come in?"

"You're really British!" Deb looked at her with enchanted eyes. "You're so skinny! Are all you British gals so skinny? Don't they feed you over there? I'm Deb, by the way. I'd shake your hand, but mine are full!"

"Come in. Right this way, please," Cathy said in the style of a maitre d', retreating into the hallway.

"I know my way around this house," Deb bragged. "I knew the family that lived here before. They moved to Milwaukee. Two cute kids, Howie and Laurie, the cutest kids in Atomic View. They loved my chocolate-chip cookies. I make them with extra butter so they spread out flat and get all crispy." She thumped the front door shut behind her with a swift, surprisingly agile kick. "These houses are all built the same, even if the outside looks different. I should know. I saw them built, every one but the two that went up before ours. Me and my husband Don were the third ones in. We just knew this was the place for us."

"Would you like some tea? I'll put the kettle on," Cathy said, hurrying ahead to the kitchen.

"You'll put the kettle on! That sounds so romantic. You could say anything and it'd come out sounding smart. British people always sound smart," Deb chattered, close on her heels. "Where should I put these? In the fridge? It's my famous Cornflake Chicken, and a side dish of Broccoli Mayonnaise, and some Apple Dumpling. I give supper to all the new neighbors, to help you through the first busy days. I brought it to Dale last year, right around this time, I guess. I think it's great he got married, just great." Deb slid the food onto the gleaming countertop, marring its surface with a shiny streak like a snail trail. Then she plucked the oven gloves from each stubby hand, round and red as match heads, and sat down on a kitchen chair, her buttocks swallowing the seat.

Cathy smiled politely and turned off the burner under the pot of bubbling peas. Her stomach rumbled but she ignored it, grateful for the banana she had swallowed just before the doorbell rang.

"Atomic View," Deb said, closing her eyes as she remembered, "was the first development in Churchtown. That was a long time ago. When I was little, Route 333 was just a two-lane stretch that connected us to Buckburg and Harristown, with lots of farms around. Now there are so many developments, you can't see where one ends and another begins. I know it's not such a bad thing—good for the economy, to have so many families moving to the area. My mother called it progress. She and my dad didn't have a TV until they were in their fifties, and I've got three!"

Cathy was staring at Deb's outfit: hot pink leggings that bunched around her ankles, topped with an oversized Minnie Mouse T-shirt, its sleeves printed with black and white polka dots. Minnie's black disc ears sat astride Deb's zeppelin-sized breasts.

"I've lived in Churchtown all my life," Deb continued, "and in Atomic View since 1968. Just about everyone here is friendly. The only ones that might not be are your neighbors across the street, the Whites. I know I shouldn't say anything, but don't go knocking at their door. They won't let you in. They kept *me* standing in the rain! It's a shame—one of their boys, Mitch, loves my Cornflake Chicken and Broccoli Mayonnaise. He and his brother used to come to the neighborhood barbecues when they were little and Mitch would fill his plate so that you'd think the bottom would fall through!" Deb hooted with delight.

The kettle on the stovetop blew its whistle and Cathy made tea in the Wedgwood pot she had bought from a Manchester charity shop. It looked like an heirloom, like something her mother had handed down to her, and Cathy pretended it was. "Milk?" she asked.

"And sugar," Deb said, watching Cathy carefully. "Two

scoops. A little bit more than that. Well, you're unpacked here, I'd say. Looks like you're a pretty good housekeeper, too," she said, regarding the new appliances all in a row, ready to go to work, the gleaming pots and pans, the smudge-free refrigerator door as yet un-decorated with magnets and postcards. "I don't mind my own mess. I'm happy as a pig in a pen, I always say."

Embarrassed, Cathy tried to think of something to say. "Biscuit?" she asked. Last night Dale had driven her to the supermarket, where she filled the shopping trolley with food she didn't recognize: Marshmallow Fluff in a jar, lard-dipped crisps—no, potato *chips*—low-fat cheese in a squeeze tube, Pop-Tarts, chocolate-chip biscuits, Cap'n Crunch, Lucky Charms, orange juice with bits of calcium, and plenty of vegetables and chicken—the only food she would eat.

"What?"

"A biscuit with your tea?"

"Like a dog?"

"What?"

"A dog biscuit? Like a dog eats?" Deb looked worried.

"I mean a cookie," Cathy said uncertainly, pleased all the same to use the silly foreign word. Had she said it right?

"Yes, please," Deb said enthusiastically. "I never turn down a cookie!"

Cathy retrieved the biscuits from the cupboard and handed them straight to Deb, who ripped open the package. Should she have put them on a plate, Cathy wondered? But it was too late: Deb had already removed three, inserting them whole into her mouth, one after the other, like coins into a slot machine. "My Don loved these. He passed away," she said through a mouthful.

"I'm sorry to hear that," Cathy whispered.

Deb swallowed. "It was years and years ago. He was killed in a car accident. I was just a baby, twenty-one years old—about your age, I guess. Of course, I never remarried. I've been a loyal wife to Don all these years."

Cathy smiled apologetically, she hoped.

"Aren't you going to have one?" Deb demanded, shoving the slippery cellophane package into her hands. Cathy hesitated—carefully she selected a biscuit, one with the least number of visible chips. She forced the treat down her throat, then sat on her hands, feeling the backs of her thighs for cellulite; the biscuit, she was sure, had immediately settled like sludge in her lower regions. Despite herself, Cathy craved another, but sitting on her hands stopped her.

After slurping every last drop of tea, tilting back her head so that Cathy could see her Adam's apple surface like a dorsal fin in the sea of flesh, Deb put down her empty mug. "I know this house inside out, but I'd love a tour anyway, just to see what you've done with the place."

Cathy led the way down the hall and into the living room where, along with the usual sofa, coffee table, and La-Z-Boy recliner, her Stairmaster stood in pride of place in the front window, its black handles wiped of sweat, pedals suspended mid-step, a white towel draped to dry over the monitor's face. She had persuaded Dale to bring the Stairmaster upstairs (the basement frightened her, being lonely, dark, and damp—how she remembered England), and he promised to buy her a telly and video (her own; he had a combined unit in his den) to liven up her exercise time. So far he had promised to buy Cathy a car, a diamond ring, a telly, and a video.

"What is that thing?" Deb asked, a suspicious look on her face.

"My Stairmaster," Cathy answered proudly. "Dale bought it for me. At the gym in Manchester they had one, but there was a twenty-minute limit on using it and they were really strict. Sometimes I went twice a day just to get my hour in. Now I can Stairmaster whenever I want, for as long as I want. I love it." It was the most Cathy had said since she could remember, and when she finished she looked surprised.

They moved through the house, Deb huffing on the stairs, exclaiming over the bare rooms. She didn't like to see a house looking so new, although she had seen them all this way at one time or another, every house in Atomic View (except the Whites', of course). She even wanted to see the bathroom, where a hardened ooze of toothpaste crawled around the sink bowl and pubic hairs swarmed on the tile floor, making Cathy blush that she hadn't wiped up after Dale.

"Well," Deb said when they descended the stairs and stood in the hall, the front door open to the hot day. "If you need anything, I'm just around the corner. I wrote my address on my Tupperware so you can bring it back to me, and I'm happy to give out any recipes. Most people ask. Oh, my oven gloves! They're in the kitchen."

Quick as a blink, Cathy had retrieved the two little grease-stained pigs. Deb slipped them on and waved good-bye, making their mouths open and close. "Welcome to the neighborhood! Bye for now!"

Cathy shut the door and leaned against it, breathing hard. She stamped her foot. "Fat fool! Silly cow! Stupid moo!" She raised her fist and shook it—she wanted to punch something. She thought of Deb wheezing up the stairs on wobbling haunches, pausing halfway to catch her breath. How could she let herself go like that? She obviously had no self-control. She worshipped her own belly, the lazy beast. It was shameful, the way she must eat! Cathy's heart battered her breast and she caught her wrist to count her pulse: 150, aerobic level. She strode into the living room and lunged for her Stairmaster, sprinting all-out on manual at Level 7 for twenty minutes, until she tilted back and flew off, landing with a thud on the carpet . . .

The smell of savory hot food woke her. Where was she? A flat field of goldenrod stretched as far as her eye could see, broken up by the polished trunks of trees, above which a smoky industrial tower rose monolithically. She caught another whiff of cooking—Cathy sat up in her new living room, with its wooden-footed furniture spaced squarely around the gold-colored wool-blend carpet, the Stairmaster looming over one shoulder. She struggled to her feet and followed her nose down the hall. She would eat it all. Her lunch was just delicious, she could tell!

But her lunch was cold on top of the cooker; it was Deb's food that smelled so good. Deb's buttery, cheesy, sugary, creamy, oozy food. Cathy rushed for the toilet with the Tupperware. She jabbed a fork into the casserole's crackling lid of melted orange cheese and cornflakes and lifted, so that it came away all in one piece. The toilet tank gurgled and

Cathy flushed, then flushed again. Hurry, hurry! Dale would be home soon, tweaking the waistband of her purple Lycra shorts, dragging her down on top of him on the floor, his hands pulling her apart and always, always something in her mouth—his tongue, his fingers, his willy, her heart.

The Atomic View Diet

She put on the weight after Don died. Before Don died, she was petite. Petite—that was her size in the shops. Don called her Bug. Don was big and strong, a football player and a wrestler who carried her around with one arm, propped on his hip. He could palm her head. Deb sat on his lap like a baby and he called her Baby Doll and Little Honey. He had easily carried her over the threshold when they moved into Atomic View, then straight upstairs where he chucked her underarm on the bed (it was just a mattress on the floor then) like he was throwing a softball. When they lay together, head to head, her toes reached his knees, her fingertips his elbows.

After Don died, she got so skinny she might have died herself, hibernating like that, but her mother came and woke her up. Her mother fixed the best lunch Deb ever had: warm egg salad with plenty of mayonnaise sandwiched in Wonderbread, Cheez Curlz on the side, and a glass of iced chocolate milk with a scoop of vanilla ice cream floating on top. She ate seconds, then thirds, before they drove off to the supermarket where Deb stocked up on food, using two shopping carts. On the way home they had to stop at Friendly's for a Jim Dandy sundae served in a fish bowl.

Deb's tongue dripped, seeing the eight scoops of chocolate and vanilla and strawberry ice cream, bright blueberries and strawberries in their jammy sauces, hot fudge, caramel, banana, whipped cream to the ceiling, and a cherry on top with its stem stuck out like a feather in a cap. She hadn't had a Jim Dandy since she was a little girl, when her dad had to help her finish. Now Deb scraped the bowl and wished aloud for another one.

Her mother laughed, happy to see her daughter so recovered. "You'll be sick."

"I'm hungry as two men. I need to fill up," Deb replied. Her taste buds had stirred to life again, like sleeping volcanoes, and her gut rumbled with pleasure. "Do you hear me purr?"

Back at home, she mixed together some brownie batter before she put the groceries away, then paced in front of the oven, having licked the bowl and spoon clean. To keep herself from diving in and eating them raw, she vacuumed the hallway and stairs until the timer went off. The brownies looked sun-baked, riddled with craters and cracks, perfectly done. Deb sped the cooling process by placing the pan in the fridge, before she ate the whole thing with a gallon of vanilla ice cream and Hershey's syrup.

Her days were hard that year. Some mornings Deb woke and didn't remember at first that Don was dead—just like when they were newlyweds and she jumped awake at the sight of the sleeping giant beside her in bed. Mornings she did remember, she would quickly think of breakfast before she started to cry, and the thought of food took Don off her mind. In wintertime she ate hot cereal cooked in milk with butter and brown sugar, and in the summer, scrambled eggs, buttered white toast, and home-fried potatoes with apples and onions, or strawberries sunk in real cream (when they were in season), and for a long time she drank hot chocolate with marshmallows instead of coffee.

For lunch Deb ordered pizza, or she drove to George's Sandwich Shoppe for a Philly cheese steak with extra Cheez Whiz and fried onions, and throughout the afternoon she snacked on Little Debbie's Snak Cakes (Devil Dogs, Peanut Butter Logs, Oatmeal Crème Pies, Star Crunches, Fudge Rounds, Nutty Bars, and Swiss Cake Rolls) while she watched her favorite soaps and talk shows. For dinner, Deb made casseroles like her famous Cornflake Chicken and Broccoli Mayonnaise, or maybe Texas Melt with spicy hamburger meat, salsa, and shredded Monterey Jack cheese. She bought family-sized tubs of Rocky Road ice cream and ate big bowls of it with pretzels in front of the TV at night, and every Saturday and Sunday she treated herself to a dozen doughnuts, all kinds, to work her way through before lunch.

Before long she had put on weight, so fast that her body ached in her thighs and hips. Her mother wanted her to diet, dropping by with pamphlets for the Grapefruit Diet, the Scarsdale Diet, the Rotation Diet, and the Cabbage Soup Diet.

"I like being fat," Deb said, laughing her new belly laugh. It wasn't a lie. Deb ate *what* she wanted to eat *when* she wanted to eat it. She didn't get upset to think she had gained a few pounds, and she certainly didn't rejoice to think she had lost the seven pounds she had been trying to lose all her life. She liked her plump, white hands, deft with wrappers and vacuum-paks, perforated box tops and pull-tabs. She liked the softened lines of her face and the pot of her belly that rested, solid as gold, in her lap.

"You're protecting yourself with those layers of fat," her mother said. As a reader of diet literature, she understood the psychology of weight gain and loss. "You're filling up on food to take away an emptiness. You think chocolate equals love. You're scared to fall in love with a man in case you're abandoned again, and if you're fat, they won't ask you out."

"Don died, he didn't abandon me," Deb said, winding the skin of a caramel pudding around her spoon. "It wasn't his choice to die. I *choose* to be fat."

"Pretty soon you'll be as big as two people. What would Don think of that? He liked you petite. There's nothing petite about you now!"

Deb winced. "Don's not here to see, OK? And there's no way he's coming back. Anyway, look who's talking—you're no Twiggy." Her mother was squat and stocky like Deb, but with an obvious waist she showed off with fancy belts, lengthening the lines of her legs with high heels that hitched up her calves.

"I'm not saying you have to be Twiggy. I'm saying look after yourself, Deb. It's harder to lose the weight than to gain it. A minute on the lips, a lifetime on the hips," she repeated, what she had already stitched into a sampler and hung on Deb's kitchen wall.

When Deb was thirty she weighed two hundred pounds. Last year, her forty-eighth birthday, she had weighed in at more than three hundred. Doctor Greaves warned her to slim down.

"You need to get your heart pumping," he said, sitting back in the familiar, creaking office chair and leaning his head against the eye chart. "Let's talk about setting some basic goals, like walking a mile three times a week."

"I do lots of walking already. I know how to get my heart pumping—I watch Tom Cruise movies," Deb giggled.

"If you keep going like this, you won't live past sixty. You'll probably develop heart disease and have worse back pain than you already have. You'll need hip replacements, knee replacements—you could end your days in bed. And diabetes, that's something to think about. You could lose your feet," Doctor Greaves said seriously, crinkling the worry lines in his yellow forehead.

Deb laughed. "My feet. I can't think when I saw them last."

"I want you to cut back on fried foods and sugar—no more fast food. And I want you to write down everything you eat for week."

"It'll be a best-seller, my masterpiece," Deb joked.

Doctor Greaves huffed impatiently. "Deborah, you have the health of an eighty-year-old man with gout."

"I'm happy just the way I am," she answered. "I don't want to change."

"Skyline Pool has a Ladies' Night every Tuesday. My wife goes there to swim and I want you to go, too."

"I can't swim," Deb stalled.

"I've known you since you were a girl and I remember

you won the eight and under girls' twenty-five-meter sprint when you were seven."

"It was the height of my career as a swimmer. I thought a shark lived in the deep end of the pool, that it was coming to get me." Deb's laugh was like an engine that wouldn't turn over.

"I'm sure you're still a good swimmer, Deborah. Swimming is like riding a bicycle: you never forget how to do it."

"Like sex. Isn't that what they say? But I can't remember *that*, it's been so long." Deb laughed so hard she wept. She covered her face with her hands and howled.

"You don't forget," Doctor Greaves said gently. "Tuesday night at Skyline, from seven 'til ten."

"I remember Pete's Pizza after swim meets," Deb sniffed, drying her eyes with her sleeve.

Doctor Greaves sighed. "No pizza."

On her way home, Deb followed the strip of fast-food outlets that populated both sides of Mother Road from the highway to Atomic View, pulling off into McDonald's Drive-Thru for French fries and two apple pies that she ate as she drove. She hardly noticed the hot apple pie take the skin off the roof of her mouth, and was surprised to find herself parked in her own driveway. Deb reached for the garage door opener with its sticky button, idly brushing her hands on her sweatpants while she waited for the door to crawl through its slow trajectory. The crumbs clung to her fingers. She brushed again. Deb was used to crumbs; she found them everywhere: in her cleavage and ears, in the rolls of her flesh, trapped in the elastic waistband of her underpants, in her bed sheets, and stuck to the shower walls. But these crumbs were different, tenacious. These crumbs kept coming back. Deb brushed. The crumbs remained. She brushed again. Crumbs, in dark uniforms, snaked up one arm and down another, crossing from seatbelt to window to cover the pane in an anti-frost, a black frost in meandering patterns. Deb screamed. Ants were everywhere in her car.

As she flapped in the driveway, smacking her belly and legs, the children across the street came out to see what the commotion was all about. They pointed at Deb, laughing, calling to their friends. "Ants," she shouted, wanting to explain. She didn't know the children's names. They laughed harder and Deb tried to laugh with them, to make a joke of herself. "Ants in my pants! Ants in my pants," she sang. She shook her fists and threatened the ants with immediate death—especially the ones that trickled down her legs in ticklish streams. Two of the children dropped to the lawn and rolled around, tangling limbs, laughing so hard they couldn't stand, while the others went red in the face, hiccupping. Deb's legs were losing their kick. Her arms flailed limply—she gasped like she was laughing, but she couldn't catch her breath. There was the sound of the sea pounding in her ears, and her muscles cramped. The fear she felt was the same as when the swimming coach threw her in the deep end when she was seven: something unknown was coming to get her, and she realized then that she would swim.

It's All in the Day's Work

Studded black leather belt looped through blue Droors, Independent wallet of black leather embossed with a red Iron Cross and chained to his Droors, black Zoo York T-shirt ("Property of the Zoo York Institute"), black Calvin Klein boxer shorts, mismatched argyle socks, Chaps roll-on deodorant. For his Zoo York team board: Thunder trucks, Spitfire Lock-ins for wheels—fast little wheels for a fast little guy—Reflex bearings, and, stowed in his back pocket, the red Tensor power tool with a three-way ratchet, axle, and kingpin sockets, 318 wrench, and reversible hardware bit.

Babo was geared up to go. He thought of Luisa's home-made guacamole and blue corn chips—his favorite snack when he was stoned—and his tongue surged, liberating the LSD from the tiny square of paper soaking there. Babo sucked the tab until it disintegrated, then sucked down a bong hit, exhaling into the towel. He heard Luisa's soft, slow tread coming down the hall. She paused at his door.

"Babo?" she called, rapping gently with one knuckle.

He didn't respond. He was loading up the bong and chewing a stem dusted in skunk crystals.

"Babo, your mama called. She'll be home late, and your dad has a dinner meeting. She said for you and Mitch to order pizza from Pete's."

As Luisa moved off, he could hear the sloshing sound her slippers made on the carpet, plus other sounds: fibrous, sweeping, pausing, worrying. She was wiping the walls with a damp rag cut from one of his father's shirts. When Babo was stoned, his hearing was acute. When he tripped, his eyesight improved and he could skate any trick as good as pros do. Babo, on drugs, felt invincible, *famous*. Sometimes he imagined a film crew was following him, recording his skating, his bass playing, his dancing, his all-around style. The whole world was watching; they knew he was cool, their man, a skate punk with all the moves. He was headed for Cali—shrimpy Babo looked great on TV! He was an instrument finely tuned, military-precise. His body was a weapon. He was powerful in his short legs and arms, fast and close to the ground, a real artful dodger. He could slip out in the middle of the night and no one heard him leave, so sly was he, his tread light in cushioned DCs, and he stuck with his shadow, clinging to walls and signposts when a police cruiser dawdled on his patch. Babo was fleet, with wheels for feet.

But first he must suck back some bong hits to get himself ready to go. Fuck exhaling into a towel, he thought, blasting the smoke from his lungs. Fuck that. Ain't nobody home to give him grief, and he turned up the music—Dead Kennedys—to ensure that Luisa would leave him alone. His family hated his music. His father called it overloud and repetitive, while Mitch just said it sucked. Who were they to judge? His father clung to his Oldies, and his brother only bought what everyone else in the world bought: fake rock for MTV. Babo, on the other hand, was a passionate listener, his record collection expanding exponentially, plus he bought records, not CDs (CDs fucking *blow*, thought Babo). He bought multicolored and marbled seven-inches and EPs, some with vinyl thick as a Thanksgiving platter, with deep, hungry grooves into which a needle could really sink. Records were carved, inscribed. They were personal, like the music he listened to. Hardcore was music with a message, underscored by rough, buzz-saw guitars played by amateurs—do it yourself, they professed—and skull-crushing, rapid-fire drumbeats. Music to make your heart hammer.

Babo repacked the bong's bowl. One more before he left for Nate's, to bring on the acid. He turned up "Holiday in Cambodia" and chanted "Pol-Pot" along with Jello Biafra, banging his head and flicking his bangs to the chorus. Today his band, Corrupted Image, had practice and Babo was stoked. Then he and Nate would drink a couple of brews and go shred Highland. A buzzing Monday night meant a slow Tuesday—recovery all day at school, more skating after to sweat out the poisons of the night before. Wednesday was half the week over, when he and Nate went on their midnight beer-stealing missions around Atomic View, targeting garages with an extra fridge for family surplus and overflow. Beer took them through the end of the week and the weekend, mostly spent out on the road on their skateboards or in Nate's basement. Kids could do anything in Nate's basement; his parents didn't care. Their house was well worn and outdated, 70s-style, the kind of place where no one worried about ruining the new furniture or chipping the paintwork. Nate's dad had specially outfitted a basement rec room for teenagers, with pinball machine, cable TV, and twin leather couches parked caddy-corner, comfy and deep. Sometimes Nate and Babo had girls over and took a couch each, turning the lights down low and turning up the volume on the TV.

Band practice was in an unfinished room next door to the rec room, C.I.'s amps and drum kit sharing floor space with Nate's mom's washer and dryer. Babo and Nate had insulated the walls with egg cartons, hundreds of them in pink, blue, and green foam, tacked on with staple guns. The Nipple Room, they called it. Tit City. On one wall hung their band banner: a red bed sheet with C.I. emblazoned in black felt Celtic script above two crossed black fists, symbolic of the band's tough punk stance. Tall, good-looking Nate played guitar and sang, with Babo on bass and Gordon, another skater with connections to Atomic View (his girlfriend Maria lived on Cosmos Drive), on drums. Mostly they played Misfits covers, but they had a few songs of their own, "Real Society" and "Change of Hate" and "In My Eyes":

"You always have to stare at me
Because I'm different, am I weird?
I don't conform to society
And that's the reason I am feared."

Corrupted Image had played out once at the Churchtown fire hall, and skate punks and punk rockers from all over the county came to the show. That's where Babo met Heather, a tiny girl with dyed-black hair and cobwebs sketched around her eyes. She was just his size. Girls were the best part of being in a band. They waited after the show and begged for Babo's wet T-shirt or Nate's guitar pick. It didn't matter how good or bad they played; the point was they were onstage. It made Babo feel tall.

Babo called Heather (who scrawled her number in black eyeliner on his thigh) and they hung out in Nate's basement one day after school, playing pinball and drinking vodka-Cokes while her friend—her ride—fooled around with Nate upstairs. Babo called Heather again and they had sex on Nate's couch, his first sex. He was grateful, feeling pangs of love for Heather, for her gingery pubic hair mismatched with her head-hair, her pale, almost invisible eyelashes and brows that disappeared on pink skin. He loved the way she stood up, straightened her skirt, found her underpants in a ball in the corner of the couch, stepped into them, then tossed the expertly knotted condom into his lap and walked out without looking back. *Punk rock*, he thought. He had found his pint-sized punk-rock dream girl.

But when he called her later that night, and again the next day, she wouldn't take his calls—or any day after that. Babo never spoke to Heather again. He heard she started going with a senior basketball player from her high school, a towering center, star player of his team. She wasn't punk; she had just been playing dress up, and now she was probably wearing pink lipstick and white sneakers. Babo was crushed. He undertook a particularly murderous kickflip frontside boardslide on one of Highland's long curved rails and cracked open his head. Punk rock, Nate said. Babo felt stupid.

Fuck girls, he thought. Girls sucked, especially Nicole, who called him names—Baby Boy was the worst for Babo— and, like Heather, chose jocks. Babo was a skatepunk. Live to skate and skate to live, that was his motto. As such, his life was very simple: two pairs of jeans, three pairs of shorts, nine T-shirts, two sweatshirts, three pairs of sneakers (DCs, the only kicks for skating), two skateboards, a bass guitar, a computer, hi-fi, and the hunting knife and German Luger he hid under his mattress. He went to school on weekdays, skated every afternoon after school, and got stoned as often as he could. At midnight, Babo skated again, mostly with Nate but sometimes alone. He liked Mother Road when there were no cars around and he could skate straight down the middle of its two lanes with all the speed he could muster, like a sprinter, sometimes hurdling moon shadows that gathered in slow, foggy mounds or raced him, de- pending on the breeze. Mother Road was too busy and risky by day, with a narrow, gravel-laden shoulder on which his skateboard's wheels skittered, or a car might swerve and swipe at his butt—what served as his bumper—and there was always a fresh litter of local road kill to avoid: mangled cats, baby foxes with flattened heads, squirrels with their guts squirted out in ketchup-colored trails.

Babo hid his bong in the closet. He sprayed his room (painted black last year, floor to ceiling, much to his satisfaction) with disinfectant and pulled the door shut behind him. He paused in the hall, sniffed twice, and lis- tened. All clear. On his way downstairs he heard Luisa in the kitchen, singing along with the Spanish radio station, her slippers shuffling on the linoleum. Babo left by the front door, his skateboard hooked in one hand, bass guitar in the other, thus avoiding the housekeeper, who sometimes acted like his mother, smoothing his hair, offering him food or a clean T-shirt. He crossed the lush front lawn, leaving his footprints in the mist rained down by sprinklers every afternoon at four. The acid leapt from his throat to his teeth and bit through the enamel to the root. Babo grimaced. It was the strychnine that did it, what they used to cut the acid. This was MIT acid, printed with rats, the very best stuff, and he paid extra for it—but there was always strychnine, no matter how good. He looked at his watch: only twenty minutes since he dosed. Normally a trip took forty-five minutes to set in, but with Babo it was half that time and he tripped twice as long, because he was so small.

Nate took one look at him and said, "You were fucked up last week at practice, Babo. Why can't you wait until the weekend like everyone else?"

"I'll dose at the weekend, too. I love this stuff."

"You'll go insane if you're not careful. I told you about my cousin who tried to eat his way out of a jail cell on acid. He didn't have any teeth. He ate baby food. They had to build a whole new mouth for him. He was all gums, man, like an old person."

"Dude, that's a ghost story. Don't tell me that shit now. You'll mess up my trip," Babo said, worried.

"It is so for real," Nate insisted. "I saw him at Thanksgiving. He could only eat the mashed potatoes and peas. You couldn't understand a word he said."

"I don't believe you."

"You don't believe things that are good for you."

"Acid is good for me. It keeps me happy. Don't you want me to be happy?"

Nate didn't have a chance to answer before Gordon banged his kick drum. "Let's roll! Some of us have better things to do."

"Pussy-whipped!" Nate snarled at him. Gordon growled and raised his drumsticks menacingly. "Plug in, dude," Nate snapped at Babo, who was watching a miniature helicopter—or a droning, dying fly—circle his head; this acid was powerful stuff, more visual than he had hoped for. "We'll start with 'Avon Lady.'"

On cue, Gordon knocked the wall behind him. "Avon calling," he said sweetly, his voice twisted up high. Then he, Nate, and Babo plunged into their music of outrage, wrathful lullabies for likewise pissed-off peers, implicating parents, police, the Pope, passive consumers, KKK members, wife-beaters, dog-kickers, and schoolteachers.

Within minutes, however, Nate strutted over to Babo's amp and ripped out his power cord, flinging it to the floor. Gordon hurled down his drumsticks and kicked his drum kit over. Only Babo played on, his eyes closed, right foot beating irregular time.

"You suck! You can't fucking play, asshole!" Nate was in Babo's face when he opened his eyes.

"I'm fine," Babo said. "I was playing fine."

"No, you weren't playing fine. You were out of time. You're supposed to be the backbone of the band. The bass player is the backbone of the fucking band!" Nate pushed Babo so that he sat down hard. Babo popped up like a Mexican jumping bean, threw off his bass (letting the guitar drop to the floor with a crash of discord), and brought out his diminutive fists.

"Adios, idiots," Gordon called as he walked out. Band practice was over. Nate thrust at Babo's gut. Babo looked at his fists and willed them to fight. His knucklebones rippled with power, the undulating bones like cresting waves, distracting him—the movement had to be repeated over and over, each time a thrill to watch, a *good visual*. He unballed his fists to study the equally fascinating creases in his hands. Here was his lifeline; now how long did he have to live? He ran a rough fingernail along the line, tickling himself. A girl in his Economics class had read his palm once and told him that he would live fast and die young, "like Jimmy Dean," she swooned.

Nate still stood his guard, ready to brawl, despite that their argument had unraveled and Babo was now busy pulling his fingers like Christmas crackers, making the joints pop. "I give up," Nate said, stalking next door. He turned on MTV, loud. "It's no use trying to play with you. You suck. You're a total asshole, a total loser. Get out of my basement."

Babo, his knuckles cracked into silent submission, was drawn to the sound of the TV. He followed Nate next door and stood right in front of the screen, watching intently, his eyes glassy and wide, the pupils reflective. "Shove over, Babo. I can't see," Nate complained.

"Shove over, Babo. I can't see," Nate complained.

"I'm learning about this stuff. These animals. You're the one who's so concerned about my brain. Let me learn."

"Your teeth. I'm concerned about your teeth because my cousin broke his teeth. Don't you ever fucking listen to me?

Anyway, it's my house. You have to do what I say," Nate whined from his corner of the big leather couch.

"It's my house as much as yours, dude. I'm here all the time. I'm going to live here one day. I'm going to buy this house from your parents and I'm not going to change anything." Babo retreated to the opposite corner of the couch and curled into a small, sleek ball. He unclenched his jaw, which had stuck. He wanted to sing along with the jingle for the breakfast cereal being advertised, but he sang a different song, half-remembered from his Mohican days: "I'm a little hunk of tin, nobody knows what shape I'm in, I've got four wheels and—" And what? "Honk, honk, rattle-rattle."

"Shut up, Babo," Nate said, bumping up the TV volume.

"Honk, honk—" No, that wasn't it. He wanted the cheer-leaders' chant from last Friday's pep rally: "U-G-L-Y—You ain't got no alibi—" but that *still* wasn't it.

Nate pressed the volume button again, while Babo concentrated. What was it? What did he want to remember? There was no need to get upset—but he was sweating, fretting. Mind over matter. Push the bad stuff out of his head. Let the acid work its magic. Nate's toothless cousin didn't exist. Please, just let him laugh right now, let him have good thoughts. "I'm bugging," Babo declared. "Got to get out of here."

"Let's drink some beer," Nate suggested.

"Let's just go. We can bring the beer with us to Highland," Babo said, grabbing the remote control from Nate's hand and smashing the off button. The sudden silence of the windowless room was as oppressive to Babo as its noise. "Come on, let's go. I want to go, Nate."

Nate shook his head. "No way, man, too many cops. Think of my cousin. If they catch us, you're fucked."

"Your fucking cousin! I don't want to think about your wasted fucking cousin!" If Babo didn't get out of Nate's basement that instant, he would never leave. His energy would drain from him, the acid heavy in his limbs like—like *formaldehyde!* Like he was dead.

"Dude, I'm telling you, you don't want the cops nabbing you for underage drinking when you're on acid. We'll drink the beers here," Nate was saying as he went to the minifridge.

"Give me one," Babo said through his clenched jaw, laced up tight with strychnine again. He splashed beer on his teeth, spattering the floor—but the few drops that seeped through to his tongue had an immediate loosening effect. Babo relaxed as the devil passed like a headache. He and Nate chugged their next beers, the way they had practiced, then retied their DCs, belching prolifically as they bent. They took the basement stairs two at a time, Nate in front, Babo hanging onto his rippling white shirttails—what were light trails to him. Midflight, he overtook; at the top of the stairs he could see a burning source, a pane of bright May sunlight, and rushed past Nate to break through first.

"Ah!" Babo was outside. All was right with the world. He was soaring again, and on his skateboard he would go higher. He would ollie the sinking sun. Skating on acid felt like God.

He and Nate lit cigarettes they dangled from their lips,

then took off for Highland, wheels thundering past fathers
tending lawns, children with baseball bats and kick balls
and soccer goals, mothers in gardening gloves. Cut grass
sweetened the air. A kite like a comet cut a figure eight,
then swerved for the telephone wires, narrowly escaping
before it crashed down to earth. Babo, so full of joy he
thought he might burst into flame, began to sing, the song
he had wanted to sing all along:

"All night long I can't get no sleep
Don't know what to do without the taste of meat
It's that smell that gets me high
I love the feel of your upper thigh
So sit on my face
On my face
Please sit on my face, Stevie Nicks."

Parental Warning: Nudity, Violence, Strong Language

Mitch crouched, listening to his parents discuss his case. By chance he had overheard them on his way to the kitchen for a snack of something sweet, and silently withdrew—barefoot, as usual—to the unlit stairs, where he could hear and see without them knowing.

"There's nothing for him to do here," his mother said, then hesitated. Mitch felt hopeful; there was something in her tone that made him think she might suggest they send him to New York after all, like they had sent him to Camp Mohican year after year.

"I won't back down on this, Eileen. He needs to take responsibility for himself."

"I think he needs help."

"With what? We've helped him enough."

"He doesn't know what he wants to do. Maybe there's a course he could take. Maybe he needs a career counselor."

"What's with this movie business? He can't be serious."

"I know," his mother said, sounding worried. "I think it's a fantasy. I don't know where he got such a crazy idea. Fantasy, pure fantasy."

Instead of hopeful, Mitch began to feel uncomfortable,

embarrassed, then angry. How dare they? What did they know what he could or couldn't do?

Mitch had a sudden inspiration: tape the scene. Record it for his reference; he could use it one day to *get* his parents. He would show them! Record it for his documentary—expose his parents to the world! He crept back upstairs, grateful for once for the wall-to-wall carpet, and retrieved the camcorder, then returned to his post. He was still sitting there an hour later when Babo came home tripping his face off. Mitch filmed as Babo strolled into the living room where his parents sat with their papers and drinks, and saluted them, his eyes spinning like disco balls. His mother asked for a goodnight kiss and, when he kissed her, she held his face with both hands, sniffing his breath.

"Jim," she called to his father. "He's been drinking. Look at his eyes."

His father looked up and nodded. It was ten o'clock. He was tired, ready for the day to be over. Babo closed his eyes and held his breath as his father put his head down and resumed reading the paper.

"It's a school night, Babo," his mother lectured. "What are you thinking?"

"I had a beer at Nate's, that's all. One beer. His dad said we could." When he wanted to, Babo could look even smaller than he was, more like four feet tall than five. Now he hunched his shoulders, sucked in his stomach, and shivered pathetically, knocking his scarred knees.

"I wasn't born yesterday. Now tell me how many beers you really had," his mother demanded, squeezing his face.

"Get off! You're hurting me!" Babo twisted free and ran out the room.

"Babo!"

"Let him go, Eileen. Not tonight, please," his father said, his voice weary and flat.

"We'll never get control if we let him walk all over us!"

"What do you want me to do about it?"

"Go after him! He needs discipline. He's fourteen—he shouldn't be drinking in the first place, and certainly not on a school night!"

"I'm tired, Eileen. Give me a break. I've had enough for one day."

She glared at Jim. "Babo, come here this instant!"

His mother's voice only gave Babo steam. "I've got to get some sleep," he called back, having reached the stairs. "I have a test in the morning."

"Great. He has a test. *Do* something, Jim," she pleaded, but his father only grunted.

Babo nearly kicked Mitch as he rushed past. "What the fuck are you doing, loser?"

"I'm filming this scene of family strife for my documentary. It's called 'Monday Night Football,'" Mitch said, aiming his camcorder at Babo. "Say something. You'll go down in history. I'll make you famous."

"Get a life." Babo looked at his brother with an expression of pure hatred.

Mitch whispered "acid freak" into the camcorder's microphone.

"Shut the fuck up," Babo said, and this time he did kick Mitch, square in the thigh.

Mitch groaned. "I'm telling," he said, grabbing at Babo's fleeing feet. "I know what you're up to, Babo!" But his brother was already gone, locked in his room, the stereo on at top volume. Mitch smelled the bong's explosion of smoke and heard Babo cough, then he was on his skateboard on the bed, practicing tricks. The skateboard clattered to the floor and Babo thudded after it. Luisa told Mitch that Babo wet the bed last weekend, and the week before he had puked in his bathtub, leaving the mess for days. He kept a gun and knife under the mattress. She was scared of Babo, she said.

"Don't tell my parents," Mitch had warned her. He wanted to be the one to tell. He would choose his moment carefully, for total effect. Maybe he would film that scene as well.

Hearing his mother stir from her chair in the living room, saying she was going to look in on her sons, Mitch, too, retreated to his room. Then, with the door locked and lights off—pretending to be asleep—he lay down on his bed to replay the tape on the camcorder's monitor. Not bad, not bad, he thought. When Babo kicked him, the shot went haywire, an authentic touch. Satisfied, he rewound further back, to a scene he had replayed countless times over the last two days: the Loser's girlfriend exercising. He watched her swing her hips, ponytail a spray of yellow fireworks shooting off above her head, her blue Lycra bra top and shorts tie-dyed with sweat. How did a nerd like the Loser— a skinny, scrawny, red-haired geek who drove a Taurus like it was a Lexus and eagerly greeted his neighbors, inserting his finger into a baby's fist to shake even the littlest hand,

acting like Atomic View was the height of the social world—
get a girl like her? What did she see in him? Mitch imagined
sliding his tongue over her soft, damp skin, firmly flushed,
a necklace of sweat at her throat. His mouth watered with
her salt. Her legs swung open to him as if on hinges. He
imagined he could charge across the street, ring the doorbell,
and take her right there in the hall. She would throw her
arms around his neck, caress his brow, kiss his eyes, lick his
lips, then attach herself to his earlobe. The words were more
breath than voice, more touch than sound: "I'm yours."

Mitch stood over his bathroom sink, underpants dragged
to his knees, watching his face as he worked himself to
climax, controlling his expression even as he came, a hard,
cold gaze he copied from porn movies. When he was done,
he ran the faucet and rinsed the sink bowl, then washed his
hands, dried them, and pulled up his underwear. In a minute
it was like nothing had happened.

And nothing, Mitch thought, nothing ever did happen in
Atomic View.

Ladies' Night

Monday night was NFL at Brandi's Tavern with her best friends, Ali and Jo, and their husbands, Joe and Chris (during the off-season they watched baseball, everyone wearing red Phillies caps). Tuesday night was Ladies' Night at Skyline Pool. Wednesday night was bingo, with a fifty-dollar cash prize to the big winner and grocery coupons, decorative pocket packets of Kleenex, or some grassy-scented Jean Naté Bath Splash for all participants. Thursday night she stayed in for the best TV of the week, gabbing on the phone to Ali or Jo during commercials. Friday night was Pizza Night at home with her friends, when they all gathered in Deb's kitchen, already crowded with fluffy stuffed animals. Saturday she visited Maureen at the nursing home, and Saturday night she did her beauty routine, trimming her nails and soaking her feet in Epsom salts. Sunday was Deb's day of rest.

Deb had always stayed in on Tuesday nights, until Doctor Greaves got her swimming. She had to buy a bathing suit of thick black Lycra with a gathered skirt, deep foam cups for her breasts, and a girdle stitched in. Deb didn't bother to look in the mirror to see how it fit. She felt that it covered her parts and supported her enormous bosom and that was enough for her. She hadn't looked at herself, her whole self, in a mirror for years. She just didn't care, or so she thought—but in the locker room at Skyline Pool, Deb suddenly lacked the courage to undress and show her body, to see herself reflected in the eyes of other women, so many of them casually, comfortably naked and chattering together.

Well, I tried, Deb thought, red-faced, stopped like a fireplug in the doorway. Rather than face humiliation in a bathing suit, she would promise Doctor Greaves to walk the circuit of Atomic View three times a week. She would never eat Chicken Lickin' again. She would cut back on sugar and drink eight glasses of water every day to flush out her system. She would do *anything,* just so long as she didn't have to strip down and let the women's locker room feast their eyes on her cellulite, heaped all over her body like meringue. Never, Deb vowed. She had her dignity. She turned to go.

"Why, if it isn't Debbie Martin!"

"Long time, no see, Debbie! Remember me?"

"It must be twenty years!"

Deb stopped short. She knew these peppy, helpful voices, she was sure.

"Debbie, it *is* you, isn't it?"

Deb held her own voice steady when she replied, gripping her towel and clean change of underwear for dear life. "Jane Deer?" Jane had been a cheerleader and homecoming queen of their high-school class.

"Jane Cook. I married Bobby. Five kids," she grinned.

"Remember me, Debbie? I'm Kate Slough—but I married

Peter Buck." Kate was their class president, another member of the homecoming court.

Deb's hand sweated into her towel. She felt like she needed some fresh air.

"Do you live in Churchtown, Debbie?" Jane asked.

"In Atomic View. The last twenty-eight years. I married Don Foster."

"Oh, but isn't he dead?" Kate said.

Deb nodded and looked down, huffing nervously. She inched backwards, reaching the door—she could feel its steel handle digging into her flesh like a knife in her back. Damn Doctor Greaves! What kind of setup was this? She couldn't bring herself to look at her old classmates, but stared at the concrete floor instead, the tumbleweeds of dust and hair, shreds of toilet paper, the Band-Aids plastered here and there, straddling cracks as if they might hold them together.

"We live in Crosswinds," Jane said quickly.

"And we're in Briarpatch," Kate said.

"I'm in Honeybrook. Do you remember me, Debbie? We always had science together."

Deb glanced up, then down again. She did remember. How could she forget the most beautiful and popular girls in her class? "You're Maryann." Another cheerleader, captain of the squad.

"Maryann High. My husband went to Garden Spot."

They fanned out around Deb, dressed in practical tank suits of navy blue and aquamarine that were low cut in the leg, squaring their bottoms. They had thickened in their limbs, and sagged in places, but each one maintained what

Deb's mother had called a trim figure. Frosted, blow-dried hair was shoulder-length; every last toenail painted dusky pink. They looked at Deb with friendly eyes directed toward the general vicinity of her face and seemed to overlook that she was overweight.

"You never come to our class reunions, Debbie. I wasn't sure if you still lived in Churchtown," Jane said. "You're not in the database."

"I'm real busy. I'm busy every day. I see Ali and Jo, I don't know if you remember—"

"Of course we remember! Are they coming tonight?" Maryann wanted to know.

"I don't think so." Both had said they would rather stay home and watch TV. Ali would be pouring out her bowls of M & Ms, peanut and plain, a half-pound of each, while Jo went for the microwave popcorn, one bag salted and one bag sweet. Deb preferred an iced sheet cake served in thick slices on a dinner plate with plenty of vanilla ice cream— but that's what she *used* to do on Tuesday nights.

"Bring them next week. We'll have a crowd, just like the old days," Jane said.

"We'd love to see them! It's been such a long time," Maryann added.

"Tell them how much fun we have here. They won't want to miss it," said Kate.

"I haven't even been in the water yet," Deb answered nervously.

"You'll love it, Debbie! Everybody does. Come on, people! Let's swim!" Maryann's strong, vivacious cheerleader call was the same as it ever was and the others nodded enthusiastically, looking at Deb, including her.

"I'll be a minute," she said.

"OK, Debbie! See you in there!" They moved off in a pack, greeting everyone they met. Young or old, fat, thin, stooped or straight, Jane, Kate, and Maryann knew their names—just as when they were in high school and were escorted through the halls by their good-looking boyfriends to a chorus of greetings.

Deb shuffled to a corner of the locker room, as far away from the crowd as she could get. She plopped down on a bench and lowered her head into her hands—already exhausted and she hadn't swum a lap!

"Hurry up, honey, we only have two hours left," a skinny granny chirruped as she passed, tucking her snowy hair into a purple-petal bathing cap.

Deb sighed, reluctantly slipping off her shoes. She slowly undressed, folding her clothes with unusual care and piling them neatly in a locker, until she stood in the black bathing suit and nothing else, her whole body flushed with embarrassment. She smoothed the suit's skirt, hoping to lengthen it to her knees, to her ankles, even. Dark sprouts of underarm hair poked out from their cave—she hadn't thought to shave. She hadn't shaved for years! What about her legs, her bulging, vein-rich, trunklike legs, no doubt a forest of thick hair? Oh, she didn't care, Deb thought glumly, wrapping an old beach towel around her middle as best she could. Grin and bear it, she told herself. She bared her teeth in a savage smile, stepping forward into a puddle of cold water, then another, following these cold puddles around the corner—she couldn't see her feet to avoid them—and through the door to the pool area, where the tiles at her feet suddenly warmed.

The air was steamy, thick with the disinfectant stench of chlorine chemicals, a cocoon of light and heat and dripping white walls sheltered under a glass atrium. The pool itself was L-shaped and painted bright blue, with low and high diving boards in the deep end. Four lanes were demarcated with lines of round red buoys strung like beads; in these lanes women bobbed or sliced their way through the water. A general swimming area bordered Lane Four, and here the water churned like a busy port of call, as swimmers jogged in place or turned somersaults or stood on their hands and scissored their legs.

Jane, Kate, and Maryann were already in the shallow end, cooing as they sank up to their necks, their fluffy hair pillowed above the water's surface. On the count of one, two, three, they dunked their heads, holding hands in a ring, laughing when they emerged again. "The water is so nice tonight," Maryann said, batting water-beaded eyelashes.

"It always is," Kate replied, and everyone around murmured agreement.

Four broad steps led from the tiled deck to the shallow end of the pool, and here women lounged, splashing gently or scooping water they dribbled down their cleavage. Somewhere a radio played tinny classical music and a few moved their heads dreamily and kicked in time.

"Debbie, come into the water," Maryann called. Deb had stalled on the deck, looking on in amazement. She remembered the pool as a rowdy bath full of knocking heads, whizzing tennis balls, and as much hollering as a speeding school bus—not this scene of oasis. Here, everyone smiled and murmured, blessedly friendly, nodding as if they shared a secret. She saw Mrs. Greaves, who waved from the slow lane. Cautiously, Deb waved back and a dozen women waved in response, beckoning her to the pool's edge.

She looked for somewhere to hang her towel. No one else, she noticed, had bothered to cover up, but sauntered out, ready to swim, as Kate, Jane, and Maryann did. A lifeguard, legs slung over one arm of her chair, sensed Deb's distress and pointed to a far wall with rows of hooks. Deb padded over to hang her sorry, ragged towel—there! Her scrap of security blanket was gone from around her waist and she stood all but naked before the crowd. Then, waddling as fast as she could, she reached the pool's edge, grasped the stainless-steel rail, and stumbled on the first step, landing with a belly flop in the Mediterranean-colored surf of the shallow end.

"Oof!" she bubbled, surprised to find herself completely submerged. She was a whale, she thought miserably, making the whole pool roil; no one would like her now—she was trouble. But when Deb popped to the surface, nobody tittered or raised an eyebrow in a pointed, practiced gesture. They just smiled their warm, welcoming smiles, Deb's wake dancing between them like a game of tag.

"The water *is* lovely," Deb heard herself saying in sweet tones as she pushed off on her back. Her skirts blossomed around her, more violet than black in the fluorescent light, and velveteen when wet. She floated easily, turning in slow circles under the atrium, her fat buoyant, weightless for once. She imagined that she was in the middle of the ocean, swimming with shadows in the deep that fluttered from her touch. She looked up through the atrium's glass to the night sky sprinkled with silver crumbs of stars that were, at that moment, twinkling. A full moon shone, flawed like silk, an unlidded eye that watched over her. There was nothing to be frightened of.

Then she was sinking, choking and scrabbling, *panicking* as water flooded her nose and mouth, before Jane dragged her up and set her on her feet again.

"I'm sorry," Deb spluttered. "I don't—" But a fit of coughing ripped upward and anchored in her throat.

Jane put a steadying arm around Deb's shoulder, over-riding her cough. "I understand. It's coming into these waters for the first time. I remember my first night—absolutely startling. It felt like birth, or what birth would feel like if I could remember. You've been baptized, Debbie. It's paradise here," she sighed.

Deb stared at Jane. She had never heard this kind of talk before.

"I like to think of Ladies' Night as a sorority, a sister-hood. Women need to get together! Don't you think so, Debbie?"

"I guess." Deb wasn't sure.

"Say it like you mean it, or don't say it at all," Jane said in her cheerleader voice. "Women should stick *together!*"

"Well, I have Ali and Jo, and they're my oldest and best friends. When Don died, they really took care of me. Is that what you mean?"

"Exactly! Exactly my point, Debbie. Friendship is what

women are all about. You have Ali and Jo, and now you have everyone here, too. We know where you stand, just by coming tonight. We know you're one of us."

"I am," Deb said, trying to sound like she meant it.

"We always want approval, don't we? For our hair, our bodies, the way we dress, the makeup we wear. Women *stare* at each other—we look other women up and down, worse than any man. Well, approval is what you get at Ladies' Night, the right kind of approval, all-accepting, unconditional. There's nothing to fear here, not age or youth or fashion faux pas. Not here." Jane hugged Deb. "Oh, Debbie, we're so glad you found us!"

"Doctor Greaves wanted me to get some exercise—"

"When did movie stars and models become our role models? My husband just *loves* Julia Roberts. He calls her America's sweetheart. It used to be that if I wanted to feel bad about myself—*if I thought I needed to lose weight*—I'd go see a movie starring Julia Roberts. But she's not a real person! I mean, she is, but she's a *projected image*. Everyone goes on about her lips and her skinny body and her beautiful hair, and you know what? I don't care! Because to feel *good* about myself, I come here, where I know women understand each other. Sometimes we just sit on the steps in the shallow end, talking about the things that concern us—pornography in advertising, how many of our teenage daughters are starving themselves. But *never* Julia Roberts. You could say Ladies' Night is our forum."

Deb nodded, dazed. She didn't know what to say.

Jane pointed to a young woman springing on her toes on the high board. "That's Susan Will. She's an accountant here in Churchtown. Every week she's up there, bouncing away until we think she's going to break through the ceiling, she gets so close."

Suddenly Jane dove forward underwater to stand on her hands and wiggle her feet. When she surfaced, she took Deb's hands, saying, "Let's have a tea party," and pulled her to the pool's bottom, where Jane mimed drinking a cup of tea and eating cookies, her pinkie finger crooked. Deb cut herself a big slice of cake while Jane poured more tea, before they shot to the surface for air. "Now I've got to swim off those cookies," Jane said, ducking into a lane. She kicked away with a tidy patter as Deb eased onto her back again.

The high board rattled. Deb watched as Susan Will folded her body into a perfect pike. Her fingertips had seemed to graze the glass of the atrium, an awesome sight.

Deb rolled to her feet and began to bob. In the water she had spring in her step, just like Susan Will on the high board. She bobbed around the pool and others joined her, cooing and smiling, weightless, like newborn babies.

Master

Cathy had a dozen sets of Lycra workout gear, color-coordinated bras and shorts in pastel hues. Stacked in the drawer, they looked like baby clothes, and she washed them on the "care" cycle to keep their softness and brightness. Cathy liked to exercise at least three hours a day, changing between morning and afternoon workouts. She ate steamed chicken, vegetables, and fruit (what she planned to eat for the rest of her life), and she was fanatical about her personal hygiene, bathing daily, moisturizing her skin from head to toe, regularly trimming her split ends with the kitchen shears, lightening her brown hair with peroxide. She had never looked so good, she thought. Getting fit had changed her life for the best. She met her husband, of course! She had fallen in love, left her job, and moved abroad. She had moved to America! She had an *American husband*. Chatty Cathy, who spoke only if spoken to, who answered "Yes" instead of the more fabulous "Absolutely!" and who never had a proper date in her life—she had become the one for whom all dreams came true. Married! With her own house and Stairmaster!

There was no chance of her throwing it all away now.

She would be good. She would stay in shape, keep her mouth shut, and be the best sex Dale ever had; she knew what to do now, and didn't he love it? Didn't he love her? He did. He did!

The night Cathy met Dale, she was wearing her lavender Next suit with a decent blouse and high heels. She knew she looked the nicest of all the girls in their Next suits, with no bulges or tense seams, her jacket's shoulders settled where they should be. Her wrists, peeking from her sleeves, were bony and delicate-looking; her legs tapered to thin ankles, even if she did think her thighs were too big as they spread across the barstool. She always hitched herself to the edge of any seat, so that her muscles dropped in a freefall away from the bone.

The bar air was thick with cigarette smoke, muggy with the central heating turned up high, and Cathy could smell the lavatory. She was with a group from work who ignored her, although they did include her in their number week after week. Cathy didn't mind. She was happy to be out on a Friday night, even with indifferent company. She perched on her stool at the fringe of the group and sipped a champagne cocktail in little nips to make it last longer.

Further along the bar, a group of Americans were drinking beer, looking bewildered by the cutting taste of the dark ale, drinking it fast all the same like it would get them somewhere familiar. Cathy didn't mind Americans. The blaring twang with its nasal resonance—the "wah-wah" her colleagues imitated when recounting key scenes from their favorite American sitcoms—didn't get under her skin.

She had never had a problem with voices or funny accents, except her own, of course.

"Hi."

Cathy clutched her drink. One of the Americans was standing next to her. "Another one?" he asked. His eyes were bold and tugged at hers—look at me, his eyes said.

She smiled shyly and nodded.

"What are you drinking?"

"Caribbean Champagne Breezer," Cathy whispered.

"Fancy drink," he said, winking. He paid with a five-pound note and left the barman a tip.

Cathy stared at the pound coin on the hardwood bar. He must be rich, or ignorant, she thought. No one tipped in England. The American said something and she looked at his straight teeth, the blunt nose with its large nostrils stuffed with brown-red fluff not unlike snuff, then up to his clipped red hair that seemed to want to escape the comb marks etched in bars of gel. He was handsome, she thought, but her colleagues would tease her for talking to a ginger-nut. Cathy didn't care. She wasn't prejudiced like that. People couldn't help what they were born with, and there was only so much you could fix—without surgery, that is. She would have liked something done to her vocal cords, some kind of snip or stretch to sweeten her voice, and definitely bigger breasts, but who could afford that?

In the meantime, a man was a man. Men had approached before, offering her a chair in a crowded bar, or wanting to buy her a drink. The offer promptly accepted, the man would launch into a description of himself, what he did, where he lived, what kind of car he drove, what kind of day at work he had endured, while Cathy gulped eagerly, nodding her head at what she hoped were the right moments; inexperienced as she was in conversation, she couldn't be sure. Sometimes a second drink was bought and the man leaned in closer, his breath making her neck sweat. By then her tongue was limber, ready to race, and she could say her name, that she worked in data entry, and she was a fan of Man City, if she had to choose.

"Sorry?" her new friend would say, his eyes widening. Soon enough he was gone, making his excuses, a girlfriend at home or a meeting with a colleague on the other side of town. In the end, every last one of them went the same way.

"Keep your gob shut or they'll scare off," the girls at her school used to say. "Just snog 'em, know what I mean?"

When she was much younger, her mother had shut her outdoors until she wore herself ragged chasing the filthy river downstream (she would fix her eye on a floating crisp packet and follow it diligently) or cycling round and round the estate. "Go and make yourself tired," her mother said, driving Cathy away with a flick of the dishtowel on her bare legs. Some nights, if Cathy was still talking, she would be locked in her room to "think about *what* she said." She began to understand that it wasn't what she said, but the very sound of her voice that made her mother wild, and Cathy learned to keep her mouth shut.

When she was fifteen, a tagalong at parties, she had trouble. The drink made her talk and she jabbered all night to whoever would listen, sometimes holding their hands to keep them by her side. Cathy found she had so much to say, years' worth—she had a whole book building up inside of her! Until one night she stumbled upon a group huddled around a notoriously cruel boy with an acid-washed face, deeply pimpled and scarred for life. No better off than herself, she had thought, but he had a gift for mimicry that made everyone laugh. He had a way with *voices*.

Cathy kept to herself after that. She steered clear of home and school, roaming the streets of Manchester and its environs, going as far as the bus she happened to board would take her. Mute by choice, she observed the world passing her by. She didn't care if she was included or not, she told herself. Life was something to get through, and then you died.

When she was sixteen, her mother, who had recently married her third husband, turned Cathy out, blaming her for the failure of her previous marriages. Not this time. Cathy could give her mum some peace and quiet, she wrote in a note tacked to the locked back door. "Not my daughter."

Cathy never spoke to her mother again. With no flatmate prospects and nothing to her name but the money in her pocket, she moved into the first of many grubby, musty bedsits and immediately took a position as a data-entry trainee at a marketing firm—work that didn't require her to speak. All day she labored at her desk, while at night, back in her room, she lay as still in bed as she had sat in her office chair, watching the tiny, secondhand television reduce the hours until work again. She would live and die like that, she thought.

She dreamed of her own flat, somewhere she could paint the walls all shades of purple: lilac, lavender, mauve, and the regal hue itself. She would keep a rack of potted plants, talking to them so that they thrived, their leaves reaching out to brush her arm or her cheek as she passed, a vine twined around her wrist as she slept. It wasn't much to hope for, was it? She never dared ask.

Five years Cathy worked, lived in bedsits, watched TV, and generally kept to herself—and then something suddenly wasn't right in her. She woke one morning feeling hot and uncomfortable, too big for her skin, like a sausage roasting in a pan. The feeling wouldn't pass. She feared she would split in two and spill her guts. The next few weeks she wore her Walkman everywhere she went, stopped drinking altogether (although she mostly drank in her room, by herself), and took up smoking for good measure. At night her teeth rattled like she was about to boil over—she woke herself shouting more than once. At work, she typed nervously, making more mistakes than not, her mouth stuffed with tissue. Still she feared the worst was yet to come, when she would lose what little bit of a life she had managed to make for herself. Desperate to keep her job and home, Cathy thought of her mother for the first time in a long time; she longed for some maternal words of advice or support, a pair of welcoming arms, a home to which she could return and hide. Instead, she remembered her mother's words: "Go wear yourself out."

Her first night at the gym, she tiptoed in. At the front desk she handed over her check and received a laminated card in return. She tentatively took the white towel she was offered, standing exactly where she was told until Kirsty, an enthusiastic blonde in a gym-logo thong bodysuit and flesh-colored tights, introduced herself. With Kirsty's help,

Cathy tugged and pushed at the free weights, breathing in and blowing out on the count of eight, then stepped onto a treadmill, catching her shoelace in the moving belt. She winced as her trainer's rubber sole burnt black, a hovering stench that followed her when she climbed aboard the stationary bicycle, on which the noise of her bare skin against the rubber seat sounded like wind. Finally Kirsty led her to the Stairmaster, reverently whispering, "I saved the best for last."

Thus Cathy began her unsteady ascent, palms slick, weak ankles inclined to buckle, but gaining confidence in her steps. By the time her twenty-minute workout was up, she had risen above the person she was when she went in. If anyone had looked closely, they would have seen that she wept as she climbed.

The gym suited Cathy. It was a place where people looked, inspecting every nook and cranny of a body, but rarely tried to speak over the loud pop music to which they beat their arms and timed their legs. Cathy tried to fit in: she cut back on smoking to accelerate her climbing pace; she counted calories and carried a bottle of water at all times; she styled her hair in a sporty ponytail, scraping back her long fringe to emphasize her emerging cheek bones, her lengthening neck. In two months, she dropped as many dress sizes.

That's when she met Dale. His eyes grazed her smoothed-out curves and easy bends, running up her legs, chasing her skirt split all the way. When he bought her a second Caribbean Champagne Breezer, she took off her suit jacket and Dale stared at her breasts through the simple cotton of her white blouse.

"You haven't told me your name," he said.

She took a deep breath. "Cathy," she squawked.

He winked at her again. "You English girls have sexy voices. Can I say that? It's the accent—it drives me crazy. I said to my friend just before I left, 'I'm going to marry the first girl that opens her mouth over there.' He didn't believe me." Dale touched her arm with his hand. "What do you think of that?"

Cathy's heart beat very fast. With the assurance of that one touch—and her accompanying silence—Dale slid his hand around to the small of her back. Then he asked if she wanted another drink.

She nodded. He told her about his flight over from America, how he had flown in business class and the man seated next to him dumped a glass of orange juice down his shirtfront—not on purpose, just an accident, but no one had sufficiently apologized to him yet, and he was going to write to the airline in the hopes of a free ticket. You had to be aggressive in this day and age, to protect your own interests. It was the only way to get ahead in the world of man against big business—and man couldn't afford to lose like big business.

"Another drink?" He was already laying a ten-pound note on the bar, ordering a shot of Jaegermeister for himself in addition to his pint of beer.

After four Caribbean Champagne Breezers, Cathy was solidly drunk. Even her hair felt drunk, having escaped her ponytail to stick to her face in sweaty squiggles. When Dale mentioned his hotel, she followed him without question. In the elevator, he kissed her, sliding one hand between the buttons of her flimsy blouse and using the other to tug at her skirt. The elevator pinged and they fell out into the endless carpeted hall, where white-tented room-service trays marked the rooms of those traveling salesmen less fortunate than Dale, lonely diners out of time zone and away from their wives and children.

Dale slammed his key card into the door and banged it open. With one arm, he tossed Cathy onto the bed—she flew like a feather—unfastening his belt with the shaking fingers of his other hand.

"You're so hot," he said. "I never met a girl as pretty as you."

Cathy pulled clumsily at her blouse, tangled around her arms. She was unprepared for this passionate scene, her first. Of course she had seen similar trysts enacted on the telly and at the cinema, and knew that it would hurt, but she was too drunk to care, or indeed direct her movements a better way. Dale, naked below his shirt, knelt over her, thrusting blindly. He tore at her underpants and their cheap nylon came apart in his hand. Cathy still wore her skirt and most of her blouse when he broke the seal guarded by her strong legs, taking her like a god, crying, "Oh baby!" in a stricken voice. A minute later he was snoring, while she passed out under his weight, oblivious to her throbbing parts. He woke the next hour and they did it again, and every hour after that—"Precious virgin," he whispered when he saw the dark, leaf-shaped stain on the sheets. By the end of the night he had declared his love and Cathy agreed with him.

They soon married in the Manchester registry office, their only witnesses the registrar's secretary and her lunch companion. After the ceremony, they returned to the hotel of their first rendezvous, but Dale was tired, having flown in from America that morning, and he fell asleep over their room-service wedding dinner of roast beef and a bottle of champagne. Cathy abandoned the heavy meal thankfully. She lay down beside him, clasping his curly head, and tried to piece together the fragments of the last few weeks: Dale's airport proposal outside Departures; Dale pressing £100 into her hand "to buy a new dress;" the long weekend they had spent together after they met, mostly in bed, when Cathy had her first sick day from the office and Dale missed his sales conference.

But before all that, before love and romance, she had the Stairmaster, and Cathy would worship it forever in thanks.

Dream Prophet

She had been dreaming strongly her whole life. She always remembered her dreams, ever since she was four years old, when she dreamed she saw a vaporous stranger at the foot of her bed. Deb thought the stranger was real and hid her head under the pillow to make him disappear. No, her mother explained when she screamed, she was dreaming all right, and there were no such things as ghosts. Her dream man had been dressed like the shepherd from her biblical storybook and Deb thought he might be Jesus. To her simple child's mind that seemed possible. She knew enough about the Holy Family to believe that Jesus could visit if he wanted to, especially if he had a message for her to share with the world. Later, when she examined a picture of her grandfather, who had died before she was born, Deb told her mother that it was he who had been in her room that morning. Her mother shivered even as she repeated, "There's no such thing as ghosts."

Deb believed in ghosts and dreams. She particularly believed in dreams, as she thought they told the dreamer something, sometimes even hinting at future events; you just had to learn to read them right. Deb had all kinds of dreams: flying dreams, sexy dreams, anxiety dreams when she resat tests she had failed in school, joyful dreams of her past, playing with the girls and boys she grew up with, her sleeping limbs transformed, potent, able to run, skip, and jump all night. Sometimes in her waking life, Deb felt like she had already done the exact same thing in a dream—*déjà vu*. She laughed, wondering which was more real, her life or her dreams, if both were happening so vividly. But as she inched toward the question of being here, or having been before, Deb stopped; she preferred to leave that kind of thinking to God. She just believed.

Growing up, Deb's mother told her not to talk about her dreams so much. "No one wants to hear about it," she scolded at the breakfast table as Deb scoured her memory, still clouded with sleep, fumbling to explain the previous night's vision. Sometimes when a dream was bad—the worst things she could conjure up—Deb had to stop the dream right there and beat the demon out from under the covers, kicking it clear of the foot of the bed before calling out for help. As a girl, she called her mother to her side; later, with Don, Deb simply had to sweat and he would wake, and he was patient as a man could be, holding her a few minutes, stroking her belly and breasts until she returned to sleep. Her craziest dreams often came in the early morning, when Don crawled from bed into the cold of the house, half-listening to him dress for work, smelling his coffee and Eggo waffles, the radio station tuned to Wink 101's Traffic Command Center. After Don had gone to work, Deb called her mother to tell her about *those* dreams.

With Don and her mom dead, and Ali and Jo protesting

they had heard enough, Deb bought a dream dictionary. From it, she learned that sight of a sailor meant she was bound for a long and exciting voyage, while a whistling sailor was good luck for her. Macaroni meant small losses, when she must economize and be vigilant in her expenses— but chocolate pudding, or any dream with chocolate, was a simple omen meaning good health and contentment. If Deb had hairy hands in a dream she would lie to harm her neighbor and benefit herself; the longer the hair on her hands, the worse her lying would be.

Her dream dictionary didn't say much about dreams of the dead, other than that these dreams often provided comfort for the bereaved. For a long time Deb tried to dream about Don, keeping one eye on their wedding photo next to the bed until the moment she dropped off to sleep. Or she sat by his grave, cloud gazing, listening to the trees shuffle their branches as she dozed against the headstone that read "Donald David Foster, Beloved Husband and Son." Generally Deb was on the lookout for signs that Don might still be active in her life, uncanny coincidences like the shock of one of his socks turning up in the laundry long after he died, or two of his favorite songs played back to back on the radio, as if he had called in and requested them, including "Only the Good Die Young."

Deb had been waiting a year before he came to her dreams, and she was scared when he did, even though it was Don—but a ghostly version of him, like the shadowy, unreal man who had stood at the foot of her bed when she was four years old. She told herself that it was only Don, her Don, whose body she had held alive and dead, as she followed him into the den. He sat down in his old recliner, just like he used to, and she faced him on the couch. The room was dark—it was night-time, real time—and Don glowed so that she could see him more clearly than when he first appeared in the hall; she had no doubt that he could see her as well, given his supernatural powers as a dead person. He smiled and made a sign with his hand like she should talk, indicating that he couldn't speak himself by covering his mouth and shaking his head. Deb asked him questions he could answer yes or no. Was he happy? He nodded. Was it nice where he was? He nodded and smiled. Was it pretty? Was he in heaven? Did he see her parents? Yes, yes, yes. Did it hurt much when he died, and so on. It didn't hurt, he said, shaking his head, which is what the doctor had told her, that he had been killed right off and never knew what hit him.

"Do you know everything?" No, Don said.

Was heaven like a baseball game, with the choir of angels looking on from above, cheering and booing the green below? Was it a field of wildflowers, scented of the most expensive French perfume, and lit by a big yellow sun that shone all the time? Was it ice cream for everyone? Were heaven's roads paved in gold? Did they all drive Mercedes-Benz? Don smiled as if it were so much more—some of her questions even made him laugh.

"I'm glad you came. You're looking good," Deb said, but he didn't look so well as when he had first appeared; he was flickering like an eaten-up strip of Super 8. Then Deb's alarm clock buzzed, and Don was yanked behind the black-out stage curtain that separated night from day.

It was a bad dream, according to her dream dictionary, a very bad dream. Dark rooms meant hardship and loss to come, plus she was upset when she woke: she was alone, when the moment before she had been with Don. Deb lay in bed all that morning, unable to rouse herself even for breakfast, crying as hard as when he had first gone. She vowed not to dream of him again—too painful. But she couldn't control her dreams like she could choose what she ate, and over the years, as she slept, she and Don met at dream parties and a dream prom, passed each other on crowded dream sidewalks, and swam at the same dream beach. It seemed like they were always waving to each other across a distance that Deb couldn't cross, and he wouldn't come to her, no matter how she flirted and called.

Then, suddenly, her Don dreams stopped. She couldn't find him anywhere, no matter where she looked (and sometimes, looking for him, she found rooms in their house that hadn't been there before, glorious, grand rooms that belonged in mansions). Deb began to wonder if he really could see just how fat she was.

These days she mostly dreamed about food—so vividly she often had the taste of sugar in her mouth when she woke—and TV. Her TV dreams were the strangest by far, the first one in particular: it was like she was watching Technicolored television, only she was *in* the television. She was on the program. She was part of a TV talk show with a live studio audience. Deb was a guest on her favorite program, *Mary Lou,* where the many problems facing the nation in the modern age, mostly domestic and sexual, were addressed every day at four—in real time, that is. In her dream, she wasn't sure of the hour.

Mary Lou was a big lady with a resounding contralto voice to match her size. She wore a string of pearls the size of golf balls and a thick layer of orange foundation that stopped at the first of her chins. Her hair was black-lacquered, flipped smartly at its tips, and her mouth was an incandescent red, with teeth white as washing powder. "Welcome!" she boomed over a burst of audience applause. "Today's show is my favorite kind of show, the kind where we do good for the world and everyone gets to feel warm and fuzzy inside. And I mean *everyone:* my studio audience, our viewers at home, but most of all the people I have sitting onstage with me, my special guests." Mary Lou beamed at Deb. Deb, overjoyed to be sharing the stage with such a great and famous lady, an American heroine of self-help, beamed right back at her. Mary Lou drew her chair closer to Deb's. She smelled of Bounce dryer sheets and hand cream—the same kind that Deb used when she went to bed. "Hello, Deb."

"Hi."

"Deb, you're a special lady. I can tell that just by looking at you. Don't you think so?" she asked the audience—entirely made up of brightly dressed women, many of them as big as Deb and Mary Lou.

"We love Deb! We love Deb!" they chanted.

Deb smiled shyly at them.

"Deb, you lost your beloved husband Don. You never had children. Your parents died before you were thirty." Mary Lou rested an oversized, pillowy mitt on Deb's hand.

Her fingernails were polished, set into squat fingertips like rubies in twenty-four-carat gold. "But you have your friends." She turned to the audience. "She has Ali and Jo, and don't we all know you're lucky in this lifetime if you have one good friend. One *good* friend."

"That's right," someone called.

"Deb, we want to introduce you to someone who says she needs you as her friend. She didn't have the courage before, but now she says she's ready. She *needs* to meet you, Deb. Are you ready?"

"I guess I am," Deb had said, but she was taken aback. What was going on? Her dream felt so real—it felt like she would wake and this had happened to her like any real thing. She looked at the audience, who clapped and hooted enthusiastically. Some were on their feet, cheering her on, while a TV camera swooped in to get a close-up of her face.

"Yes, yes!" the audience cried out. "Meet, meet!"

What else could Deb say? It was a dream, and crazy things happened in dreams—but she knew, too, that she could always wake herself if things got bad. She nodded at Mary Lou, who turned with a flourish of wobbling underarm flesh to the curtain behind them that swiftly split. "Come on out, Maureen," she called to the shrunken woman cowed there, turning her face from the lights so that Deb couldn't see who she was.

Maureen scuttled toward them and sat down in the chair next to Deb, still hiding her face behind one arm. She was unnaturally stooped, her mousy hair a mushroom cloud that hovered just above her head. Maureen glanced at Deb, briefly showing herself, and Deb caught a glimpse of protuberant front teeth like Jimmy Carter's (like Chicklets, Deb thought, her mouth watering), a pointy nose that dripped. She quickly turned away again—but there was something familiar about her.

Mary Lou shushed the audience as Maureen curled into herself and tucked her chin to her chest. "There, there, none of that," Mary Lou said, taking her hand. Maureen flinched. Mary Lou patted her hand anyway, talking a mile a minute. "Deb, I think you remember Maureen. You're not sure just yet, but I know you know her. Think about Atomic View and all the people who have come and gone. Think about your neighbors, Deb, and those who have moved on. You keep in touch, sending Christmas cards, don't you? Of course you do. That's the kind of person you are. Who haven't you heard from, Deb? Who's missing from your list? Who did you forget?"

Then Deb did remember: Maureen Parker had lived with her husband Mike in a mint-green rancher on Jetstar Drive. She remembered that Mike drove a Mustang that he hand-waxed every weekend, and that the couple were childless. When they moved, they moved fast—vacating the house overnight, practically, which made the neighbors talk. Deb hadn't had the chance to get their new address for her Christmas card list, and no one she asked knew where to track them down.

"Last year Maureen wrote to me and said she needed my help. 'Mary Lou, if anyone can help me, it's you. I need you to broadcast around the world, to go beyond this physical world into the fourth dimension, beyond the stars, beyond the heavens, beyond *time*. I need you to help me find a family. I'm all alone, Mary Lou. I need help. I don't know what I'll do, but it won't be good.' So I found you, Deb. I found *you*."

The audience was silent, the stage still. Deb skipped a breath, and then another—her heart tripped. Maureen's glassy eyes popped in horror as Deb's lungs lacked and wouldn't fill themselves up again. Something obstructed her throat, something real but not real, like a cut jewel, or a Werther's Original, lodged in the butter-soft flesh of her fat-clogged gullet. Had she swallowed a tooth? In the wide O's of Maureen's eyes, Deb could see her dying self: the gray tint of her skin, head like a water-soaked log. Was she having a heart attack? If it happened in her dream, then did it really happen? Would she die if she saw herself die in her dream, on TV? She was on *Mary Lou*, wasn't she?

Mary Lou gripped Deb's arm and gave it a good shake. "Breathe, Deb!"

Deb slipped from her chair to the stage floor and lay there, paralyzed, like a tumbled tin soldier shot point-blank with a rubber band.

"Breathe," Mary Lou whispered. Her voice was low and resonant as she engulfed Deb in the voluminous folds of her print dress, the plentiful flesh of her lap. Mary Lou's sweet-smelling sleeve drifted back and forth across Deb's face, ever so gently, soothing her, making her sleepy. "That's it, Deb, sleep," Mary Lou cooed. When she was sound asleep again, the show resumed, Deb back in her seat as if nothing had happened, the live studio audience gazing at her, the camera zooming in again.

"Maureen needs a friend now, more than ever before. It's

all so tragic," Mary Lou said, a trickle of tear slipping from the fleshy pocket of her left eye. "Her husband left her two months ago. What friends she had, she shared with her husband, and they're her friends no more. They've shown her no loyalty—no one has proved faithful to Maureen in her life. She needs you, Deb. I won't ask you twice. Will you be her friend?"

Deb looked at Maureen, who looked back at her expectantly; she knew she could count on Deb. Deb took Maureen's hand. Mary Lou beamed and the audience thundered their applause, waking her once and for all.

She hopped straight out of bed and down to the kitchen, where she cut herself a thick slice of carrot cake with double cream cheese frosting. She didn't sit to eat, just pushed the cake into her mouth in three big bites, then cut another slice for comfort, and another for strength, before she reached for the phone book instead of her dream dictionary. By chance, there was a listing for M. Parker in Buckburg, just ten miles south-east.

By the time Deb arrived at Maureen's house the next afternoon, her old neighbor was half-expecting her—that is, she was hoping someone would come and rescue her, take away the drink and give her something to eat. Maureen had been drinking vodka straight for two weeks with nothing to line her stomach or give chase, no toast or tonic, nothing but drink.

Deb drove to her house and knocked at the door like it was natural she should come to pay a Sunday afternoon visit, the way a minister would do. She knew she was in the right place, and it wasn't just her gut telling her: a wooden plaque that read "Parker" in burnt cursive letters swung from the lamppost and a weather-battered pickup truck with a "My Other Car is a Mustang" bumper sticker parked in the yard. When Deb knocked (the bell didn't work), Maureen didn't answer, didn't call out "Who's there?" like it was all a joke. Deb looked in Maureen's front window and there she was, lying on the floor in her nightgown, looking fast asleep except that her leg was kinked at a funny angle. Deb found a neighbor to call 911 and the fire department broke down the door.

Thirty-six bottles of vodka in all were stashed conveniently around the house in various stages of drunkenness, with two more cases stacked up in the garage. Maureen would have died if Deb hadn't come—and in the meantime she drank so much she gave herself a wet brain. She would never walk again. It had something to do with thiamine, Deb learned, like her system needed antifreeze, but it was too late; everything had frozen. Now Deb visited her at the nursing home once a week on Saturdays, giving her all the news of Atomic View. A dream prophet honors her dreams, she promised Maureen.

No Body to Bury

"Mitch." His mother tried his locked bedroom door, forcing the knob. "Answer the door, Mitch."

"Yes?" he croaked.

"It's Dad's birthday. Did you forget?"

"No," Mitch lied. He had forgotten. She could tell he was lying: he answered with the taunting edge she remembered all too well from when he was a teenager and regularly missed his curfew.

"We're going out to dinner. We leave in ten minutes. We're going to DeZing, so look nice."

"I'm not hungry."

"Come on, Mitch. You know your father hates to be late. It's his birthday." Eileen still had the doorknob in her hand and she gave it another twist. There had been too many times she regretted their decision, when the house was built, to fit every door with locks. She and Jim had wanted their privacy; they hadn't thought they would be locked out from the lives of their children!

"If you force me to eat, I might throw up. All over the table, in front of everyone," he added.

"You won't. Now get dressed and downstairs in ten

minutes." Humming no tune in particular, Eileen retreated to her bedroom where she hung up her suit, dropped her shirt into the laundry basket for Luisa to deal with, freshened her armpits with deodorant, and changed into a dress for the occasion, waistless navy blue silk with a white Peter Pan collar. She patted her throat with perfume and ran a comb through her short hair. It was the least she could do, with Babo refusing to bathe or change (despite that he had spent the afternoon skateboarding and had fresh wounds on both elbows and bloody drips down his shorts) and Mitch playing difficult. Thankfully, she had given Jim his birthday presents that morning when they were alone at the breakfast table: a new camera for their trip to Italy—"*Buon compleanno!*" she had written in the card—and three Italian guidebooks, signed in her hand from Babo. Jim had gone off to work in a good mood, kissing her more passionately than usual; he only pulled away when they heard Luisa's husband's Nova rev up the drive.

As Eileen passed Mitch's room on her way downstairs, she heard him moan. She rapped at the door again. "Hurry!"

But when Mitch appeared in the kitchen, he wore greasy jeans and a T-shirt streaked with grime—it looked like one of Luisa's dusters, rescued from the cleaning bucket. He was unshaved, his long hair a bird's nest, his feet shoeless. "Happy birthday, Dad," he said weakly.

"Thank you, son," his father said. "You better get dressed. We're leaving in five. I'm going out to warm up the car."

"I feel sick, Dad. I don't think I should come. You don't want me to get sick in the restaurant."

"Talk to your mother about it," Jim sighed, heading for the garage.

"Now look what you've done," Babo said. "You pissed off Dad on his birthday."

The two boys glared at each other. There was no apparent brotherly love between them. Their mother blamed the gap in years—Mitch was furious when Babo came home from the hospital, old enough to understand that he had lost the run of the house to an infant's perfection and demands. Luisa had to keep Babo with her at all times, lashed to her back to protect him from Mitch's murderous assaults, including, variously, sitting on Babo's soft skull while watching television, dipping his curious fist in hot coffee, burying him under his cuddly crib toys, pushing him down the stairs. The doctor assured their mother that this was normal sibling rivalry—in fact, he knew of worse cases where the baby had actually been crushed, scalded, and suffocated. Interfering would show favoritism. Babo would learn to protect himself, the doctor said, and Mitch would eventually lose interest in destroying him. Besides, a little competition in families was healthy and made for thriving, achieving children. Leave them be, the doctor concluded, so she left them to Luisa.

"What's going on here? Where's your father?" Eileen asked, coming into the kitchen.

"Ask Mitch. He did it," Babo said.

Eileen studied her sons, both rigid with the desire to hurt the other. If she had not been standing there, one would have struck out with a kick or a fist, then both would drop to the floor, raining blows like a magician rains doves, their rage seemingly pulled from thin air. They were such angry boys, she thought.

"You look nice," Mitch sneered at Babo. Babo wore a black sweatshirt printed with a red Iron Cross, baggy blue shorts, and ratty sneakers. Greasy black hair hid one eye completely. His left ear was pierced with a shard of sharpened chicken bone. He reached inside his sweatshirt and scratched himself. "I bet you're hungry for some birthday dinner. Got the munchies, Babo?"

"Fuck you," Babo muttered, looking away from his mother.

"Babo," she warned. "Watch your mouth. Mitch, you can't wear those clothes out."

"I'm not going. I'm sick."

"It's your dad's birthday, Mitch. We're having dinner together as a family."

"I'm not." Mitch leaned closer to Babo. "You stink, shrimp. You smell like you're dead. You make me want to throw up on your head. Actually, it looks like someone already did."

Babo blinked at Mitch. "I'm not eating with this loser. And if he doesn't have to go, then I'm not going either. It's only fair," he declared.

"You're both coming," Eileen said. "Mitch, upstairs. *Change.*"

Mitch crossed his arms defiantly. "You can't tell me what to do. I'm a big boy, remember? That's what you said."

Before she could reply, he walked out of the room, stamping his bare feet—but his tantrum's effect was muted on the carpeted stairs, no doubt enraging him more. Eileen

133

heard his bedroom door slam. Mitch crossed the room to his bed, the headboard scraping the wall as he threw himself down, then nothing.

Jim blew the BMW's horn in the garage, an echoing report that marked his imminent departure. Eileen looked at Babo. "Go sit with Dad in the car. Give him some company. Tell him we'll be right out."

Babo shrugged. "I don't feel like it." He opened the refrigerator door and began pawing a plate of bean burritos, leftover from Luisa's lunch. "I'll eat here."

Snubbed, Eileen faltered. Surely this kind of behavior was a joke? Yet the pang she felt—the split, the disconnection from her children's way of thinking, which was supposed to reflect her own—was absolute. Babo stood there, defiantly chewing a mouthful of burrito, showing her it was true. "What's wrong with you two? Look at me when I speak to you, Babo. You're coming out to dinner and that's final, so let's go."

"Don't feel like it," Babo said through another bite. He turned his back to her, burrowing in the refrigerator, where he found cold pizza, tapioca pudding, and a jar of deli pickles.

"Then we'll eat alone," Eileen huffed, walking away from the situation, head high, chin set deliberately like a ship's prow still on course through a storm. She didn't want to yell. She only yelled when she lost control, and she hadn't lost control, she reassured herself.

"Where are they?" Jim asked. "We're going to be late."

"They're not coming. I'm sorry. I don't know—" What had just happened? What about her plans for a happy birthday celebration, like they always had? She thought it was *understood* how everyone was expected to behave in this family, at least on special occasions.

"I think we should have them tested for drugs," Jim said, accelerating unnecessarily out of the garage, screeching the BMW's tires, then a sharp left onto Quasar Lane so that Eileen had to grab her door handle to keep from toppling over. "I don't hear of other people's children acting this way."

He was furious, she could tell. Given the opportunity, he would drive as fast as his racing pulse. She needed to calm him down—it was his birthday, after all. "Oh, I don't know that it's drugs. I think it's the usual bumps of being a teenager."

"Mitch isn't a teenager. You saw him—he looks like he's on drugs. He's a mess."

"I don't know," Eileen said helplessly. She really didn't.

The rest of the journey was passed in silence, except that Jim cleared his throat repeatedly, as if he was about to say something very important, a nervous tic he usually suppressed. Eileen sighed in response. Jim's throat-clearing drove her nuts, but she held her tongue. She held it, too, every time he blasted his horn when the car in front showed its brake lights. Finally they pulled into the restaurant's parking lot, when she said, "Let's try to forget about what just happened."

Jim simultaneously cleared his throat and jerked the car to park. Eileen was thrust toward the windshield, her seatbelt catching her as it locked with the brakes. "It's not my fault!"

she cried. "It's nobody's fault! Children have their own minds. I want them to act right as much as you do!"

Jim stared straight ahead. "I know it's not your fault. I think they're on drugs. There's no other explanation that I can think of."

"I'm sure," Eileen answered, quickly recovered, "that it's nothing."

"That's what you always say. Part of the problem is that they know you're a pushover—you always have been. You're soft on them. What the boys need is the hard line."

"What do you want me to do? Hit them?" Eileen asked angrily.

"Sometimes I think that's what they need. Teach them to show a little respect. They should be *afraid* of me."

She gritted her teeth. Eileen had never laid a hand on her sons. She didn't believe that it accomplished anything, while Jim used his belt from time to time. "We'll continue this inside. Let's not be late for our reservation," she said, opening the car door—but Jim grabbed her arm.

"I don't want to discuss this in a restaurant. I refuse to discuss our private business in a public place," he hissed.

"Fine. We'll have them tested for drugs. Next week," Eileen agreed, too easily. She simply wanted this conversation to be over. Anyway, he would soon forget his threats, she told herself—even though she knew he wouldn't. Jim didn't forget anything. He kept score, and his scorecard went back tens of years.

She got out of the car, as did he, checking his door lock by lifting the handle several times, then they set off in stride across the parking lot, both silent, not touching, hurrying so they wouldn't be late. But a young couple, kissing deeply, their eyes shut, oblivious to the Whites' approach, blocked the door to DeZing. Jim cleared his throat as he and Eileen were forced to halt.

"We're celebrating," the man offered in explanation, wiping his mouth. "My wife just arrived. She's British. Aren't you, honey?" he said, prodding her with his elbow. She nodded. He wore a red carnation in the buttonhole of his gray suit; her red-beaded cocktail dress—far too dressy for dinner at DeZing, Eileen noted—showed off pale, bare legs scalloped with muscle. She was much too thin. "Hey, you guys look familiar. Are we neighbors?"

Jim and Eileen instinctively shook their heads. Jim cleared his throat again. His right wrist, on which he wore his watch, twitched with an impulse to check the time.

"I'm sure we're neighbors. We live in Atomic View, on Quasar Lane. I'm Dale Manley and this is my wife Cathy." Dale stuck out his hand.

"Then we're neighbors," Eileen agreed.

Dale Manley waited, but no names or hands were forthcoming. "Well," he said. "Funny we should meet here, of all places. I've lived in Atomic View for more than a year and I thought I'd met everyone."

Jim glowered at him. "We're late," he said, pushing past. Eileen followed without a word.

"What an asshole," Dale said. Cathy said nothing, just stared after them.

The Whites were immediately seated at a spacious round table in the bay window of the well-known restaurant, much to their relief. It didn't matter that the table was much too big for the two of them; they were there, they were on time, and they hardly needed to consult their menus, eating out so regularly that they knew the mushroom risotto was the DeZing house specialty. It was Jim's birthday, so he ordered the risotto, while Eileen asked for a chicken Caesar salad, hold the anchovies. She didn't have much of an appetite, she said. It must be the heat.

"Or the boys," Jim said; he couldn't let the subject drop.

"Please, Jim. They're just acting up. It doesn't mean anything."

"Our family life isn't normal. If it were normal, our sons would be with us right now. Babo's always been rebellious, but at fourteen I can understand. He just needs someone to say no to him. But Mitch," Jim shook his head. "He was fine when he was Babo's age, just like everyone else. So what happened?"

"You talk about him like he's some kind of criminal."

"I happen to think it's criminal to waste our money on such a large scale, Eileen, and I'm worried if you don't think the same. We held up our end of the bargain. We gave him college."

"He hasn't wasted it yet. He's finding himself. Some kids take longer to decide what they want to do with their lives. If we just give him time—"

"There you go again! Always defending him. Listen, what's Babo supposed to think of the value of a college education? Is he going to think it's party time, too? That you don't have to *do* anything?"

Eileen was silent. She picked at a dinner roll. "God knows

what Mitch gets up to when we're at work. I asked Luisa and she said he stays in his room."

"Drugs," Jim said quietly, checking to make sure no one had heard. "I told you. They could be using anything. I think the signs are here for us to act."

"I don't agree. We *explained* law and sentencing for drug offenders, we warned them how severe it was. They're not stupid. They're boys acting like boys. Frustrating, yes, but not criminal."

"Next thing, we'll have the police at our front door just like what's-his-name's son around the corner last year. How old was he? Fourteen? Fifteen?"

"He was sixteen. Dealing marijuana from his bedroom, but I think he was only charged with possession."

"Only? That's enough. Depending on how much he had on him, that can carry a mandatory minimum sentence of some form of incarceration and at least a couple thousand dollars in fines. The charge stays on his record for the rest of his life. That's his life ruined, not to mention his parents' reputation. I don't want my kids in drug court for everyone to talk about. We've got to crack this now." Jim bent over a dinner roll with his knife, cutting the roll into four slices.

"Here's our food," Eileen said gratefully.

They were served with due recognition by their waiter (who knew them to be generous tippers) and, as they ate, turned the conversation to their workdays. At no point did they notice their neighbors at a far, dark table in the corner, drinking champagne toasts and kissing as passionately as they did at home.

Back in the car after decafs, buckling in for the drive, Eileen said, "I hope you had a nice birthday, Jim."

"It's just another day, isn't it? Birthdays are for kids. When you get to be our age, it's just another day done."

Eileen looked out her window, watching the scenery of developments go by. "I guess you're right. Another day done," she sighed, and now she was thinking of her children. "But you don't get them back, do you? When they're gone, they're gone."

Phoenix

In bed that night, Dale was still talking about their neighbors, while Cathy worried about what she had eaten and drunk. *All that food* remembered in gaudy detail. First, champagne when they sat down at their table, and Dale had insisted she order a starter as well as a main, plus pudding, and, last but not least, deep cups of milky, sweet coffee. They had drunk a *whole bottle* of champagne, ordering another bottle of wine with their meal, and her drunkenness—and Dale's insistence—ensured that she ate what was on her plate, and ate well.

She started with prosciutto-wrapped spears of asparagus dribbled with hollandaise, while Dale spread deep-fried lumps of chevre dressed with tomato vinaigrette on crispy garlic bread. Salad was included with their mains, drenched with honey-Dijon. Then Cathy ate penne with scallops dressed in pomodoro sauce, Dale the veal filet, fried again, with creamy Parmesan dumped on top, and both wiped their plates with the warm, doughy dinner rolls, requesting a second basket. For pudding, Cathy ordered chocolate parfait layered with crème fraîche—the chocolate dense, leaden, the cream light as breath—and Dale polished off a slice of chocolate-chip cheesecake, which he ate one-handed, the other hand buried in Cathy's lacy underpants. He paid the bill while they drank their coffee, left an exact ten-percent tip, then drove home wildly, crooning like a legend along with the radio while she worked an imaginary brake pedal.

As soon as the garage door touched down, Cathy was sprawled on the hood of the car, clinging to the windshield wipers to keep from sliding off. After a few frantic minutes, Dale tried to carry her into the house—but his arms were soft, and he was drunk. Together they sagged to the cold concrete floor, Cathy's spangled dress a lasso around his neck. Dale lurched off, braying that he needed to pee, leaving her a bundle of shame. When he didn't return, Cathy crawled after him—only to have him jump out from behind a corner, yelling "Boo!" so that she yelped in fright. Then he was chasing her down the hall, roaring with desire. She tried to cover her (she imagined) dimpling thighs with her hands, but he slapped them away. He pushed her down on the stairs and they did it there, bumping up one step at a time, Dale lifting her with the force of his hips. They humped all the way to their bedroom, where Cathy was pinned to the carpet, burning her back. She bit her tongue so as not to cry out—what sounded, she knew, like the slaughterhouse yowl of a cat in heat.

But before the drink and food and sex, before they were seated at the fancy, candlelit table, Dale groping her under the tablecloth, pretending to talk about his forthcoming business trip, and she with her hand lashed to the bulge in his trousers, pretending to listen—before they even got through the door of the restaurant, something had happened to make Dale upset.

"Who do they think they are?" he complained. He lay in bed with his arms folded behind his head and his ankles crossed, a white flag of toilet tissue crumpled around his willy. Cathy's cheek rested on his furry chest, which she backbrushed with her fingers, fanning the strawberry hairs so that they stood on end and the freckles were revealed. Where he wasn't freckled or haired, Dale's skin was the color of bleach. He was colored like a Bengal tiger, but he was skinny and flaccid from sitting at his desk or behind the wheel of the Taurus, covering the tri-state area for Smart Cups. Cathy didn't care that he was out of shape—although he had sniped about *her* weight once or twice. Right now she was trying not to look at her belly, a rumbling, bulging, high-pressure area, painful to touch, unused to the surfeit of butter and cream. She curled carefully around it, distracting Dale with her fingertips. He mustn't see how fat she was!

"Just because they're rich doesn't mean they're better than us. Rich people always think they're better, like they're cleaner or something. Well, we all shit and we all die in the end. Dust to dust, the Bible says. Just because that guy drives a better car, he thinks he's too good to shake my hand. I'll be earning twice what he earns in five years. I'll have three Cadillacs in the garage and he'll be shining *my* shoes then!"

Cathy felt the calories surging through her body, flowing up and down her arms and legs. She wiggled her toes enthusiastically, wishing that the calories would filter out and be lost, like Dale's seed, to the sheets.

"They're not perfect," he continued. "Their kid is out all hours on that damn noisy skateboard, and he looks like a freak. You know the one I mean. Real short, always wearing those weird clothes. He's a dwarf, right?"

Cathy nodded absently, remembering how Dale hadn't been able to carry her in from the garage. She was sure she was putting on weight, getting fat on love and marriage. Just because she had some security didn't mean she could let herself go. How did she think she got what she had? Cathy stroked Dale's hairs at a faster rate, aware that she was panicking. She mustn't panic; panic made her blurt. She couldn't be Fatty *and* Chatty Cathy at the same time!

"That kid keeps the whole neighborhood awake at night. There's no supervision there. It just goes to show what happens when a mother works. You won't work when we have kids. My wife doesn't need to work. I can pay the bills just fine. You don't want to work, do you, baby?"

Cathy shook her head vigorously and for too long, burning calories. She was even beginning to feel up for more sex. She could work the insides of her thighs, give her stomach a workout with mini-crunches if she was on top. Sex burned six calories a minute—as much as a brisk walk. Cathy slid her hand toward Dale's groin, tugging at what he called his treasure trail, the bit of orange fluff below his belly button. But Dale and his penis were sleepy, despite her insistent touch. He pushed her away, muttering, " . . . like we're trash . . . my hand's not dirty . . . lawyers are liars, my daddy always said . . ." His arm was a five-pound weight around her neck and in a few minutes he was snoring.

Cathy slid noiselessly from the bed. Naked, she crept downstairs. No tattling floorboards here, no whispering radiators or groaning pipes like in England; this house was tight—watertight, Dale had said, like a boat. You could set this house on the Atlantic Ocean and it would float.

Cathy tiptoed to the Stairmaster and touched the monitor with one finger. It lit up like a house on fire at her touch, whirring with excitement. "That's right, we're going for a ride," she whispered. "Now shush."

She climbed gingerly at first, aware of Dale asleep upstairs, but soon forgot herself, sprinting over the pattern of hills. She leaned forward into summit after summit, the Stairmaster singing high-pitched encouragement to her— what sounded, to her ears, like a mating call. Racing toward the beast she loved, she sang as well, her voice a bleating, flat A. Every two minutes she rode the hard crest of a mechanical climax, and on the sixth peak—the last and most difficult—Cathy's heart threatened to fly out of her chest. Her mouth parched, her whole body burned, pumping legs fanning the fire that consumed her. Without ceasing her pace, she took her pulse: 190, the redline rate for her age and weight. Firing hot in the heat of her own kiln, becoming unbreakable, Cathy finally transcended her body, a blazing bird with talons and a beak of jewels. She flew out the window, into the macadam-colored sky, evaporating clouds that were nothing to her flames, spinning constellations with the bellows of her wings until she was quite lost in the black dust . . .

Then the machine was guiding her home. She picked her way down the steep approach marked out with the posts of the nether regions' monsters, through the mountain pass that ran between the poles, cooling her heels in the aquamarine waters of the Earth, and the waters bubbled and sighed as they quenched the last embers of Cathy's flight to the stars. There was nothing of her night out with Dale left inside. She sank to the floor in a rubbery heap, feeling blissfully empty.

But when she slept, she dreamt of ice cream by the gallon, summer fool, rhubarb crumble dressed with brown sugar and double cream, custard doughnuts, buttered hot-cross buns, thickly frosted chocolate layer cake . . .

A Matchstick for the Devil

"Long time, no see, Mitchie. What have you been up to, buddy?" Steve's voice swaggered across the telephone line. Mitch flinched. Steve sounded so arrogant. He had always been confident—confidence Mitch had envied and tried to emulate, bred from prep school, lacrosse, and summers sailing the Atlantic seaboard with a likewise sandy-haired, carefree crew. Now Steve worked for Lehman Brothers in New York's financial district, ascending the heights of the World Trade Center every morning at eight, part of a fleet of recent college grads determined to become big money men, just like their dads. Steve's brother and father had gone before him, Mitch knew, and Steve's legacy landed him the job in the end.

"I'm good, I'm good. You?" Mitch said, straining to sound alert, casual. He lay naked on top of the unmade bed; he had spent the last day and a half undressed except for when he left his room to grab food: bags of chips, pierogies, slices of cold pizza, frozen hamburgers nuked in the microwave. When Steve called, Mitch had been whispering to his main fantasy these days, Scarlet, the Loser's girlfriend from across the street. "What are you thinking?" he asked her, stroking his own arm, kissing the mouth his forefinger and thumb made.

"I want you to take me to New York and share me with your friends. They don't know how hot I am. They'll love me and they'll love you because of me," Scarlet said. Her mouth was swollen and red, vague around the edges. She had been sucking him off, or so he imagined as he arched into his Vaseline-lined fist, when Luisa knocked at his door and said there was a phone call for him.

"Who is it?" Mitch choked as his hard-on instantly deflated.

"Your friend Steve. He says it's important."

Mitch grabbed his room's extension, the ringer of which had been turned off a few days before when he didn't want to be interrupted in his fantasies—not that it rang lately. "I'm spent, hung over in the worst way," Steve said. "We're out every night, partying like rock stars."

"Yeah, I'm busy too."

"That's great to hear, buddy." Steve sounded like he was doing something else at the same time he was talking to Mitch.

Mitch raised his voice. "A hottie hardbody moved in across the street. She's on her Stairmaster all day, practically naked, and I've got a room with a view."

Steve snorted. "A hottie hardbody in Hicktown? I bet she's something special to see. Hold on a sec, buddy."

A few minutes passed with the detuned scratching noise of Steve's restless palm over the receiver. Why had he called if he was going to act like this? What did he want? To remind Mitch how far away he was? But Mitch didn't need reminding, and finally he shouted, "Yeah, I need to get out of here!"

"What's that? What did you say, buddy?" Steve was back.

"I said, I've got to get out of here."

"You want to make movies, right? A director should live in New York. All the hot artists are living in Alphabet City. You know, learning their ABCs." Steve laughed at his own bad joke. "Tell your parents that. They'll eat it up." He muffled the phone's receiver again while he talked to someone else.

Mitch thought about hanging up.

"Hey, Mitchie, guess who's sitting right here? Alex Fitz, buddy, my new colleague. He says what up. He says you're missing the *killa* city life."

"Alex is there?" Mitch hated Alex Fitz, who had slept with his ex-girlfriend Jenna before she was his ex, forcing the collapse of that relationship. "He's working there?" Mitch hated the whiny sound of his voice when he asked.

"Just started two weeks ago. Hey, Big Al wants to know when you're coming into the city next. We should all hang out."

Alex seemed to have forgotten his encounter with Jenna just weeks before their graduation from Conn College, provoking Mitch to accost him one night in a bar. Mitch had been drinking steadily for three days, depressed by Jenna's blatant deception as well as their imminent departure for what adults kept calling the real world. He swung a punch that landed badly, passing through Alex's Bermuda-bleached hair.

"What are you so upset about?" Alex had said, steadying

him with one hand clapped to Mitch's sagging shoulder. "It's all in the family here. Bitches are bitches are bitches, buddy, like a rose is a rose. The sooner you get that into your head, the better. Here, this will help," he said, retaliating with a hard drive to Mitch's left eye, blackening it sufficiently so that on graduation day he still bore a jaundiced socket ringed in violet. He had to wear sunglasses throughout the ceremony and celebratory meal at the over-priced brasserie fully booked by Mitch's friends—but only the Whites had sat silently at their undersized table for four.

Now Mitch was enraged to hear that Alex worked at Lehman Brothers, when he had repeatedly asked Steve for the same favor. "My dad says he just can't do it right now. I'm lucky to have my job and I'm the boss's son. Anyway, you're too smart for this work, buddy," Steve had told him. "You're a creative—you're the talent of our crew." As always, Mitch believed whatever Steve said. How he wanted to believe he would go far in the film world!

Steve hooted into the phone while Alex said something about the night before in the background.

"That's funny," Mitch said, pretending he had heard.

"Listen, Mitchie, I've got to go. People to do, places to know."

"Yeah, me too." Scarlet would be back on her Stairmaster soon—he didn't want to miss her workout.

"So when are you coming to visit?"

"How about this weekend?" Mitch said impulsively.

Steve drew his breath loudly through his teeth. "We're all going to the Hamptons for Memorial Day. I got a time-share with Alex and a bunch of people for the summer. It's the first weekend and everyone's going out. And I mean *everyone*. Anyone who's anyone has a place in the Hamptons this year. The city will be a ghost town come Friday night."

"Sounds great." A weekend in the sun might be just what Mitch needed to shake his slump. He had never been to the Hamptons, although he had a pretty good idea what kind of scene it was: Jay Gatsby hanging around with the *Bright Lights, Big City* crowd. The best houses were in Sag Harbor and Amagansett, and the best surfing was in Montauk, but sometimes there were sharks. He knew that Steven Spielberg had a massive pad, and so did Billy Joel and Calvin Klein.

"Why don't you call Lily Kay? Her parents have a place in Quogue—megabucks there, buddy. Someone should snag that girl."

"What about your place?" Mitch asked.

"No room at the inn, buddy. We've been booked for months. We found our place in December."

Then why hadn't Steve mentioned it before? Why not include Mitch as well? Because he wasn't *there,* he thought. He had to get to New York immediately, before he missed another minute of life being lived to the hilt. "Give me Lily's number. I'll call her as soon as we hang up."

"I've got her number in my Rolodex. Just hang on a sec," Steve said. He grunted with the exertion, like it was too much trouble. "Buddy, I can't find her number right now. Let me get back to you this afternoon after I've made a few calls."

He was lying, Mitch thought. Why was he lying? "Yeah, OK. When are you guys leaving for the Hamptons?"

"We're catching a late Hampton Jitney on Friday night, after cocktails at Lily's. You remember her place, right by Sotheby's on East 72nd. The one with the awesome pool table. Buddy, she's having a *bar* put in, and she just got one of those poles like they have in strip clubs. It's a *killa* pad."

"Great, great, sounds great," Mitch repeated feverishly. "Just make sure you get me her number today, OK?"

"Got to hang up now—here comes my dad."

"Call me. Don't forget!"

"Who, me? Forget about my little country buddy?" Steve laughed.

Mitch felt sick when he put down the phone. He wasn't one of them anymore. He definitely wasn't one of them. But they had to let him back in—if he went to them, he was sure they would. They *liked* him. They had liked him for four years at Conn College, so why not now? He closed his eyes. Why not now?

Remembering Scarlet, Mitch crawled to his bedroom window where he knelt, the same old T-shirt thrown over his torso (which was the color of a peeled potato, lumpen and sallow), the tip of his hard-on brushing the wall. He used his father's binoculars to watch Scarlet in close-up. She was dressed in a white Lycra bra and shorts, quickly soaked to the bone; he only knew that time passed by the saturation of her outfit. He could see the red discs of her nipples, the dark corner of her pubic hair. Sweat drained down her cleavage in steady rivulets. Mitch strummed. Scarlet scratched her crotch. Mitch's eyes bulged. She replaced her hand possessively on the Stairmaster's arm—then she was tugging her shorts to the side, that is, to the very center of her body, her core, her piffy, her poonanny, to reveal the first real-life pussy Mitch had seen in more than a year, or since Jenna slept with Alex, effectively ending their relationship. Scarlet scratched long and hard as he coordinated his masturbation to climax.

Satisfied, she fixed her shorts and battered her Stairmaster at renewed pace, while Mitch collapsed on his bed, postcoital, or so it felt. He muttered sweet nothings to the pillow before he slept, thinking he would just close his eyes for a few minutes before the phone would surely ring and it would be Steve calling to make plans for the weekend.

Stakeout

The Powerwalker was jogging in place. She had nearly finished her first circuit of Atomic View when she returned Deb's floppy wave with a broad smile, so grateful was she to have an hour to herself while the babysitter fed the baby lunch. That one spontaneous grin was all the encouragement Deb needed; she had been out in her car all day, had driven miles, and still hadn't spoken to a soul—properly spoken, that is. She hadn't told someone her news and heard news in return. Deb pulled up alongside the Powerwalker in her Town Car, angling the hood with its prickly ornament so that the Powerwalker was forced to halt.

"Tonight I'm meeting my friends Ali and Jo and we're going out for a nice big meal. The last supper," Deb joked. "My doctor says I have to get in shape, like you. Maybe we could walk together. I go swimming now, at Ladies' Night at Skyline Pool—you should come with me, every Tuesday from seven 'til ten. Normally I would stay in tonight—Thursday night is the best for TV—but I made an exception since everyone's going away for the weekend. I can tape my shows and watch them in the morning. Ali and Jo are both going to the shore—well, actually, Ali's going to the shore and Jo's going down to Maryland. She and her husband Chris just love Maryland blue crabs. I think they look like hairy spiders. I can't touch them," Deb shuddered. "Even with all that melted butter. I *love* melted butter. Chris eats their guts. He calls it the mustard."

The Powerwalker flapped her arms and shuffled her feet.

"My last big meal," Deb sighed. "I'm not going to have big meals anymore. I'll have to keep busy somehow. I need some projects, or maybe I'll travel. Two weeks ago I went down to the Baltimore Aquarium, and you know what? I'm so glad I went: I thought since I was swimming that it'd be good to go look at some fish. It's easy to get there—just a straight shot down the highway. It only took me an hour and a half to drive. There's parking at the aquarium, no trouble to find. My favorite was the rainforest that you can walk through. They offer an umbrella, but it's only a little thing, too small for me. They said I could take two, but I said forget it and just got damp. I'm not fussy or hard to please. I took pictures and they came out OK, not great, but OK. I used a disposable camera. I'll show them to you, if you want to drop by some time."

The minutes seemed hours to the Powerwalker. She mourned the loss of her walk as Deb continued, having shifted her car into park. Sometimes the Powerwalker wondered if Deb lay in wait for her, so often confronted was she by the enormous car and her equally huge neighbor hanging out the window. "How's your house? My house was just painted. I have it painted every five years. Blue, but I guess you can see for yourself that it's blue. The old shutters are off, and the new ones are on my living-room floor. I hope to get them put up next week—the painter left them and told me he'd be back, but I haven't seen him since! Mick McCoy, if you want to know his name. My house is a disaster zone, stuff all over. I'm trying to get my summer flag hung and my flowerbeds planted and nothing is finished. A lot started, but nothing completed. I hate when I do that, but it happens a lot, I'm sorry to say! There's always tomorrow," Deb added.

Tomorrow will be too late, the Powerwalker thought furiously. Tomorrow I don't have a babysitter. Tomorrow I have the baby to myself all day and he'll scream when I get out the stroller to walk. She thought *she* might scream if Deb didn't move her car and let her pass. The Powerwalker started a countdown from sixty in her head, like when she ordered the baby to pick up his toys.

"Once my Fourth of July barbecue is over, I can breathe. I've been having fun with my plans. Wait until you see what Sue Martin suggested for the centerpieces. She certainly is creative—she makes her own paper in a bucket and lays it out on a plastic sheet to dry in the sun. She's making me some nice flag placemats. Great news about your baby, by the way. Sue told me you're having another one. On *Mary Lou* the other day they were talking about test-tube fertilization and all the wonderful ways they make babies these days. I wish I'd taped it now. Did you see it?"

The Powerwalker shook her head. "I think I left the stove on."

"Thanks for the offer to bring a friend to your Flag Day picnic," Deb continued as if she hadn't heard what the Powerwalker said. "I'm deciding who I'll ask. Jo can't come, she already said, and I'm not sure Ali would appreciate it—she might fall asleep. That's what she does when she doesn't know anyone."

"And the baby is in the house. Sleeping."

"I better let you go! Bye for now!" Deb tooted her car horn.

The Powerwalker back-pedaled and rerouted herself at triple pace, while Deb reversed three driveways until she reached her own mailbox. She pulled the pile of circulars and donation envelopes onto her lap, eased the car up the driveway, into the garage. Five hours later, at five o'clock, the sun still a floodlight outside, grass singing with the high-pitched frequencies of gnats and bees, Deb, having watched her soaps and *Mary Lou*, was backing down the drive again. It was her third trip out that day; sometimes she made six or seven trips in her car, the tangle of highway—one strand of the Medusa head that was the Dwight D. Eisenhower System of Interstate and Defense Highways—there for her to cross with little effort and everything in the world to gain. People had to drive if they wanted to go somewhere in Churchtown. That's why the four-lane highway (a popped-up blood vessel compared to the Interstate's aorta) had been built, to connect them to all of America, to take them where they wanted to go. Deb knew that she could go anywhere, that she wasn't *nowhere*. Why, her house was just a half-mile from the entrance/exit ramp!

This evening she wasn't in a hurry. She had plenty of time to enjoy the drive in her big Town Car with its extra-long, extra-strength hood, plenty of elbowroom, and all the amenities of home: warmth or cool air, entertainment, butterscotch drops in the glove compartment. She didn't mind the highway billboards or brutalist bridge supports, the spouting pollution and white noise of the passing cars, or the shrinking open space corralled by concrete noise barriers. These obstructions had been there so long that she couldn't really remember what the land was like before. Now, as she drove, Deb mentally checked off a list of sights—the full-service Mobil filling station, McDonald's, Taco Bell, Howard Johnson's, Burger King, all the standardized food and gas stops, predictable and safe—to reassure herself that she was in the right place, the same person as the day before.

Taking 333 to the Steak-Out, where she would meet Ali and Jo, Deb hummed along with the radio, the air-conditioning up high and her windows rolled down, observing the highway speed limit of 55 miles per hour. Inside the restaurant, Ali and Jo had already been seated—but Deb wasn't late. She was never late. They were early, in plenty of time for half-price Happy Hour drinks with free bar snacks, drinking frothy pink Love in the Afternoon from frosted daiquiri glasses and crunching nacho chips. Deb joined them in their booth, squawking at Jo to shove over and give her some room.

"Did you see *Mary Lou?*" she demanded, blotting her brow with a dinner napkin.

"Some of those women were disgusting," Jo said, scratching the bottom of her glass with the cocktail umbrella provided.

"Help! My lover weighs six hundred pounds!" Ali hollered, pounding the table, she laughed so much.

"Well," Deb said seriously, "I think we could all use some help in that department."

"What are you talking about?" Jo lifted a chip precariously balanced with cheese, guacamole, salsa, and peppers to her gaping mouth; as soon as that chip was in, she reached for another one, this time dropping salsa in bloody clots onto the plastic red-checkered cloth. "Whoops-a-daisy!" she exclaimed, scooping up the mess with one finger and depositing it on her tongue.

"Sometimes I have half a mind to go on that show myself. Maybe I should drag you two with me," Deb said.

"To talk about what?" asked Ali.

"To talk about our weight problem."

"Since when is it a problem?" Jo said belligerently.

"You know I've been swimming. Well, this is my last big meal. It's time for me to slim down." A waiter wearing a baseball cap paused at their table. Deb pointed at Ali and Jo's empty cocktail glasses. "Get me one of those, and while you're at it, we want three sixteen-ounce steak dinners, well done, with baked potatoes, sour cream, and coleslaw. Our usual."

Ali whooped. "Go, girl!"

But Jo said, "This ain't normal. Something's not right."

"All I'm saying is, I want to lose some of this excess baggage." Deb indicated her belly—an extension of her bosom that melted into her thighs.

"We're all in the same boat, hon," Ali said as *her* belly bumped the table, making the glasses and silverware jump. "What makes you think you got to do this now? Why not enjoy life? Live the way you want, that's what I say. You can't make everybody happy, but at least you can make yourself happy."

"I'm not respecting my body like this," said Deb. "You know, I think I tried to stop certain things from happening by getting fat."

"Like what?"

"Like falling in love again. I didn't want to love anyone else but Don, but I thought something was wrong with that."

"*We* never said you should get married again," Ali said.

"That's right," Jo agreed.

Deb hesitated. "I know I didn't have to marry someone else just because I'm a woman and that's what women do. I was lucky. I had my own house and some money. Not every woman is so lucky. Some don't have that choice. They can't do what's right for them. There's lots of women that like to live alone, but people don't accept that. It doesn't fit the stereotype."

"Huh?" Ali said.

"You're fat. So what? So's everyone," Jo said. "Don't make a big deal about it. You just like to eat. If Don was still alive, he'd probably be fat, too."

"Yeah. Everyone we know is fat," Ali agreed. "Why do you want to be different? Are you going to be on a *diet* from now on? Are you going to have to eat special food?"

"Why make things complicated?" Jo grumbled, snapping her cocktail umbrella in half.

"It's not that I'm unhappy with my appearance," Deb said. "I still love food. And I'm definitely not going to diet. Diets don't work—diets are a conspiracy against women.

Did you know that young girls are more afraid of getting fat than they are of nuclear war, cancer, or losing their parents? Isn't that just crazy?"

"What are you talking about, Deb? You're not making sense. I wasn't going to say so, but you been saying crazy stuff like this for a couple of weeks," Jo declared.

"Ever since you started swimming," Ali echoed. "Don't you think, Jo? That's what started all this. Swimming. You're like some kind of exercise freak."

"The water makes me love myself. I'm beginning to feel like I *own* my body," Deb said.

"You're talking like a nut! Are you some kind of nut?" asked Jo.

"Oh, Lord." Ali rolled her eyes. "She's been converted!"

"Why are you ganging up on me? I just want to help myself," Deb protested.

"We're not ganging up! We're your friends. Our duty is to be honest with you. We're just being honest, Deb."

"We don't know where this crazy talk is coming from, that's all," Ali said.

"It's coming from my heart," Deb said. "I'm not feeling so well."

"What's wrong with you? Are you sick?"

"I just feel—" Deb stalled. What did she feel? What did she want them to know? That she wanted them to be in this together, as they always were, or as she hoped they always were, for she knew Ali and Jo saw more of each other than they saw of her. They talked on the phone for hours every morning—early, before she woke, after they fixed breakfast for their husbands and children and sent them off to work and school. They double-dated on Saturday nights, and twice they had gone on vacation together without her, united as families, once to Maine, in search of three-pound lobsters, and once to Disney World, where they bought Deb's beloved Minnie Mouse T-shirt. She knew they would do anything to help her, and yet there was only so much they could do. Above all, Ali and Jo refused to join her at Ladies' Night, no matter how she begged them to go. "I feel like I have to make some changes. Doctor Greaves says that if I keep on like this, I'll get sick and die. Mary Lou said it today on her show: obesity kills. I don't want to die."

"No one ever died from being a little bit fat," Ali scolded. "You're not obese and you're surely not dying, Deb. It's all in your head. You been watching too much TV. That *Mary Lou* show is all made up—it's just entertainment. No one expects you to believe it. Most of those guests are paid actors! And Mary Lou is fat. Why would she say you'll die from it? That's like saying *she's* dying. It's more crazy talk!"

"You have to enjoy your life," Ali insisted. "You enjoy good food. There's nothing wrong with that. I'd rather die happy and fat than skinny and miserable—and *hungry.*"

Deb listened to her friends. Ali took her hand and squeezed it. Jo motioned to their teenage waiter for another round of Love in the Afternoon and asked why their food was taking so long. They were starving! They were having an emotional crisis! They needed *food.* More bar snacks, more nachos and chicken wings and mozzarella sticks. This is what friends were for! To sit around together and eat sympathetically.

"I can't have another one of these," Deb groaned when their drinks arrived. "I won't be able to drive home."

"Sure you will. You know these roads like the back of your hand. Just close your eyes and steer. That's what Chris always does," Jo said.

Ali nodded. "Joe too. Hell, Joe takes a drink in the car with him. A road soda, he calls it." They all laughed as their steaks were set before them, lengthened with fat until they tipped the scales at sixteen ounces, seared like a tic-tac-toe board, served with steaming hot baked potatoes cooled by dollops of sour cream and coleslaw.

By the time they finished their apple pie à la mode, Deb's crisis was over. There was nothing like sugar to sweeten experience, she thought. She reached for the check. "Let's see what the damage is. Jo, you're the best at math. You figure out what each of us owes. Don't forget to add in the tip. You always forget to add in the tip—and don't skimp on it, either. Regulars have to tip right. If we don't tip right, they won't serve us well the next time."

"That's what you always say, and the service is always bad," Jo said.

"They can't keep the staff, is why," Deb said. "That's what the manager told me. We got to chatting."

"You always get the story from people, Deb. I don't know how you do it," Ali said admiringly. "No one can keep anything from you. It's like you got some kind of power over people."

Deb flushed at the compliment. She felt better after the big meal—deep down, she had known she would. Outside in the parking lot, she hugged her friends. "You're my real pals. Bye for now!"

But driving home, her good mood darkened. What was she going to do? Food was her *thing*. Didn't everyone have their *thing* in life, the one thing they couldn't see beyond? If Deb gave up food, what was left? Alone in her car, it seemed an impossible task: to not eat so much, or so often, never again to graze the kitchen counter with its bountiful jars and canisters of sweet things and salty fried treats. She felt a weakness in herself that might never be cured—and her anxiety about not eating made her hungry, despite the big meal. As Deb drove, digesting steak, potato, and apple pie, the headlights of oncoming cars were like the reflections she saw when she looked up from just under the surface of Skyline Pool, her eyes full to overflowing—but these were tears, not water, and the pain in her heart was nothing romantic.

Memorial Day Weekend

The twins waved their parents off with the usual promises: "No big parties, just a few friends, we'll clean up."

"No skating on the ramp after ten o'clock, Nate," their mother added.

"Ma," Nate whined. "But I just finished building it."

"Think of the neighbors. OK? I don't want the police coming here again and telling me I'm a bad mother. Do you hear me?" She jabbed her pointer finger in the direction of Nate's chest.

"Say OK," Nicole muttered when Nate hesitated.

"I wasn't talking to you, Nicole," their mother said. "Nathan?"

"OK, OK!" Nate agreed hotly.

"Just keep the noise down. And be good. Clean up your mess. I'm tired of picking up after you and your friends."

Nicole kissed her parents goodbye. "We'll be good," she promised, but Nate turned his back on them.

His mother shrugged. "Suit yourself."

When they had driven off, Babo popped out of an evergreen shrub by the back door. "They're gone?" he asked suspiciously.

Nicole lit a cigarette. "Yeah," she exhaled. "Finally."

"Christ, I thought they'd never leave." Babo was already chewing on the corner of a sheet of acid printed with American flags.

"Mom can be such a bitch," Nate moaned. "It's like she doesn't want us to have any fun."

"She just doesn't want us getting busted. You remember the last time. She had to go in to school and practically beg the principal not to expel us," Nicole said.

"That was bullshit. They have no rights over us when we're not in school."

"I think *school* called the cops. I think they heard about our party and called to report it," Nicole said. "I bet it was that asshole Mr. Keller. He's so uptight. He got all religious during health class the other day. He says God is his life."

"I wouldn't be surprised," Nate said. "Hey, share the wealth, Babo."

"It's Memorial Day special," Babo said, offering the sheet to Nicole first.

She snorted smoke. "No way. I'm not going to fry my brain."

Nate grabbed the acid, tearing off two squares. He sucked his tongue hungrily, eyes closed, concentrated on pulling as much bug juice (one of Babo's friendly nicknames for LSD) as possible down his throat. Nothing of the drug must be lost, same as with weed: use everything, chew on stems, plant seeds. Then he smacked his lips and tore off another two squares.

"Nate, take it easy! You'll never come down," Nicole said.

"Shut up, Nico," Nate growled.

"That shit catches up with you, you know. It screws with your DNA. You'll have genetically modified children. Look at Babo—he's totally growth-stunted. His parents must have been on drugs." Nicole cackled at the thought of this, nudging Nate with her elbow. "Can you imagine Babo's parents on *drugs*? No wonder he's so messed up."

Babo stared hatefully at Nicole. She was evil. She was so evil she looked ugly. "Shut up. You don't know anything."

"Yeah, you don't know what you're talking about. You sound like the fucking Just Say No campaign. Completely fucking ignorant," Nate agreed.

"I've dosed forty-five times. I'm a specimen of perfect health," Babo said, thumping his compact chest. "You don't get much better than this. I'm positively Olympic. I'm the champion of trips. Twice a week for the last six weeks. I'm smarter than I ever was," he bragged. "I see what other people don't see. At school, all my teachers say, 'You're so perceptive, Babo. You read into things.' I'm brilliant. I'm not kidding."

"You are the stupidest person I've ever met. What do you think of that?" Nicole didn't give him a chance to answer, stalking off to her room to finish her cigarette.

Babo turned to Nate. "She's mine."

"Shut up. She's not impressed, Babo."

"She wants to look after me. She's concerned about my health."

"She hates you, man."

"She loves me. She's showing she loves me by hating me. If you don't have feelings for a person, then you're indifferent," Babo proclaimed. "But if you hate someone, then you love them. It takes passion to hate. It takes a whole lot of energy. It's tribal. She's acting all tribal and shit to get my attention. I just have to show her my caveman tactics and she'll be all over my dick."

"Don't say that about my sister," Nate warned.

"What I have to do, right, is show her who's boss around here. You know, put her in her place. Make her fetch me drinks and shit. Nicole! Bring me a Coke, bitch!" Babo hiccupped with laughter. "When she gets out here, I'll pull her around by her hair."

Nate didn't laugh. He never laughed when Babo talked about Nicole. "That's what she does to *you*, Babo. It's cave-*woman* tactics!"

"See? I told you she loved me."

Nate shook his head. "You know something, Babo? You're not living in the real world. You just don't live in reality. I'm starting to think you're taking too many drugs."

"Fuck you very much," Babo grinned. "I'll take that as a compliment."

"You would."

In succession, six cars passed with coolers and bicycles strapped to their roof racks. As Atomic View emptied, three hours away was a beach that was quickly filling with people and umbrellas, where small children kicked their feet in the shallows of the shoreline or lay beached on their bellies and pretended to swim, spooning up handfuls of sand. Once Babo, Nate, and Nicole had swum with them; now they wanted to stay home with their friends, preferably without parents. By the time night fell, these teenagers would all but have the neighborhood to themselves.

"Listen, we got things to do before this shit kicks in." Nate handed Babo the sheet of acid.

"Yeah, like your sister. I've got to do your sister," replied Babo, folding the acid carefully in half. He placed it first in a plastic sandwich baggie, then into the envelope it had arrived in that morning, via the U.S. Postal Service: to Babo White from MIT. The envelope went into his wallet, always chained to whatever jeans or shorts he was wearing, and he licked his fingers clean.

"I'm talking about the keg, asshole. Tim Johnson said he'd buy the keg for us."

Babo looked startled. "Johnson? Did I hear you say Johnson? *Tim* Johnson? Like, the biggest Johnson of them all?"

"Yeah, he's home for the weekend."

"I can't stand those dudes, Nate. They're the spawn of the devil. They're not human. They're some kind of super-jock Frankenstein experiment, big and dumb, programmed to follow the bouncing ball. Dude, those guys *suck.*"

"He's the only person we know who's twenty-one, besides your loser brother who doesn't come out of his room."

"I can't believe you asked a fucking Johnson! The last thing we need at this party is a Johnson, and now I bet we get them all, every single Johnson in the world. Every dick-head ever born. Thanks to Nate!" Babo bellowed.

Nate was defensive. "Dude, you got to do what you got to do. We got to get a keg. What's more important, Johnsons or beer?"

"This is ramp debut night, Nate! Tonight's our fucking

ribbon-cutting ceremony, and you fucking invited the fucking Johnsons to drink our fucking beer!" Over Nate's shoulder, upstairs, Babo could see Nicole smoking out her bedroom window. She gave him the finger. He flipped the bird right back at her—but Nate grabbed his finger, twisting until it popped out of its joint cushion. Babo snatched his hand free, shaking out the injury. "You fucker, Nate! That fucking killed! First you invite the fucking Johnsons, then you try to maim me! Fuck you! What's your fucking problem, you traitor?"

"Leave her alone," Nate barked.

"Tell the Johnsons to leave *me* alone!"

"It was the only way I could think of to get beer. I saw Tim on the street and I didn't think it was a big deal to ask him."

"Dude, the Johnsons have been beating up on me for years. They beat me worse than Mitch ever did. You *know* they kick my ass. What have I ever done to them?" Babo asked plaintively.

"They like you, dude. I know they like you. It's just, you know, what they do. They like to get a rise out of you." Nate didn't say, "It's because you're little." He didn't have to. Babo knew. The Johnsons were the ones that took a family nickname—Baby Boy, Babo—and made it something awful. He had always been an easy target, until he got his skate-board and could escape the Johnsons or anyone else who picked on him. "Just chill out tonight. They'll leave you alone. No one's sweating anyone. Everything's cool."

"It's all on you if they sweat me. You better throw their

jock asses out of here when they show up. I thought this was supposed to be a *skater* party."

"No, it's *my* party, is what it is. Mine and Nicole's. My house, my ramp, and I'll throw *you* out, asshole."

"I helped you build that ramp!"

"You hammered one nail."

"Dude, I *designed* it."

"It's a ramp, not brain surgery, Babo."

"Ramps demand true design prowess. You're just a grunt."

"It's my ramp. Do you want to ride it or not? Because I might not let you ride if you keep talking this shit."

"Dude!" Babo was outraged. "I'll *dominate,* believe me."

"Whatever you say, Babo."

"Face it, I'm the better skater here." Babo had recovered himself, talking about skating, and stood up taller than his five-foot frame.

"Let's just get the keg. We need beer for tonight. That's what's important."

"I'll rock you any day, dude."

"I said let's split," Nate said, grabbing his skateboard. "I told Tim we'd be there at four."

"That's what I thought. You know the truth and the truth will always prevail. *I* will prevail. I'll be king of your shitty ramp." Babo strutted around Nate's driveway, cocky and proud. He kicked the ramp for effect. "Piece of shit."

"I'm not fighting you, dude. I just want to get the beer." Nate sounded tired.

But Babo shook his head. "You go. I'll stay here. I'm not riding in any Johnson car. He'll try to kill me. He'll drive us through a red light or something. That's just how Johnsons are."

"I need you to help me with the keg, Babo. You never help me with anything," Nate complained.

"I'm your inspiration. Isn't that enough?"

Nate put out his hand, palm flat up. Babo plucked his wallet from his pocket and counted all the money he had into Nate's hand, eighty dollars in remarkably new, neat bills—his allowance, doled out in weekly twenty-dollar increments. Nate stuffed the money into his pocket and skated off without a word, while Babo unwrapped the acid he had spied in his billfold. He tore off one gummy corner and let it soak on his tongue. He didn't care about money. Money wasn't shit to Babo.

Nicole was in the kitchen microwaving a Lean Cuisine lasagna and drinking Diet Coke through a red-and-white-striped straw. A cigarette burned on its roost on the edge of the countertop. She had changed her clothes when her parents left, and now wore tight black jeans and a black tank top that showed her tanned midriff—the real thing, not orange from a bottle, spread in streaks.

"You look like a TV commercial," Babo said.

"What?"

"You look like a Diet Coke commercial."

"Where's Nate?"

"He went to buy beer."

"You didn't go with him?"

"Didn't want to," Babo shrugged. He still felt the ache where Nate had yanked his finger out of joint. He wiggled the finger, which tickled his ears. He did it again. The two were definitely connected. As Nicole watched, sipping Diet Coke, Babo laughed, tickling himself. Oh, the world was good on acid. He loved the wavy carpet, melting walls, the kitchen bulletin board that was a television. He loved it all. He loved the way Nicole's cheeks were filling up—her cheeks were two balloons. Nitrous! He wanted a toot on her straw. Babo loved nitrous too! Nicole's shiny straw (or was it a Christmas candy cane?) flickered and winked, and those red stripes were fire, licking her fingers and lips. Babo dug into his wallet again and pulled out the acid. Too eager to get to it, he ripped a hole in the plastic baggie, then tore off a two-inch strip of blotter. He wasn't bothering to count doses tonight. Babo just wanted to eat.

"Are you taking more of that stuff? Haven't you had enough?"

Babo opened his mouth wide to show her the pulpy mash compacted in his molars. "Ah!"

"You're a real fuck-up, you know that?" Nicole's voice was sinister, taunting. She dragged on her cigarette, grinning maliciously, crocodile teeth glittering, pink tongue a rasp over her lips.

Babo backed away.

"What's wrong?" she hissed. "Are you tripping out? Are you having a bad trip?" She dragged another bellyful of smoke from her cigarette, drawing the ember halfway to the filter.

"I didn't know you could do that," Babo whispered.

Nicole belched smoke in twin columns that curled around her head. Her narrowed eyes flared red. "Do what?"

Babo's jaw locked open and he stared in terror.

"What?" Nicole bellowed cruelly. She scratched her arm so that dry scales hung off in a yellow crust, exposing the raw skin underneath, bubbling with life. The pulse points at her throat surged with excitement. Her ears drew back. Nicole was an alien predator!

Making Tea for the
Tupperware Lady

Cathy scratched between her legs: dried sweat, she thought, and too much sex. She had been scratching for two days. Dale was at her three or four times a night, leaving her blinking in the dark when he dropped off. She couldn't seem to sleep—jetlag, he reassured her—and had taken to exercising while he snored away upstairs. She stole through the house, her naked body the color of moonlight. Once astride her Stairmaster, she climbed mountainsides where the lingering mist dampened her skin, finally peaking above the clouds, triumphant again, beating the demon that chased her every time. By day, her Lycra shorts bagged at the waist, her cleavage a pinch of skin between grasping fingers, and Cathy was elated, even if Dale said she was too skinny, complaining that she felt like a spider when they made love.

But Dale was away now, through the end of next week. He had left early that morning, kissing her goodbye passionately ("Oh baby," he groaned, grinding against her like a teenager), and when he was gone, Cathy threw out the junk food he liked to eat: Cool Ranch Doritos, tubes of beef jerky shrink-wrapped in plastic, cheese-in-a-can to spray in flourishes on Saltines. Dale traveled a week of each month for Smart Cups, driving around in the green Taurus or flying to the Midwest, the West Coast, and Europe, where he talked up the latest lines of paper and foam to his service industry clients. Dale was good at his job, although the more successful salesmen drove Cadillacs. He was confident he would be driving a Cadillac in two years—not a foreign car, like their neighbors, but something made in the good old USA.

Cathy scratched. She really should get into the shower; she had finished her afternoon workout an hour before, then eaten a leisurely lunch of boiled corn. She reached inside her shorts, scrubbing so hard she winced—but at least the pain took the itch away. Cathy was still scratching when the doorbell rang.

Deb held out a letter. "This is for your husband. It came to my house by mistake," she said.

Cathy plucked the envelope from Deb's squat fingers—was that chocolate smeared on one knuckle? Ketchup rimming her nails? "Thank you."

Deb remained solidly in Cathy's doorway. "While I'm here, I thought I might as well pick up my Tupperware."

"Tupperware?"

"For my Cornflake Chicken, Broccoli Mayonnaise, and Apple Dumpling," Deb explained.

But Cathy had put the containers out with the rubbish rather than face the enormous cow returning them. "I think Dale threw them away," she lied.

"He threw away my Tupperware? Why would anyone throw away Tupperware? I have Tupperware that's twenty years old! I never heard of anyone throwing away Tupperware before. Never, in all my years," Deb said, shaking her head in disbelief.

"He didn't know they were yours."

"But he returned them last time," Deb said. She remembered she had snatched back her precious containers, thanked him shortly, and shut the door in his face. She didn't want anything to do with Dale Manley. She felt sorry for his wife, having that kind of man for a husband. He was a sex maniac! Dale had attacked Deb when she took her Cornflake Chicken, Broccoli Mayonnaise, and Apple Dumpling around the first time, inviting her into the kitchen, where he suddenly kissed her, filling her mouth with his tongue while his hands seized on her breasts, kneading and squeezing them. He pushed her against the counter, his arms banded around hers, so that she felt the hardness in his pants. When she struggled, he laughed.

"Come on, fatso. I bet you don't get much of this. I've always wanted to do a great big fat lady. Come on, make me a man," he said, and slurped at her mouth again.

Deb had finally pushed away his thrusting hips, his too-wet lips, and run from the house to the safety of her car. She hadn't told anyone what happened and she had been sure to steer clear of Dale ever since—although when she heard that he had married and that his bride had arrived from abroad, her generous instincts overcame her fear. Deb couldn't resist a new neighbor, although she approached in the safety of daytime when she was sure that Dale was at work.

"Never mind about my Tupperware. I have plenty to

spare," Deb said kindly. Cathy was a foreigner, after all, and she might not know better. "Can I come in anyway? It's hot out here."

Cathy hesitated. She was desperate to scratch herself.

"I could do with a drink," Deb wheedled. "On such a hot day."

Reluctantly, Cathy nodded, and the fat lady nudged into the hall, filling it up with her bulk, expanding while Cathy contracted. There wasn't enough oxygen for both of them in the confined space—Deb sucked it all in, more than her fair share. She was greedy, a glutton in every way, the stupid pig. Cathy panicked. Was she going to faint again? She had fainted twice in as many days, both times when she was home alone, but she hadn't told Dale; she didn't want to bother him. The familiar black cloud seeped behind her eyes. Not now, she willed herself.

"I know the way," Deb said, waddling down the hall to the kitchen, more at home than Cathy was.

With Deb out of her airspace, Cathy's head cleared. Quickly, she scratched, her little finger biting at the itch.

"Are you coming?" Deb called. She had already seated herself, perched on one buttock on a chair.

"I was just about to make some tea," Cathy said, coming into the kitchen.

"Iced tea would be great."

"Iced tea? I don't think—"

"I'll take instant. I like it strong. Sometimes I put a whole scoop into one glass," Deb confessed.

"That's right," Cathy said, putting the kettle on to boil.

"The water doesn't have to be hot."

Cathy looked at her. Idiot, she thought. Of course the water has to be hot.

"Where do you keep the tea? I'll make it myself, that way I can get it just right."

"The tea is in the larder," Cathy said.

"Where?"

"The larder." Cathy pointed to a yellow cupboard as tall as she was. "In the white jar."

"That's the pantry, or that's what we call it over here, anyway. I guess we have lots of different words, even though we speak the same language," Deb said, her face solemn with this profundity. Heaving herself from the chair with great effort, she found the tea jar and unstopped its cork lid. "So you make it the old-fashioned way. Of course you do—you're British. But do you have any instant? I like the taste better."

What? Cathy thought about it: but tea *is* instant. It only takes a few seconds to brew. "Would you like a cup of tea?" she asked, beginning again.

"Yes!" Deb cried. "But I'll make it myself, if it's no trouble to you. Just give me a glass of water and some ice."

"Tap water?"

"That's fine with me. I'm not fussy about my water the way some people are."

"Ice?"

"Of course. For *iced* tea."

"Iced tea?"

"Haven't you ever had iced tea?" Deb asked in amazement.

Cathy shook her head.

"A whole country of tea drinkers, and tea in the afternoon, and tea parties, and tea sandwiches, and you've never had iced tea?"

Cathy shook her head more vigorously. Her itch had raised its sleeping head.

"Ain't that something!" Deb grinned and clapped her meaty hands—like two worlds colliding, Cathy thought, with a fallout of biscuit crumbs. "You're missing out on a real satisfying taste treat. Put Lipton Iced Tea Mix on your shopping list. You can get it Low-Calorie with Nutrasweet. That's what I always get," she added.

Cathy nodded. She was distracted by her need to scratch. She grabbed a dishtowel and held it in front of her, a curtain behind which her fingers—and their formidable nails— longed to dance.

"If you don't have iced tea, do you have any soda pop?" Deb asked.

Cathy grimaced and shook her head. She had thrown Dale's soft drinks out with the junk food—let him think she drank it. Let him think she ate and drank like he did, that she wanted sex all the time, that she sounded like everyone else. Her itch surged. Cathy clenched her teeth.

"Then I guess I'll have a glass of water."

"I'll get it."

Deb dropped back onto the kitchen chair, which creaked uneasily under her weight. "They say it's going to be a record hot weekend. Do you have any plans for the holiday?"

"Holiday?"

"It's Memorial Day this weekend."

"Memorial Day?"

"Don't you have Memorial Day in England?"

Cathy shook her head. "What is it?"

Once again Deb was amazed. "No iced tea and no Memorial Day. What else don't you have over there? Do you have washing machines?"

"Of course," Cathy said. She was up on tiptoe, rubbing herself against the Formica countertop's sharp edge.

"Well, I don't know, do I? I've only ever been to New Jersey and Maryland. I've never even been to Canada, although I do plan to go one day. I'm going to drive up with my best friends Ali and Jo, and we'll sail over Niagara Falls in one of those bucket boats. Just like the cartoons," Deb chuckled. Then, spontaneously, she sang: " 'To race the falls they took a ride on the steamship *Maid of the Mist.* She forgot the Falls she was so busy being hugged and kissed.' That's the old song about Niagara Falls. I remember learning it when I was a Girl Scout. I bet they don't have Girl Scouts in England!"

"What's Memorial Day?" Cathy asked again, trying to steer Deb back to the subject. They would be here all day at this rate, taking detours to talk about the most inane things. Deb talked just to hear herself talk!

"It's the official beginning of summer," Deb said. "People go to the shore, and have barbecues and picnics, and the outdoor swimming pools open for the season."

Cathy handed her a crackling glass of ice water. "What is it a memorial for?"

Deb didn't know, she realized. "Something to do with war. A memorial for soldiers, I guess. Didn't your husband tell you about Memorial Day?"

"He's away," Cathy said.

Deb looked shocked. "Don't tell me he went off and left you alone on Memorial Day weekend!"

"He's away on business. He couldn't help it."

"But you only just got here," Deb protested.

"It's business," Cathy repeated, which is what Dale had said. If it was business, then he was looking after her, even when he was away. He was looking after their financial future. There were mortgage payments on this big house, plus all the luxuries a wife should have, like dresses and manicures, a nice car, and a diamond ring worth two months' salary. He couldn't just sit at home all day, watching TV—although he wouldn't mind. But *someone* had to earn the money to keep her in this country, and no wife of his would work.

"On Memorial Day weekend? I never heard such a thing. I guess times have changed," Deb sighed. "I hope he's somewhere good, at least."

"New Jersey?" Cathy guessed. She didn't know the geography of America yet. She knew she was somewhere on the East Coast, in the town of Churchtown, in the state of Pennsylvania, and that was it. Dale had promised to buy her a United States atlas so she could get a sense of where she was and just how big an area he covered for Smart Cups.

"Did he say where in New Jersey?"

Cathy thought for a minute. "Wildwood?"

"Wildwood is a seashore town," Deb nodded. "It'll be busy this weekend. I went there once, a long time ago, with Don. We rented a raft and lay on it all day, floating like a couple of castaways. When we finally sat up and looked around, we'd drifted too far from shore to get back by ourselves, the current was so strong. The Coast Guard had to rescue us, and when I climbed into their boat, I stepped on my bathing suit straps, which I had pulled down around my shoulders to get some sun. I was bent over like this, trying to get in the boat—" Deb leaned forward in her chair, but her tubby belly stopped her from going far. "And my whole top came down! Boy, how Don and the lifeguards laughed. I can laugh now, but we never went back there again."

Cathy gritted her teeth and tried to smile politely—but she didn't care about beaches, or iced tea, or Deb's Tupperware. She hated the fat lady who wouldn't shut up, who made a nuisance of herself, dropping by when she hadn't been asked. Cathy wanted Deb to leave now. She wanted to scratch properly, to get her shorts off and get down to the skin, dig into her flesh with her fingernails, a hairbrush, anything rough. Desperate, she opened the door to the basement and started down the wooden stairs, grabbing at herself.

"Where are you going?" Deb called after her. "I didn't mean to make you upset. I'm sure Dale has to work, just like you said."

"My washing," Cathy lied. "I should check on it."

Deb followed her to the top of the stairwell. "It's dark down there. Here, let me help," she said, flicking the light switch.

Just in time, Cathy withdrew her hand from her shorts.

"I'm fine," she muttered, going back upstairs. She shuddered as she chafed Deb's panting side.

"Are you OK?" Deb asked.

"Yes."

"You know, you don't look so good," Deb said.

"I'm fine."

Deb cleared her throat. "OK, whatever you say. I've got to go to the supermarket before the hamburger gets bought up. They always sell out on Memorial Day weekend. You'd think the stores would learn by now. I've tried to tell them. I know Bob, the store manager. He offered me a job once, based on my feedback." Deb looked pleased with herself. "If you want to stop by my house this weekend, you're more than welcome. I'll do us a barbecue. Ribs and Sloppy Joes and foot-long hotdogs on the grill. My doctor told me not to eat so much, but it's Memorial Day, and if you don't have your fun, what do you have?" She rubbed her belly. "Tonight's Pizza Night, if you want. I always order from Pete's Pizza on Fridays. They make the best stromboli in town."

Cathy nodded, glaring at Deb's feet.

"Really, I mean it. I'll get enough for both of us."

Cathy didn't say anything.

Deb trotted for the door, the short spirals of her dark curls quivering. "Whatever you want is fine by me. Bye for now!"

When the door was shut and locked, Cathy dragged her shorts to her knees, scratching frantically. Something escaped—she felt a tickle on the back of her hand and lifted it to inspect. A tiny rust-colored mite scuttled over the bridge of one finger, around to the soft palm. She turned her hand over. The mite wiggled and tried to burrow into a crease of skin. Some kind of bug, probably dropped from the ceiling, Cathy thought, glancing up at the corners she had hoovered of cobwebs, the wiped walls, thinking of the revolving strip of flypaper Dale had hung in the kitchen. Her palm twinged with a familiar itch. Cathy stepped into better light, drawing her hand close to her nose. It looked just like a crab, pincers and all, a disgusting critter the color of blood—she screamed and clutched at herself, raking through her pubic hair. That wasn't the only one she found.

Villain by Necessity

Mitch opened his closet door to reveal the black Gucci suit
he had purchased for his college graduation. A fine silt of
dust had collected on its subtle shoulders, and the suit
needed dry cleaning; he had thrown up on himself the last
time he was in New York, after a long night of drinking.
Mitch had sat on Steve's brand-new couch and barfed into
his cupped hands in front of his former classmates, most of
whom were also dressed in suits, having come from work,
while he had endured yet another unsuccessful interview.
He winced, remembering. He hoped everyone had forgotten
by now. He thought of the Pisser at Conn College, who
peed on Steve's CD collection one night after she followed
him home from a bar; she said she couldn't find the bathroom when Steve found her crouched over the Grateful
Dead. Had his friends come up with a name for Mitch as
well? What would he be greeted with? "Hello, Chuck!"

Mitch scraped the suit's lapels. The specks of vomit that
remained he sponged off with the toe of a sock dribbled
with spit. It was three o'clock already; at five sharp his
parents would return from work and they had agreed to
drop him at the bus station on their way to dinner. Mitch

would arrive in the city shortly after eight, race to Lily's party, surprising everyone, then off to the Hamptons at last, and life after that.

Never mind that he hadn't informed Steve that he hoped to crash on his couch for a few weeks, until he found a job and his own apartment, probably in Alphabet City. But Steve hadn't returned his call yesterday as promised. He was working, Mitch reasoned, and he always went drinking after work, staying out late, all night if he got lucky. He might still call today. Either way, Mitch knew the plan and where he was going. Of course his friends would be happy to see him! They *wanted* him to move to New York. They always said so. He tried not to worry as he packed his treasured castoff Louis Vuitton duffel bag (from Stephanie, the only daughter of a telephone company chairman, his first love at Conn College) with enough clothes to get by. Once he was settled in, he would send for the rest of his things, or he might just start all over again, with new clothes, furniture, and CDs, a whole new Mitch.

Yesterday, while Luisa was vacuuming downstairs, he had crept into his parents' neat bedroom, with its average antique pieces and elaborately draped tapestry-print curtains. His mother's jewelry box, which alone adorned her bureau, had been a gift from her mother. The plain mahogany box was lined in raspberry velvet, its lid mirrored inside, and Mitch avoided his eyes when he removed his grandmother's diamond earrings—the sole tenants of the box, for whom it had been specially made. He was ten years old when his mother showed him the earrings for the first time, the diamonds in their white gold settings larger even than her own large engagement ring from his father.

"They're bee-ooo-ti-ful," Mitch had breathed. "Why don't you wear them?"

"They're not for me. They're for you and Babo when you get married. You'll each have an earring for your engagement rings."

Mitch had nodded solemnly as she told him about her deceased parents, neither of whom he had met—but instead of listening to that privileged bit of family information, he was intent on the earrings. They were fine, covetable jewels like he had read about in detective stories, the kind that were always being stolen or smuggled across borders in a child's teddy bear.

Before they were shut away, the diamonds had winked at him as if to say, "Come play with us!" He had marveled at them many times after that day—once, he weighed them on a set of metric scales he swiped from the science room at school: 800 milligrams. Now, seeing them again after so many years made Mitch breathless with anticipation, the two insoluble ice cubes tinkling like dice in his cupped hand. He threw them down on the bureau top. "Snake eyes!"

His mother had never worn the earrings, had never even had her ears pierced. She was too impatient to fuss with earrings or any jewelry other than her plain gold wristwatch and wedding and engagement rings, which she never took off. She had work to do, she always said, and work was law. The housework, gardening, and cooking for her family, dressing up to go out—these chores she left to others who could, she admitted, do a better job. When Mitch was born, she was studying for the bar with an associate position lined up. Babo popped out nine years later, and Luisa, who had been their twice-a-week cleaning lady, signed on for a full-time week with the White family.

Mitch had an idea of the diamonds' value, of what they might be worth on the street, but he didn't understand just *how* valuable they were: the future of two sons. He knew his mother as unsentimental and hardworking, lacking social grace, dress sense, and a comfortable maternal instinct. The earrings wouldn't be missed, at least for a while—and not by a woman who scorned frippery, he thought. If the diamonds *were* discovered missing, he could always blame Babo. But no, Mitch reassured himself, his mother wasn't likely to open her jewelry box anytime soon. Maybe he wouldn't even need to sell the earrings when he got to New York. Maybe things would work out for him.

Meanwhile, today was the day, his last day at home, at long last, and it was time to get washed and dressed. Mitch's neglected skin was like sandpaper, crackling when he scratched himself. His hair was stringy, too long, catching in the sticky corners of his mouth. Styrofoam-like plaque clung to his teeth, and the thin, sensitive skin of his gums was swollen almost to splitting. His nose was stubbled with blackheads. Even his eyebrows had grown, their hairs thick and black, gathered like devil's horns. In the shower, he lathered his head three times with the clotted contents of an ancient bottle of herbal shampoo. He sniffed—rosemary, lavender, and mint. So this is aromatherapy, he thought, already feeling more like his confident old self. He scrubbed and rinsed and scrubbed again until the water ran clear down the drain. Finally, with his pores yawning from the steam, he stepped from the shower, wiped the mirror, and squeezed his nose clean. He brushed his teeth, spitting pink, and combed his hair, slicking it back Wall Street trader-style. He would have it cut in New York, he thought, feeling inspired, at Vidal Sassoon, perhaps by the man himself.

Mitch had pulled the dusty Louis Vuitton bag from his closet shelf the night before and buffed its vinyl to a clear shine. Now he taped his grandmother's earrings inside the bag, then packed three pairs of Levi's 501s and the staple white T-shirts he had taken to wearing in college, stuffing in as many pairs of underwear as the zipper could hold. He had decided against taking his camcorder; it was time he got a real movie camera, a professional model. He dressed in the Gucci suit trousers and a starched white collared shirt borrowed from his father's closet. He looked at his watch (just now found in his suit coat pocket) and saw that he had an hour to kill. What to do? There was never enough to do at home.

He went to the window and looked out. No sign of Scarlet across the street. Her Stairmaster waited patiently for her return, as Mitch had all week—but now he was getting out of here! He would meet plenty of girls in New York, all tangible and real, girls that he could reach out and touch, his fingers grazing their coat sleeves as he passed them on the street, his elbows electric against theirs as he ordered a drink in a bar. Steve said that there were more women than men in Manhattan, sixty percent versus forty percent, like at Conn College—and the women were horny and liberated. They didn't care about commitment, and if they did get pregnant, they went straight to the abortion clinic and paid for it themselves. One girl had already had four abortions when she met Steve, and talked openly about her terminations like she was going to the dentist, he said.

Mitch sat down at his desk out of habit, despite not having accomplished anything there during the last year. He opened the drawer and fiddled with a chain of paper clips he had linked the other day, then re-inked his name, carved into the drawer's bottom when he was ten and acquired the desk: MITCH in tall, red letters. He decided to write to his parents, telling them of his plans to stay in New York. He would leave the note on his pillow so Luisa might find it and pass it on when she stripped his bed (a rare opportunity to launder his sheets was never missed).

He stared at the blank paper, uninspired as usual. His eyes dried out from staring and he dropped his head into his arms. This instinct, too, was familiar. How many exams had he slept through at Conn College after a late night? How many all-nighters, down to the wire with an essay due, had Mitch had a good night's rest instead? Now, as he slept, he dreamed he was outdoors, stretched out in a field of wildflowers. He smelled rosemary, lavender, and mint. The sun was warm on his face. A cooing dove waffled on and he let this peace roll over him . . .

A car horn blew, jerking him awake. He knew where he was in an instant (Atomic View was *hell*) and knew he had somewhere to go. His father's horn brayed impatiently. Mitch groaned. When had he last seen his parents? He remembered watching from his bedroom window as his father weeded dandelions using a sharp knife; he held each weed aloft triumphantly, the ganglion roots dripping milk-blood. His mother he had passed last evening, stooped over a spread of paper at the dining room table. At first she hadn't looked up, still mad, he guessed, about his father's birthday. But when Mitch broached the subject of visiting New York, she thought it was a good idea for him to see his friends—they might have a positive influence on him, she said, and besides, it was time for him to dip his toe in the job market again. He should make sure to bring home a New York Times classifieds section. Mitch had sighed with relief and almost kissed his mother goodnight.

Now this one last encounter to brave and he was free, indefinitely free. His father's horn rang out again, held down, furious. Mitch grabbed his bag and suit coat. It must come clear and hard, the voice, when it comes, when it tells you to go.

Secrets Explode!

As they passed Deb at her mailbox, one of the Johnson boys was overtaking the Whites' BMW in his hopped-up Rabbit. The Powerwalker tucked and rolled onto the Rothmans' lawn across the street, saving herself, as the Rabbit skipped from one side of Cosmos Drive to the other before streaking off, the Whites on its tail.

"Did you see that?" the Powerwalker called out to Deb. "They almost killed me!"

"They *were* driving fast," Deb said, rolling down her car window for a chat.

But the Powerwalker was already on her feet, two fingers on her pulse, ready to tear off again. "This neighborhood is changing," she huffed, beating her arms and wagging her bony rear end as she disappeared around the bend.

Well, Deb thought, she's right, maybe. Deb was starting to feel like people didn't want to talk to her. They sped past in their cars when she hailed them, and kept their lawnmowers running when she stopped to ask the latest news. Daily, she circled Atomic View, looking for somewhere to drop in and visit, but more often than not she ended up back at home in front of the television. People just weren't neighborly like they used to be. They cut in line at the store, or tailed each other bumper to bumper on the highway, swearing and sticking up their middle fingers like it was a natural thing to do.

A stench of burnt rubber lingered where the Rabbit had marked its trail in the road, and Deb rolled up her window to get away from the smell. She did the loop once more in her car—it was a hot day, maybe too hot for people to be out and about—before parking in the shade of her garage. Back in her kitchen, she restlessly opened every cupboard and drawer, lingering in the cool air of the refrigerator. She tried to listen to her belly, like Doctor Greaves said she should. Was it hungry? It wouldn't answer. Was it lonely? Bored? Did it want something to do?

Deb slammed the fridge door and reached for the phone.

"What's wrong? Did something happen?" Maureen was always a good listener. She loved Deb's stories, loved to hear about Atomic View; like Deb, she loved the neighborhood, remembering it as a happy time in her life. She often wished aloud that she could live there again.

"I don't know what's wrong," Deb said.

"Are you sick?"

"I'm hungry."

"Then eat something!" Maureen laughed.

"I'm trying to be healthy. I'm not really hungry, I just think I am. I don't want to eat—but I'm so hungry. I'm starving!"

"I don't understand why you don't just eat if you're hungry. Your body knows the answers, Deb."

"I guess I'm not making any sense. I'm not hungry—

but I am. I mean, I know I'm not, not really, I just think I am." Deb paused, then was silent. It was unusual for her not to say anything.

Maureen picked up the slack. "I just had my lesson with the girl from the teaching college. I wrote a poem. Do you want to hear it?"

"OK."

"Here goes. It's called, 'My Name is Not Mo':
'My name is not Mo,
And please don't call me lazy, good-for-nothing, slow,
Slut, stupid, or boring.
You may call me Maureen.' "

"That's nice, Maureen. I like that. I wish you could show that one to Mike. Show him how smart you are."

"How could I show it to him? Mike's dead."

"Mike's not dead, Maureen."

"Mike's dead," Maureen answered stubbornly. "To me, he's dead."

"That's not right. You can't just pretend someone's dead when they're still alive."

"Why not? It's what gets me through. Isn't that what's important? What gets you through? I can see him dead and buried in my head. I can see the stone at his grave. 'He was a good husband,' it says."

"He wasn't a good husband to you. You know that," Deb said.

"He wasn't half bad. Poor Mike. Now he's dead. Hey, I bet Mike and Don are friends in heaven. I bet they go to the game together. Don't you think? They would like each other—I mean, they were married to us, and we like each other. Right, Deb?"

"We're a couple of fruitcakes," Deb sighed. "They'll put us away."

"They already put me away," Maureen giggled. "I'm so nuts that you're the only one who comes to see me. Everyone else steers clear. Maybe they think what I've got is catching."

"You're lucky you've got me. And I'm lucky I've got you," Deb said. She turned on the TV, keeping it mute; it was time for *Mary Lou*. She waited out the commercial break, listening to Maureen chatter about last night's AA meeting—and couldn't believe her eyes when Cindy Hart appeared on the screen.

"Maureen, I've got to go," Deb said, interrupting.

"Are you coming to see me tomorrow?"

"I always come on Saturdays, don't I?"

"You're a good friend to me," Maureen said happily.

"I'm your sister, Maureen. That's what we agreed, remember? We're sisters, and we need to stick together."

"That's right!"

"OK. See you tomorrow. Bye for now!" Deb pressed hard on the volume button, turning the TV up loud so she wouldn't miss a word of the program.

"Today's show is called 'Secrets Explode!' and our next guest is Cindy." Cindy was a Churchtown girl who worked as a cashier in the supermarket where Deb shopped. She was a favorite among customers, her bottle-blonde bangs teased into a tidal wave three inches above her forehead and sprayed until starched—a real rip-curl of hair. She smelled of raspberry bubble bath and the menthol Kools she smoked, the pack stashed in her register next to the twenties in case a quiet moment came, when Cindy would hit the "no sale" button, catching the drawer with her hip, grab her cigarettes, sling the drawer home again, and dash out front to smoke. In between smokes, she cracked gum vigorously, and sometimes did both at once. She lived with Lawrence Caper, her high-school sweetheart, in a trailer park called Conestoga Wagons. Cindy's parents were Christians who didn't approve of her living with Lawrence before they were married, but Cindy had always been rebellious and fast. Deb knew these personal details because Cindy and Lawrence were big news in Churchtown two years back. The particular *Mary Lou* she was watching was a repeat—Deb had a tape of it somewhere, of course: a local girl on national TV, bravely telling her story to millions!

Before Cindy met Lawrence, she was good and pure, her parents said, a virtuous Christian, a volunteer. It was Lawrence who changed her. Lawrence wanted Cindy to dress sexy and dye her hair blonde. Lawrence wanted Cindy to quit school so she wouldn't get too smart. Lawrence punched Cindy in places that wouldn't show the marks, making sure she listened to him.

Then Lawrence started seeing another, younger girl on the side, just fourteen to his and Cindy's seventeen years, and he broke Cindy's heart. Her blonde bangs stuck up more for being unwashed and a bad night's sleep, like she buried her head in the pillow and wept, and she didn't bother with makeup. She was quiet at her register, her eyes downcast when before she challenged anyone who walked past, and she packed Deb's groceries badly, putting the laundry bleach in the same sack as the meat, cans of peaches in syrup on top of the eggs and bread.

"Lawrence is the love of my life," Cindy declared on TV. "We've been together since we were kids. I know Lawrence loves me. I mean, he says he does."

"What happened?" Mary Lou asked.

"When I came home from work the other day, Lawrence's car was parked outside our house. I walked in and he was in bed with that little bitch. *Our* bed! They both just looked at me. They didn't even stop at first!" she wailed. "They kept *doing* it!"

The audience groaned in chorus. "Come on, girl! Wake up and smell the poontang!" someone called out.

"Lawrence says he's done with her anyway. He says that was the last time. He says that she *made* him do it, that she raped him, practically," Cindy explained.

"Do you believe him?"

"All I can say is, if he ever goes with her again, I'll kill him. I'll kill her first!" Cindy balled her fists.

The audience whooped their approval.

"Cindy, calm down, or you'll be in trouble before you know it," Mary Lou warned.

"I can't live without Lawrence!"

"It doesn't sound like Lawrence is good for you. If he disrespects you now, he always will. There's no changing other people, that's what I always say on my show."

"I want to have his babies," Cindy begged. "I want us to have a nice house with a two-car garage and a little boy named Lawrence Jr. and a little girl called Pearl."

"Cindy, if you lock yourself into Lawrence now, it's a life sentence. Once you have kids and a house and everything else that comes with making a family, you're stuck. You'll stay and try to make it work, no matter what. I know you will. I've met a lot of girls like you, and they always find a reason not to leave. He'll be your warden, Cindy. You better be sure you want that life—I know I wouldn't. No man is worth this amount of trouble and heartache, especially a two-timer like Lawrence."

Cindy sniffed and looked at her hands. "I guess you're right."

"I *know* I am," Mary Lou said, and the audience applauded. She shuffled a pile of index cards. "Cindy, I think it's time you met someone. You've seen her before, during the unpleasant incident you mentioned to us just a minute ago. She's trouble to you, but we need to get to peace here. You two need to talk to each other and that's what I do: I get the truth out. You only get the truth on my show. Isn't that right?"

Again, cheering from the audience, while Cindy looked nervously around, checking over her shoulder, squinting into the dark depths of the stage wings.

"Are you ready, Cindy?"

"Yeah," Cindy said uncertainly.

"Are you ready, audience?"

The audience clapped heartily.

"Michelle," Mary Lou called. "Come on out."

Michelle charged onstage, ready to fight despite that she was the smaller girl by far, and the audience responded with a chorus of boos. Her blonde pompadour of bangs—a good two inches taller and prouder than Cindy's—crowned a pinched, pink face screwed up like a wash rag, and she flailed her skinny arms, staggering on high heels to her seat. "Go to hell," she told the audience, gesturing obscenely.

"Michelle, sit down, please."

"Go to hell!" she screamed.

"I won't ask you again, Michelle," Mary Lou warned. At the front of the stage, her security guards—overinflated beefcakes, identically dressed in red muscle shirts, trained to sit, heel, and roll over—readied themselves.

Michelle sat and crossed her arms defiantly over her flimsy bust.

"Do you two know each other?" asked Mary Lou.

"No," Cindy replied hotly, tossing her blonde head.

"I know who she is," Michelle muttered, her chin jutting defensively. "She's my boyfriend's ex."

Cindy gasped and turned her head to meet her challenger's stare. "Liar!" The audience leaned forward in anticipation.

"Who's your boyfriend, Michelle?"

"Lawrence Caper."

The audience whooped and beat their hands together. "That's a lie! You little bitch!" Cindy shouted, leaping to her feet, fingers reaching for Michelle's hair in which, if they had the chance, they would entwine mercilessly. But no such luck: Mary Lou's guard dogs rushed the stage and lifted Cindy back into her chair, where they held her, one on either arm, as the audience roared appreciation.

"I'm no liar!" Michelle screeched, as two more of Mary

Lou's security team appeared to ensure she stayed in place. "Lawrence is *my* boyfriend!"

"He loves *me!*"

The girls lunged and spat like rattlesnakes. Mary Lou fanned herself with her index cards while the audience hollered, "We want Lawrence! Bring us Lawrence!"

"He's been cheating on you all this year with me!"

"Well, he *lives* with me! We're getting married!"

"It's me he's going to marry!"

"You're his whore! You're so easy!"

"Don't nobody want you! You're butt-ugly! You're a smelly old shoe!"

"We want Lawrence! Bring us Lawrence!" the audience chanted.

"Open your eyes, girls—Lawrence is a liar to *both* of you," Mary Lou said.

"He's a dog!" someone called from the audience.

"He is *my* man!" Cindy defended hotly.

"If he's your man, why's he coming to me? You're not woman enough, is why!" Michelle retorted.

"Shut your fat trap! You are going to pay!" Cindy cried, pounding her feet on the stage.

The audience whooped. They were there for the dirty stories of other people's lives, admittedly worse than their own. They wanted to verbally wallop the doomed, their cruelty endorsed by the television network as deserved by those who willingly placed themselves in Mary Lou's chairs. The audience wanted the public confession, wanted to know when the first speck of darkness set in and the bad cell began to migrate and multiply. They wanted to hear every last detail of the departure from childhood incest to promiscuity at twelve years old to the crack pipe and jail. Most of all, they wanted to see blood.

"We're going to take a break," Mary Lou said to the camera.

The next time Deb had seen Cindy in the flesh, she was wearing Lawrence's engagement ring. She flashed the chosen hand to anyone who cared to look, as well as those who didn't, displaying its thin gold band with a diamond chip tacked on. Her bangs peaked on her forehead like a rooster's crown.

A week later, she and Lawrence killed Michelle. The teenage girl was found with her throat cut, just inside her own front door. Michelle had greeted Lawrence with open arms, then, from behind him, Cindy swooped, and it was Cindy who wielded the bread knife while Lawrence held the surprised girl down.

For the first time in her life, Deb turned off *Mary Lou*— it was a repeat anyway, but more than that, it troubled her now. She wondered if the show's producers knew what horror followed the girls when they left the stage. If they had sat and analyzed the tape afterwards, as Deb had done, looking for clues as to what was coming. If they had looked back and thought, I should have known, I should have done something when I could.

Carriages Without Horses
Shall Go

Before they even left Atomic View, they almost crashed in the car. Mitch's father was a reckless, heavy-treaded driver, a speeder, and a tailgater—a surprising glitch in his otherwise law-abiding character. Once, after collecting eleven-year-old Mitch and his friends from the Water Buggy waterslide, his father had driven the entire way home on the highway's shoulder when traffic backed up from a car accident. "There's no need to tell anyone about this," he instructed the spellbound boys.

"Cool. That was so cool," they had proclaimed, Mitch loudest of all.

His mother often had words with Mitch's father before any kind of family outing. If he still drove like a road-guzzling salesman, she warned him quietly and firmly. If the situation worsened yet, she hissed, "Slow down!" with the sibilant S like heat coming off the macadam in fuel-colored jet streams.

That Friday, when Mitch threw his Louis Vuitton bag onto the BMW's backseat and followed it clumsily, limbs just awake, his father had barked, "We're late. *You're* late. Now we'll have to hurry." He accelerated before Mitch could shut his door, and the impetus of the car's lunge forward meant the bivalve part nearly crushed his exposed ankle (Mitch never wore socks, not since his arrival at Conn College).

"We have plenty of time," his mother said.

Mitch looked at his watch. "No, we don't. My bus is in fifteen minutes. I don't even have a ticket yet."

"What were you doing that you couldn't be outside waiting? I asked you to be outside, didn't I?" his father demanded.

"Jim," his mother said. "Just stop now. There's no need to take it out on Mitch—"

"I'm not taking it out on Mitch."

"You *are* taking it out on Mitch."

"What happened?" Mitch asked.

"Are you blind?" his father snapped.

"*Jim.*"

It was only then that Mitch saw his father's hands were bandaged, that he held the steering wheel gingerly in gauzy white mitts. "Jesus, Dad, what happened?"

"A client's dog bit me."

"On both hands?"

"What does it look like?"

"He spent the afternoon in the hospital," his mother said. "He had to have stitches."

"How many?" Mitch asked.

"Twelve," his mother answered. "But he won't let me drive."

"It's just a couple of stitches. It's not like they cut off my hands."

Mitch whistled. "Pretty good, Dad. Whose dog?"

"He can't say," his mother said.

"Mrs. Weatherly," his father answered in an icy voice.

Mitch could imagine the scene: his father, never a lover of dogs, bowing stiffly in his navy suit to pat the offender's head. The widow, Mrs. Weatherly, brooches pinned all over the front of her food-spotty dress, would have warned him that her baby was suspicious of strangers. Another lawyer might have cracked an anti-lawyer joke, something like "I'm no stranger—I know everything about you. I may steal your money, but I'll do it to your face, ha ha ha." Mitch's father would never make a joke like that; law was his vocation, not a get-rich scheme, and he was reverent to its practice and propriety. The dog would have scented his stuffy discomfort as he reached out with a bone-white hand—and the sound he made when bitten was like a squeak-toy, wheezing and yelping.

"Surely you're due some kind of compensation, Dad," Mitch said. "I mean, you can't just let her get away with it. I bet you could win a big chunk of money from this old lady. Both hands! You've definitely got a case." If only that dog had bitten *me*, he thought, then my troubles would be over. He knew Mrs. Weatherly was a rich woman whose husband had owned the farmland on which the mall, Park & Shop City, was built.

"We'll see," his father said, glancing in the rearview mirror. "Now what's this?"

A battered VW Rabbit had thrust itself at the BMW's rear bumper, just missing contact. Its driver was clearly laughing—Mitch could see that it was Tim Johnson, his old playmate, who gave him the finger by way of greeting. Next to Tim, looking somehow small in his bucket seat, looking apprehensive (despite that he, too, was a big boy, often approached by the high school basketball coach), was Babo's bald, best friend Nate.

Mitch's father accelerated, too late. The Rabbit's muffler roared as it struggled to pass, using will and nerve to beat the BMW at the race.

"Slow down," his mother ordered over the noise of battling engines. "This is crazy!"

The Rabbit swerved in front of them, blasting its horn triumphantly. Mitch's father swore and slowed. When the Rabbit snaked onto Mother Road, the BMW followed.

Mitch's mother breathed out a long sigh of relief to be on the busy road, self-regulated by a steady traffic flow. "It's not a race. Whoever he was, he was showing off. You don't have to compete—you're not a teenager, for God's sake. I bet you don't have any grip on the wheel in those bandages," she scolded. "We can be a few minutes late. They won't give away our table."

"What about my bus? If I miss my bus, I'm screwed," Mitch said.

His mother shot him a look. She despised the casual use of obscene language, especially by her children: it reflected badly on their upbringing, she said. Fuck that, Mitch thought. He was using the language of the world *he* knew.

"It does matter if we're late, Eileen. It matters to me. I've had a terrible day. All I want right now is a nice dinner with my wife, some easy conversation—no politics, please— and a good night's sleep."

But traffic on 333 was heavier than usual, the road packed with cars headed for the shore. "Well," Mitch said, "if I miss my bus, looks like I'm stuck with you. Where are you guys eating tonight? Anywhere good?"

"If you hadn't been late, we wouldn't have this problem! You'll sit in the car and wait for us if you miss your bus," his father exploded, nearly bumping the car in front.

"Jim," he was warned again.

They sat in silence until the traffic suddenly broke, the source of the bottleneck revealed: a fender-bender, two cars pulled off on the road's shoulder, their drivers shouting abuse at each other, wives by their sides to back them up— or, perhaps, ready to take on each other as well. The muscular four-by-four was undamaged; the Ford Escort's back window had shattered, its rear bumper shorn off, its trunk rendered a flapping gap-toothed smile, corroded by rust. In both cars sat families, the children of the four-by-four mute and scared-looking, strapped into their seats in the air-conditioning, while the Escort's clan wandered freely, hanging out the open windows, Kool Aid rings around their mouths, chucking handfuls of broken glass.

"A bunch of rubberneckers. That's what the problem was. A bunch of rubberneckers," his father muttered, picking up speed.

"Just goes to show you the benefits of driving a bigger car," his mother said. "Look at that Escort."

"It's a shitty car anyway," Mitch said.

His mother turned around to look at him again. He sniggered. She sighed. "What are your plans for the weekend, Mitch?"

"I'm going to hook up with a bunch of people and go out, I guess."

"You're going to party," his father said, giving the word "party" a disapproving twist.

"What's wrong with that?" Mitch said. "I haven't been out of the house in months. I'm young. I should be having fun. It's no fun living at home, I'll tell you that. No fucking fun," he added for his mother's benefit.

Sure enough, she glared at him, before his father braked sharply and she quickly faced front again. "That's all you boys think about," his father said. "Parties. Where's the party. Party, party, party, all the time. You don't think about the real world or what your lives are going to amount to someday. You have no ambition. You only care about having fun."

"Babo is very motivated about his skateboarding," his mother said. "That's something. He told me he could be a professional, with sponsorship. Some of them make a good living."

Mitch couldn't help himself—this might be his last chance to say it. "At least I don't sleep with a gun. Babo's got a gun!"

"Where do you come up with this garbage?" his father said, pulling into the Churchtown bus station—a ticket box in a diner parking lot. An old horse cart was parked in the lot, its flatbed filled with colorful pansies and impatiens, a hand-lettered sign reading "Welcome to Churchtown" where its driver should have been.

"Hey, I need some money," Mitch said.

"What?" his father barked.

"I don't have any money. Remember? That's why I'm living at home."

"I'll get it, Jim," his mother said quickly, opening her purse.

"Give him a hundred dollars."

"New York is the most expensive city in the world," Mitch protested, taking the money. "This will barely feed me." Was it enough to get to the Hamptons? He didn't know how much the weekend would cost. He had counted on his parents giving him two or three hundred dollars, as they usually did when he went to the city. Mitch didn't want to have to borrow money from one of his friends. The only people who could get away with borrowing money were people everyone knew were rich. *Really* rich. Then there was no problem—not that they paid the money back, because most often they didn't. They forgot, it was assumed. Money wasn't something they thought or talked about; it was just there for them to spend.

"Then eat at McDonald's," his father said.

"I hate McDonald's. I can eat at McDonald's anywhere. I want to eat good food in New York." Mitch saw his mother's hand flutter over her wallet and he leaned forward hopefully—but his father stopped her with one white paw.

"A hundred dollars is enough," he insisted. "Teach the boy a lesson about economizing."

Mitch slammed the door hard when he got out, so that the car vibrated with the blow. "Asshole!"

His father rolled down his window. "Mitch!"

Mitch kept on walking. He joined the short line at the ticket window before he looked back, pointed at the waiting

bus, and shrugged. His father motioned to him with a bandaged hand, but Mitch stayed put. He bought a ticket—one
way—waved goodbye, and boarded the familiar Greyhound, joining the other passengers with their cardboard
buckets of fried chicken and oversized Cokes, their pro-
motional duffel bags of cheap nylon printed with an
insurance company's logo, their bad haircuts, mullets and
home-cooked bubble perms with teased bangs, scalped little
boys ready for the summer heat. He found two empty seats
next to each other and settled in, placing his bag on the
window side, his arm protectively through its leather
handles. As the bus began to roll, he offered one last prayer
to Churchtown: that his father's white-hot moment of anger
would melt into a slow burn, like indigestion, and ruin his
meal.

Christmas

Babo fixed his gaze on the bush's timbered ceiling. He inhaled the balsam scent, like smelling salts for the faint-hearted, and thought of Christmas. Christmas was a comforting thought when things went wrong on drugs. Babo loved Christmas. When he was very young and had piano lessons, he played Christmas carols year-round; in art class his favorite color of construction paper had been blue, on which he drew white crayon snowflakes (haphazard stabs and dashes) and a fat red Santa Claus zooming over the moon, led by eight reindeer with silver-glitter hoofs.

Christmas. *Christmas.* Babo whispered the word and hugged himself. He curled on his side on the floor of what he imagined to be a friendly forest, not far from the North Pole. He tucked his knees to his chest and lay his cheek on a pillow of soft fronds. The late afternoon sun pushed a finger down the evergreen's spindly trunk, winding round until it lit on Babo in a visor of golden light he wore on the crown of his shiny black head.

In the world beyond the bush, a helicopter crackled and sirens shrieked in the distance. Babo pictured a fragrant six-foot Douglas fir resplendent in glass bells and tinsel in the

Whites' living room window, his parents in repose in their massive wing chairs like the King and Queen of Christmas, encouraging the unwrapping process. Christmas morning at the Whites was spectacular, with thousands of dollars of gifts for the boys, skateboards and roller blades and bicycles and computer software and designer clothes. Luisa baked muffins freckled with cinnamon and raisins and chocolate chips, cookies smudged with jam buttons with which they stuffed themselves. In the background, the radio was tuned to a local station devoted to Christmas carols, while the TV displayed a popping, snapping log fire, perfectly built and maintained seemingly without the interference of man. At noon, his mother slid the turkey Luisa had dressed the day before into the oven. His father made creamed corn, and Babo sliced the roll of cranberry sauce that slithered from its can. Even Mitch beat the mashed potatoes to a frothy pulp, adding plenty of butter—the real stuff—and salt.

Babo shivered. He had taken too much. His eyes burned—he squeezed them shut until tears leaked from their corners. He set his mind on his Christmas list, images of wondrous material things whizzing past like a slot machine: a Sims racing team snowboard, a Tag Heuer watch, more Droors, a new turntable . . .

I'm Gonna Wash That Man Right
Out of My Hair

Prioritize, Cathy thought after her third breakdown in an hour. She had immediately employed Dale's electric razor, flinching from the tickle of the quivering blade, then scraped herself clean with a disposable and Dale's forest-scented shaving foam. Then strong soap, the green bar of Fels Naptha with its rough surface that smelled of disinfectant—she considered washing, even douching with laundry bleach. At last the itch subsided, replaced by a steady sting. Perhaps she had got them all. She picked through the hair in the sink, a nest of crabs and their crumb-sized eggs that suckled where blood surged, night after night, in arousal. Cathy lit a match and touched it to the fuse of a curly pubic hair. Immediately a fiery hand, its arm a column of smoke, reached up to slap her face, and she had to jump back to save herself from burning. When the fire waned in strength, she threw in her panties and all her Lycra workout gear, then everything else she had brought with her from England, blouses and skirts, trousers, and lastly, the red-beaded cocktail dress she had bought with the £100 Dale gave her when they met. It was contaminated, wasn't it? A conflagration flared; the smoke detector in their bedroom shrilled its battle cry, and Cathy wept too, watching her precious bits burn. Her freshly shaved pubis welled and dripped and she blindly blotted the nicks with tissue.

What if they were inside her? What if the bugs had crawled up her vagina and set up home on the plain of her uterus? What if they were cinched to her cervix? Wallowing, bloated, in her Fallopian tubes, tethered by nasty claws?

Cathy ran a bath, then collapsed over the side of the tub, wailing along with the smoke detector. The hot water might force the crabs further up. She considered the blow-dryer and other measures, like a spoon to scoop them out, ant spray, or weed killer. The smoke detector reached a higher pitch yet, its ultimatum, and Cathy yanked out the battery. She stood there, trying to think. She had to call Dale. She would call and confront him. She didn't want to, but what else was there for her to do?

Stairmaster. She could Stairmaster until she was calm and didn't want to scream anymore. But even as she thought this, the familiar itch gave a little twist, a corkscrew turn, and Cathy charged downstairs to the phone.

Of course she dialed wrong and had to be corrected by a superior recorded voice; it was her first time using the phone in America, and Dale's handwriting was hard to read, the letters squashed, with scattered dots and crosses like a bug stamped out on the pavement. Her finger shook as she dialed again and soon the phone was ringing somewhere in New Jersey. How different the ring sounded in England!

"Yeah?" a woman's sour voice answered.

"May I have Dale Manley, please," Cathy said, her voice breaking up with nerves.

"What?"

Cathy cleared her throat. "Dale Manley."

"You got the wrong number," the woman said, and she put down the phone.

Cathy studied the number Dale had scribbled, then redialed carefully, twice starting over. "Dale Manley, please," she said when the line connected. "I need to speak to my husband, Dale Manley."

The same voice answered as before. "Lady, there's no Dale here."

"Wait!" Cathy cried. "But I was given this number."

"I don't care." The line hummed.

Cathy stared at the phone in her hand like it was a loaded gun. Should she try again? What if the same woman answered and shouted at her? She thought she would cry if she did—but she didn't know who else to call. After a moment she dialed "O" for Operator, which is what they always did in films and books. "I need the number for Smart Cups."

"I'm sorry, ma'am, I didn't hear," the operator said.

"Smart Cups! Smart Cups!" Cathy bleated.

"I'll connect you with Directory Assistance. Please hold," the operator said mildly, unflappable.

"Directory Assistance, what listing?"

"Smart Cups."

"What?"

"Smart Cups," Cathy said, and then she spelled it out.

"You mean Smart Cups. What department?"

Cathy had to think. "He's a salesman?" It was a question, not an answer.

215

"Then you want sales."

"Sales!" Cathy gasped.

"Please hold for your number."

Cathy dialed Smart Cups. A recorded message told her the offices were closed for the holiday weekend and would reopen on Tuesday morning at nine o'clock. It was Friday evening, six o'clock. She couldn't wait that long.

She broke down for the fourth time, staggered by Dale's betrayal. He had been with another woman since he was with her, she was sure. He might be with his lover *right now*, and meanwhile there was no one for her to call, nowhere else to go than this house. What a trap it was! What a double-cross! Cathy threw the phone at the kitchen wall and its antenna fell off. "Rubbish!" She leapt across the floor to pick it up, her foot catching on a kitchen chair, knocking it over. She laughed a terrible rabid laugh that frightened and exhilarated her, before she overturned the kitchen table, trapping the other chair, whose two front legs snapped off like teeth. Next, pouncing on the heavy wooden chopping board, she threw *it* to the floor so that it split in two, and the sharp crack, the feeling of letting such a solid thing drop from her hands, was more satisfying than she had hoped for. Moving to the sink, Cathy turned on the tap full blast, water filling faster than it could drain. She opened the cupboards, seizing crockery and glasses, easily shattered, music to her ears. When the lot was smashed at her feet, she reached for what little food remained in the refrigerator and freezer: green grapes, broccoli, tomatoes, carrots, bags of frozen peas and corn she tore open and scattered like chicken feed. She would starve this weekend if she had to!

She would never eat again! Dale would be sorry then! Cathy laughed her terrible laugh and grabbed a knife.

In the living room, she slashed the upholstered furniture until its stuffing spilled in coils of foam entrails, then got down on her knees and savaged the carpet, slitting, cross-hatching, pulling it up in slices and trapezoids, marking out a rough-hewn trail to the dining room. There, she threw the chairs at the walls, scored deep grooves in the table, and pulverized the picture glass of a scene of fat bulldogs playing poker. She dragged the curtains from their rails, rending them triumphantly, then draped the rags over the broken chairs like cobwebs. She left the knife speared in the tabletop and sprinted down the hall to Dale's den, where she toppled his giant TV with a terrific bang that sent sparks racing along its power cord. Spying his putter in one corner, she swept it up to smash the den's cabinetry, revealing a stash of hard liquor and his video collection. She pulled out the silky black tape in fistfuls, tossing the streamers every which way like a party, celebrating with the Kahlua bottle, shot after sweet shot. Reclaiming the knife for one hand, the putter in the other, Cathy headed upstairs, hooking lamps, chipping drywall, denting the hardwood baseboards.

In the bedroom, she swung at the bedposts until they came down like felled trees in a snowy tangle of eyelet canopy, then smashed the bureau's mirror and hauled open its drawers, dumping their contents to the floor. She dragged Dale's clothes from the closet, tearing sleeves from shirts, splitting trousers down their seams. His ties shredded easily, beautifully, in enviable ribbons, and his shoes' soles cracked in her hands. She slashed at the mattress—their marriage bed was no good to her now! She headed for the bathroom to find the matches she had used to torch her pubic hair—she would burn their bed to hell, where Dale could screw for eternity!

But Cathy stumbled as she ran, twisting her ankle on a stump of bedpost, bumping her head when she landed. Sprawled on the floor, the flesh around the joint began to cook, and there was a sound in her ears of waves crashing, the dark water coming down on her, before a voice calling out brought her back. The voice was her own. It couldn't be heard by anyone else, not above the thundering surf pouring from every faucet in the house.

Bad Brains

Babo's tonsils vibrated like bees to a hive with their sugar-treasure—he could *feel* them when he talked, and the sensation was beyond ticklish, his nerves jackhammered by a million tiny buzzes. He kept cracking up. "Your sister turned into an alien!"

"Dude, when I came home, you were in the bush and the bush was twitching like it was alive. Like it had a power within—Moses and the Ten Commandments, dude. You *are* the bush. Your word is law," Nate babbled. "I'm tripping my face off."

"This trip is the bomb," Babo heard himself saying, although he wasn't sure if he believed it yet.

"I want to trip for*ever,*" Nate sang.

Babo dropped onto his back in the grass, looking directly at the sun. Let it bore a hole in his head—what his brain needed right now was oxygen.

"Don't do that, Babo," Nate said, standing over him, blocking his view. "You'll burn your eyes out."

Babo squinted up at Nate, his favorite tripping buddy and his best friend, whose bald head—freshly shaved for the party—glowed like a bright idea. They had played together since they were six, when Nate and Nicole moved to Churchtown from Tennessee. Nate had a burr cut then, unfashionable in the North but practical in the steamy South, and at school he and tiny Babo were the odd men out. They stuck together over the years, more like brothers than friends. Babo would do things for Nate he wouldn't do for Mitch. "This acid rocks my world," he said more confidently, beginning to believe it—to *feel* it. "I'm totally psyched on this shit. I'm the pinball wizard. I work for the rock and roll federation."

"That's right," Nate said.

"Are you clairvoyant?"

"You were losing your gourd back there for a minute, but you're OK now, little buddy. Nate's here and we got beer. We got a whole keg of beer to drink."

Babo laughed gratefully, with relief. "Dude, your sister's face melted before my eyes."

"You were curled up like a baby. I thought you were crying at first."

"I'm thirsty," Babo croaked.

Nate trotted into the garage and came back with two webbed lawn chairs, their wooden arms dried out like old sponges, flecked with peeling orange varnish. "Keg chairs," he said, unfolding them. Babo crawled into a chair, while Nate set about tapping the keg with professional gusto. Then he went into the house and returned holding two glass mugs scummed with frost, bought at a garage sale on Jetstar Drive (for their fathers, they told Mr. Silverman, who had refused to sell them to the boys otherwise). Nate pumped the keg, filling both mugs to overflowing. "Stay young until we die," he toasted Babo. If a trip was coming on heavy or too fast, then drinking helped. A blot of drunkenness was a lot more liquid than a drop of acid, and Babo and Nate, tripping harder than they ever had before, concentrated on their dripping mugs.

"Dude, imagine if we were sitting poolside right now. I'd dive in with my clothes on and float," Nate said.

"If I had a pool, I'd drain it and skate it," said Babo.

"Yeah, that's cool. I'd punch a frontside one-eighty."

"I'd bust an alley-oop."

"Dude, we should move to Cali. That's where the pools are. We can skate all day and party all night and sleep with beautiful California girls. We'll use their hair for covers. People will read about us in *Thrasher*."

"We *have* to, dude. We should go right now," Babo said.

"We'll take your mom's car. We'll go in *style*. A loaded BMW—dude, we'll pull girls from coast to coast."

"No way. My parents are bastard lawyers. They'll sue me 'til I'm nothing and stick what's left in a juvenile detention center," Babo said.

"Fuck that—you're old enough for real jail. You'll be in there with murderers and shit. You'll be in with that guy who knifed his girlfriend in the throat."

"What guy?"

"Lawrence Caper."

"Dude, his *girlfriend* knifed his *other* girlfriend. He just watched. Like a threesome—a *menage à trois*. I want to have a *menage à trois*."

"You want to kill someone?"

"Yeah, you, dude. I want to kill you," Babo grinned. "I

have a knife. I could do it. I'm all fucked up right now. That will be my defense."

"My cousin went to that guy's school."

"Your cousin with no teeth?"

"That's right."

Babo shuddered. "I don't want to think about that right now."

"Think about Cali."

"Oh yeah. *Cali*. Fuck my mother's BMW—we'll *steal* a fucking car. We'll go all the fucking way. We'll be outlaws. They'll have warrants on us in every state."

They high-fived, laughing so hard their beers sloshed into their laps. Then they refilled their mugs while the keg was still their very own, watching the sun cross the sky like a watch hand passes time as they told stories and jokes, drawing each other into disingenuous arguments from which they recovered with great hilarity.

By eight o'clock their fellow partygoers had begun to arrive in packed carloads, girls sitting on boys and boys sitting on girls, the cars shaking with bass and the friction of the sexes. VWs, SUVs, various convertibles, as well as the usual dun-colored heaps heavily stickered on their old-fashioned chrome bumpers, were parked this way and that around the neighborhood. In Nate's backyard, the party reached critical mass and Babo dosed as many as he could, doling out tabs for five dollars a pop. Inside the house, hip-hop beat on the living-room hi-fi, shaking the walls with talk of the ghetto and street-life. The basement was thick with bong smoke, and someone was playing "Stairway to Heaven" on Nate's acoustic guitar, while the Red Hot Chili

Peppers' tour video rolled on TV. Upstairs, young couples hastily undressed for bouts of furious sex, and in the bathroom someone was taking a bath; she leaned forward so that her friend, shirtless, wearing a black lace bra and an oozing, swollen, brand-new Tinkerbell tattoo on her right shoulder, could soap her back, the acid making her moan with simple pleasure.

The keg had been dragged to the middle of Nate's open backyard, preventing bottlenecks at critical junctions. The yard itself was bedecked with hoop-skirted evergreens, woody hydrangeas, and two overgrown peonies; should the police raid the party, kids would hide in the shadowy greenery, or crash through the branches to the neighbors' yards. For now, no one was thinking about the police—but they never did, until it was too late.

Nate, in his chair, kept watch over the keg, dangling a sleeve of plastic Smart Cups, while Babo, at his side, conducted business. He had nearly sold out of acid.

"I'm walking on the moon," Nate said dreamily. His cheeks and his shaved head were rosy, his belly full of beer, and he had just eaten an oversized ham sandwich lovingly prepared by Missy, the girl he hoped to score later. Nate could always eat on acid, while Babo could only chew on the insides of his cheeks and suck his tongue for its flavor. "I can see all these floating rocks and shit—boulders, man. They're huge. It's some kind of monster pool table, all this shit knocking around. Whoa, I just stepped into a crater. I'm out, dude, I'm out. I'm the fucking pocket ball."

"I always want to feel like this," Babo declared.

"This American flag is the best I ever ate in my life," said a voice from the crowd.

"Yo, Babo ate half a sheet," Nate boasted, jerking awake.

"Yeah, right," someone jeered.

"You should have seen him earlier. He was foaming at the mouth. He's a fucking vampire when it comes to acid. He can't get enough," Nate said.

Babo belched and smiled.

"Good appetite," Nate said.

"I thrive on this shit," Babo bragged. "I should have an odometer for my brain, it's moving so fast. I could power a nuclear plant. Dude, they should sign me up for scientific research. I *am* science."

Everyone laughed. Encouraged, Babo dug into his pocket, producing his wallet on its spangly chain and from it, the sheet of acid—or its grubby remains, the size of two postage stamps.

"Anyone? Anyone?" Babo waved the acid over his head. An arm shot out from the crowd. Babo tore the paper in half—and stuffed both pieces into his own mouth. "Sucker!"

Nate looked worried now. "Take it easy, man. You're going to make yourself sick if you don't stop."

"I'm done. It's gone," Babo said. "No more left." He showed his empty hands, his empty mouth. His eyes glittered with secrets—briefly, they rolled into his head so that only the whites showed, and Babo's body flinched with spasm, just once. Then he was back again, grinning, full of himself, same as he ever was. "I'm fine, I'm fine," he repeated.

Kenny Johnson, the youngest of the four strapping

Johnson boys, marched up to the keg with an empty pitcher. A belly roll poked out from his T-shirt, jeans cut off with pinking shears at the knee—the new jock uniform for the summer. Sunburn scorched his cheeks and the back of his neck. "Fill me up," he demanded.

"No way, no pitchers," Nate said. "That's the rule."

"My brother bought the beer."

"Like we give a shit," Babo said. "We paid for it. *I* paid for it. If it's anyone's, it's mine."

"Yeah, but my brother *bought* the beer. Get it? Like, it wouldn't exist if it weren't for my brother."

"Babo, butt out," Nate said. "Give me your pitcher, Kenny."

"No way!" Babo stood up and blocked Kenny from making the pass to Nate as best he could, but Kenny simply tossed the pitcher over Babo's head, then moved in with an agile cut, his left shoulder angled down, football player-style, to stand by Nate's elbow, guarding him while he poured. "You're giving him all our beer!" Babo wailed.

Kenny turned and winked at him. "I'm a big, thirsty guy. I just can't help it. It's in the genes, you know. Hey, where's your Dixie cup, Baby Boy? I'll fill you up." He took the full pitcher from Nate and held it over Babo's head on a tilt, so that beer slopped the spout and threatened to spill out in a downpour.

"Fuck off," Babo growled. He ducked his head and tried to get away—but Kenny followed him with the pitcher, making airplane noises.

"Cut it out, Kenny," Nate warned.

"I'm just teasing, right, Baby Boy? We're playing a little

game. It's all fun. Hey, Dan and Rob are on their way over," he called back as he lumbered off.

"Did you hear that? Did you see? That guy was ready to dump his beer on me. Did you see his face? He looked like a fucking pit bull. I could see *all* of his teeth. You fucking traitor, Nate! I can't believe you invited them to our party!"

Nate looked guilty. "Forget about them. We can still have a good time. This acid is the bomb, right?"

But Babo couldn't relax now; he crouched on the edge of his chair, ready to attack or flee, whatever was required. "They're giants compared to me. They're fucking ogres. Those guys look at me like I'm a cocktail sausage."

"Relax, Babo. They're jocks—they've got tube socks for brains."

"Your sister likes them. Nicole goes out with jocks. She *likes* tube socks."

Nate didn't say anything.

"Seriously, dude," Babo said, his brow knitted anxiously, "I think that guy wants to hurt me. I don't think it's a joke. We might have to call the cops."

"Hey, check it out. I think it might be time for some cherry popping. Those skaters look like they might riot or something if we don't get the ramp going," Nate said, abruptly changing the subject.

Babo fell for it. "Do you feel like you can skate?"

"Don't you?"

Everything was blurred to Babo, a mixture of what was real and what was strange. He shook his head no, as if to clear out his brain—and then he began to know, somewhere in the confusion of his stimulated senses, that he could skate.

He could always skate, better than anyone. He was the best skater in Churchtown. He could make it happen. Babo nodded to Nate.

"All right." Nate stood, abandoning his keg post. "Let's do it."

"Let's skate. It's not too late. Let's skate. Nate, let's skate, it's not too late," Babo chanted to himself.

Nate pushed strongly through the crowd toward the ramp, Babo tumbling after him. When they reached the red ribbon that held the skaters back, Nate cleared his throat with an exaggerated racket. "After many months of hard work, with no assistance from my faithful friend here," he warbled, resting his elbow on one of Babo's shoulders. "Scraping and stealing and sawing and hammering—"

"Dice the fucking string, asshole!"

Everyone laughed, pressing in, wanting to be first on the ramp.

"Fuck you very much," Nate retorted as he bent over the ribbon and torched it with his lighter's flame—but already Babo was airborne, launching an indy to fakie.

"Let's skate!" he screamed.

"Whoop ass, Babo!"

"Hubba, hubba!"

The ramp rumbled with noseslides, frontside Cabs, McFlips, and kickflips over the coping, executed to applause and jeers. Bloodthirsty bats dove for mosquitoes, flitting their wings at the moonlit heads of oblivious teenagers. The Johnson brothers took to the trampoline and bounced high and hard, spraying the girls who trailed them with the last gulps of their pitcher, calling out for a wet T-shirt contest.

The girls squealed, shielding their made-up faces and hair, letting their tops soak through so that the lace of their bras showed. Inside, a forgotten pizza burned in the oven, while the hi-fi seized on a bass line, shaking the whole house.

Babo and Nate were four hours into their trip—peaking, elated, irrepressible. "Dude, it's the best trip, the best ramp, the best night," Babo said, hugging his friend. He was slick with sweat and left the imprint of his face on Nate's red T-shirt. "I love you, dude."

The Friday Night Movie

Deb was sacked out in her La-Z-Boy, ready for the Friday Night Movie. She had eaten her regular pepperoni pizza and four-meat stromboli from Pete's Pizza, then made s'mores in the microwave. She ate alone, with the television for company, and now, digesting, her chin bobbed, then she was treading the quicksand between TV and dreams, unsure where one ended and the other began . . .

"Tell me what happened. It's time we got the truth out. You only get the truth on my show." Deb recognized this contralto, with its mellow tone of universal concern, and looked up to see Mary Lou dressed in a purple muumuu, a lei of passionflowers at her throat, addressing her usual TV audience. Next to her, a girl in a soft pink dress held her head in her hands, the hair that hid her face a mass of big curls and hairspray flourishes. The girl's shoulders bucked with sobs. "You're OK," Mary Lou said. "Talk to me. Tell Mary Lou what happened."

The girl lifted her head, revealing a punctured lip, two blackened and bloodshot eyes, a dripping gash on one cheek, and a nose that had been pushed to the side. When the murderess Cindy Hart opened her mouth to speak, she was missing her two front teeth. Her left arm hung limply from its socket, cradled in its twin.

The audience laughed at Cindy. "Cry-baby!" She was pelted with ballpoint pens and packets of chewing gum, eye drops, Chapsticks, the kind of objects that came easily to hand from a woman's pocketbook. The light of the studio changed from yellow to green, tinting everything, and the atmosphere thickened, making the air soupy so Deb could feel it slurping her skin; it reminded her of pond swimming when she was young, the algae slop up her nose and streaming through her fingers. Frightened, Deb called out for the only person she knew could rescue her—there she was, as she always was, as Deb had known she would be: Mary Lou stood in the aisle by Deb's seat, extending her microphone like a helping hand. "She says she walked into a door. What do you think?"

Cindy was waving to the camera with her good arm. She smiled now. "Hi, Mom and Dad," she slurred through the mess of her mouth, a juicy trickle dribbling down her chin. As Deb watched, horrified, Dale Manley appeared behind Cindy onstage. He swaggered around, unbuttoning his shirt and slowly drawing down the zip of his pants, teasing the audience, who urged him on. Dollar bills were waved, lewd offers of beds for the night shouted. Dale, down to turquoise bikini briefs, took Cindy in his arms and carried her into the wings. He flashed a knowing, naughty grin while Cindy beat her legs playfully, screaming like she loved it, like she was riding a rollercoaster. When they disappeared, the audience, as ever, roared for more.

Babo appeared then, through a split in the curtain. He

just stood there, weeping, while the audience, suddenly indifferent to their subject, chattered incessantly among themselves, everyone talking at once. Where was Mary Lou to stop them? Deb craned her neck—there she was, propped up in a front-row seat with a bag of potato chips, looking bored by everything, while someone touched up her makeup.

"Please help me," Babo sobbed. His gruff teen voice cracked with the effort, but no one noticed. "Help, help," he wept. Deb heard her own cry blare like an alarm clock—she was awake, sweating, the credits rolling on the Friday Night Movie.

There was no time to waste. Deb hurried to her car, with its long hood shaped like a shield and bearing the motor company's coat of arms. She nearly tore through the garage door in her haste. She was a dream prophet, she told herself. She was being shown events before they happened. She had a special gift, a talent. She could *save lives*.

At the end of her driveway, Deb flicked on the turn signal—tick, tick, tick like a watch's second hand. Hurry, she thought, switching on her high beams. She rolled down the window and breathed the first scent of her trail: fresh-cut grass. She pressed the gas pedal, keeping the speed needle at five miles per hour, scanning the breadth of Atomic View. Looking for Babo.

Stones in His Shoes

He arrived in the city at eight, as planned. The bus discharged him into the fume-infested cave complex of Port Authority's underground station, and Mitch gripped his duffel bag, pushing through the crowd with aggressive determination. He felt, each time he arrived in New York, his heart rate quicken, while his face hardened to a look that was more—he hoped—cool and imperious than nervous. Stepping out onto Eighth Avenue, he hardly noticed the neon signs and lights: SUNNY DELI. CHECKS CASHED. GIRLS. ATM. BATHROOM FOR CUSTOMERS ONLY. WE HAVE STARBUCKS COFFEE. JOIN THE JESUS ARMY.

Mitch hurried, despite the choking heat. He knew not to head north and find himself in the steaming galley of Hell's Kitchen, where prostitutes and slaphappy johns trolled for business and used condoms squelched underfoot, the stench of uncollected garbage mingling with the chlorine reek of urine. Instead, he turned south one block, so as to avoid the line for taxis policed by a belligerent Port Authority security guard. He confidently saluted the street and a taxi was immediately at his side. Mitch strictly took taxis in New York. His trips to the city were short enough that he had no time to waste getting lost on the subway. He wanted to be dropped off exactly in front of his destination in a decent state, no fooling around trying to get oriented or plodding against the flow of pedestrian traffic. "The Upper East Side," he ordered the driver.

In the taxi, he discreetly counted his money (one hundred dollars minus twelve dollars' single bus fare made eighty-eight dollars, plus a pocketful of quarters for any phone calls), then slid one hand inside the duffel bag, checking for his grandmother's earrings, which were still in place. The cash wasn't much to go on, he thought bitterly. At Conn College, he always went out for a night of bar hopping with at least a hundred dollars in his wallet, but New York required more cash than that, much, much more. Mitch sighed. He would just have to be careful, that's all. This was his last taxi until next week, he vowed—unless someone else was paying. Once he met up with his friends, he would be fine for rides.

Mitch looked up through the smear of the window, but the sun's glare drove back his gaze, the hulking skyline more felt than seen. He might have rolled down the window to let in the pandemonium of Times Square, but his taxi driver had already hollered at him that the air-conditioning was on full and he better not try anything stupid. The city was livid with heat; it hovered like dread in the minds of those who remembered last summer, who hadn't been lucky enough to escape to the Hamptons or upstate.

"Where you going?"

"The Upper East Side. Right by Sotheby's."

"Yeah, but what street?"

"I can't remember," Mitch explained. "I'll remember when we get close." And soon he was in more familiar territory, among the giant apartment buildings of Park Avenue, the blocks peopled by legions of dog walkers, delivery boys on bicycles, and black Lincolns parked bumper to bumper, double-parked, their waiting drivers eating or dozing or yapping on cell phones. Mitch liked what he saw. "You can let me out here," he said as they pulled up in front of the auction house.

"That's what you said. You said Sotheby's. I took you to Sotheby's," the driver bickered pointlessly.

Mitch waited for his change, the driver for his tip, and both were unhappy with what was left when they parted. Mitch counted in his head: he had eighty dollars. It was going to be a tight weekend.

He stood at the corner of 72nd Street and York, gathering his bearings. He had bluffed to Steve on the phone; Mitch didn't remember at all the exact location of Lily Kay's apartment, as he had been very drunk even before he arrived at her cocktail party. He was sure he would recognize the building, however, having stood outside for a long time, drawing deep breaths of air in an attempt to settle his stomach. That was another night he had thrown up in front of everyone, this time making it to the bathroom, but leaving the door ajar. Not only that, he stayed in there for hours, so that guests had to go elsewhere. Potted plants, the kitchen sink, a neighborhood bar—Mitch remembered that someone had threatened to use *him* as their latrine, but that didn't happen. Still, he blushed, remembering. He was just out of practice, he thought. He would get his drinking stamina back soon, just like everyone else.

Mitch took off his suit coat, rolled up his sleeves, and began his search for Lily's apartment building, ever hopeful that he would find the right place or see a familiar face. As he stalked the blocks, the duffel bag grew heavier, and he passed it back and forth from hand to hand every few seconds like a basketball. The sky was dimming, city lights aglow against the purple haze, although it was still furnace-hot. What time were Steve and everyone getting on the Jitney? What was it, a train or a bus or what? Where did it leave from? He needed to ask—but the Chinese delivery boy didn't know what Mitch was talking about, nor did any other menial straggler he saw, and the Upper East Side was otherwise deserted for the holiday weekend. Everyone had gone to the Hamptons, he guessed.

Back at Sotheby's for the third time, he used a payphone to call Steve; the phone's receiver was spread with ketchup and Mitch handled it carefully to keep the goo from his ear and hair. Steve's machine answered. He tried Zack, Ian, Melissa, Adam, Katie, Sarah, Jason, and John. Each number he called, an answering machine picked up, until there were no names left in his address book. The heat was getting to his brain. He was dehydrated, panting, and he couldn't think straight. Sweat dripped inside the stovepipes of his black trousers, and he wished he had worn socks; as his shoes filled, his feet farted.

South, he would head south, Mitch decided, and set off at a crawling pace.

A teenager, whose legs were lost in oversized, flapping jeans, jostled him.

"Watch where you're going," Mitch warned.

The teenager stopped, a vicious look in his eyes, his lip curled. "What'd you say?"

Mitch walked away fast, praying he wouldn't be followed.

"That's what I thought!" the teenager hectored, laughing at him, at his fearfulness.

To get away from the boy's jeers, Mitch started to cross the street without the "walk" sign, causing a legion of taxi drivers, gunning for the green light, to blast their horns. Startled, a drunken man dressed in filth for a shirt and ruined trousers tumbled over the walleyed toes of his shoes, spilling blood from a split in his skull, a growing puddle Mitch jumped to avoid. He kept walking. He walked until he couldn't go on, when he hailed a taxi, barely able to lift his arm.

The driver waited several minutes for instructions, holding the car at the curb. "I guess Alphabet City," Mitch said finally. He had given up on finding his friends. He would catch up with them when they returned on Monday, but in the meantime he would have to get by on his own, and Mitch had never been on his own in the city for more than a couple of hours.

He watched the taxi's meter with growing anxiety: four, five, six, seven dollars and counting. Mitch needed to conserve his money for a hotel room for the night. It was too late to sell his grandmother's earrings; he would do it in the morning. He would go somewhere nice, Cartier or Tiffany. He would do the job right.

"I changed my mind. You can let me out here," Mitch told the driver, and then he was slamming the door in traffic, another car's exhaust pipe burning his trouser leg through to the tender flesh of his calf. He cried out with the pain—branded, he had been *branded,* he thought—but no one paid any attention, so intent were they on the light that was about to change. On the sidewalk, limping slightly now, his back to the Empire State Building as the north point of an improvised compass, Mitch reeled along, staggering somewhat, in the thick of it at last, with night about to descend. His first night as a citizen of New York, and all he felt was sick with the heat. He kept on walking. He walked straight into the heart of the East Village, St. Mark's Place, with its sunglasses stalls and war-wounded preachers lining the sidewalks; another two blocks east and he was in Alphabet City, home of guitar-strummers and stand-up comics, actors, radical dressmakers, DJs, deadbeats, writers and waiters, bartenders, bus boys, and kitchen chefs—where Mitch's friends thought he, the artist, should live.

The tenement buildings that exclusively made up Alphabet City sagged and crumbled, leaning on one another like a grieving family over the grave. Rainbows of fairy lights glittered like cheap jewelry on the drooping fire escapes; a junkyard obelisk built of clutter and bric-a-brac—the contents of Grandma's attic—dominated a community garden on one corner. The gutters streamed with filthy runoff. On the whole, Alphabet City looked needy, strung together on a shoestring, its residents dressed like refugees in thrift-shop castoffs. The streets were crowded as if for a carnival—obviously no one *here* had gone to the Hamptons for the weekend.

He paused outside a cafe on Avenue A that offered two-dollar breakfast all day. He was hungry, he realized. He hadn't eaten for a long time, since early that afternoon. Some food might help him get a grip, then he could figure out where he was going to stay for the night—preferably somewhere far away from Alphabet City, maybe SoHo, maybe Tribeca, but somewhere downtown; he didn't think he could afford uptown prices, or the taxi to get him there. Mitch sat down inside the cafe and ordered breakfast for dinner: two fried eggs, two slices of toast, homefries, and coffee refill. The food was bad, the eggs hard and the toast cold, the potatoes and coffee scorched, but he ate every scrap, wiping the plate with the last bite of crust. Then he left the waitress two dollars exactly under the sugar shaker.

But when Mitch stood to leave, the Louis Vuitton bag safely in hand again (he had kept it between his feet while he ate, a chair leg through the handles), triple-checking to be sure he left nothing behind, he saw a sweater on the opposite chair that he hadn't noticed before. It wasn't his, he knew that—he hadn't thought to bring a sweater with him. He picked it up. If it was nice, he would keep it, he thought—and that's when Mitch saw the knife on the chair, a nine-inch hunting knife with a thick black rubber handle. He froze, transfixed, as if the knife might suddenly levitate of its own accord and dive for his throat, prune his ears and nose, make sashimi of his more tender parts and serve them up for the delectation of some pervert. Mitch didn't wait to find out.

Back at Port Authority after another taxi ride, he left a message on his parents' answering machine, telling them that he was on his way home. He had almost two hours to wait for the next bus. In the meantime, Mitch hunched on the floor of the terminal, head down. He didn't want to be rescued now, nor seen by anyone he knew. His lip shook like a motorbike's throttle, and when the bus arrived, he sat in the very back where he quietly snuffled into his hands, the only crying he would allow himself.

His father was waiting for him at the bus station. Mitch slumped into the back seat without a word. "Why are you sitting there? Do you think I'm your chauffeur or something?" his father asked rudely, looking for a fight, furious that he had been called out in the middle of the night. His bandaged hands glowed against the black leather steering wheel, and he steered with the heels of his hands, keeping the gauze mitts stiff. His fingertips, poking through at the top, were inflamed, too swollen to bend, nails like luminous watch dials. He grimaced as he turned out of the parking lot, jerking the car onto the empty highway, and Mitch, seatbelt-less, slid across the back seat—he didn't even try to stop himself from sliding. "Is that what you think? That I'm here to ferry you around?"

"I don't feel like talking," Mitch said.

"You never talk to us."

"Look, I've had a bad day. I burned my leg in New York, really bad. Maybe you should take me to the hospital."

"Is that why you came home? So I could pay your hospital bill? Do you think your *burn* is worse than this?"

his father asked in a shrill, unnatural voice, holding up his bandaged hands.

"No," Mitch said sullenly. He sighed, then drew a deep breath. He noticed the sweet, medicinal scent of bourbon that permeated the car's interior.

"What happened in New York, Mitch?"

"Nothing."

"What happened?" his father persisted.

"Nothing happened. I just didn't want to stay."

"I don't get it. It doesn't add up. You were desperate to get to New York. Something happened that you're not telling me."

"I didn't have enough money to do anything good," Mitch replied in a snotty voice.

"You won't go anywhere in life, Mitch. You'll always need our support or a place to stay. Isn't that what you expect? It's like we've had no influence on you whatsoever, to show you the right way to live. I think it's pathetic the way you take the opportunities we've given you for granted. You're *pathetic.*"

"At least I'm not a stoner like Babo," Mitch shot back. "The kid's practically living on drugs and you don't even know it. I'm not the problem—*he's* the problem! He's got a fucking gun!"

"I'm not talking about Babo, I'm talking about *you,* Mitch. Don't try to change the subject, telling lies about your brother. You only sound more pathetic."

"I'm not fucking lying!" Mitch kicked the back of his father's seat.

"Hey! I'm driving! That's dangerous!"

"Oh yeah?" Mitch punched the headrest of the passenger seat this time—where his mother usually sat. "Is that less dangerous for you?" His father turned around and swiped at him with a bandaged hand. Mitch punched his father's seat. "Am I hurting your *car*, Dad?"

He didn't even have time to shake out his fist from that ultimate blow. The BMW flew up the exit ramp to Mother Road, aimed for Atomic View. The rear of the car swung outward as it cornered, the tires clawing at the tarmac as Mitch's father oversteered into the curve and lost control.

Electrickery

"Babo!"

Nicole was calling him. He heard her from the safety of the crowd of skaters watching Aaron Linnen launch a disaster. Babo turned his head slowly, cautiously, to see where she was, feeling every muscle and tendon in his neck flash with electricity. A strong current moved through him, making him anxious. He might short-circuit and blow off an arm or a leg, wires and bone popping out the raggedy end that once boasted an attachment.

"Babo!"

He inched his head to the left and there she was, her arms open, a look in her eyes of concern, of *love* for him.

"Babo," Nicole said urgently. Her jaw throbbed like it always did when she was upset—Babo could see the same milk-blue charge pulsing through her that pulsed through him. They would make a connection! They would fuse skin, burning against each other, one person. He twisted his mouth to smile at her. He moved, careful not to jolt his limbs and make them spark, very slowly in the direction of Nicole, who was shivering with current. Nicole, his positive.

"Come here," she said, pulling him close. She was so

warm! He put his nose to her neck and sniffed: cigarettes and beer, Nate's house, flowery perfume, suntan oil. That was Nicole. Now he knew. "Babo, come with me," she said in a gentle, mothering voice.

He had waited years for this. He couldn't believe his luck! He was finally in Nicole's arms and she was leading him away from the others, around to the front of the house. She wanted to be alone with him.

But something was wrong. Out front, Nicole let go, moving off to stand apart with her arms wrapped around herself—she was crying! A police officer took hold of him instead.

"Are you Jeremy White?" the police officer said.

"Babo," Nicole babbled. "His name is Babo. Everyone calls him Babo. It's short for Baby Boy. It's because he's so little. He's my brother's best friend."

Why was Nicole crying? Babo was frightened. Cops! The pigs! Run, Babo thought, but his legs wouldn't respond. His nerves had shorted out on him—he had taken too much! Babo bit his lip, drawing blood. He wanted to throw up. He felt for his wallet, following the chain's loop to his pocket. He knew he had put the acid in his wallet (somewhere in the back of his mind he knew), along with a careless wad of five- and ten-dollar bills from what he sold at the party. Was there any acid left? He couldn't remember—and now Babo laughed. Busted for sure! He couldn't help laughing about it. In a minute he would hit the ground, howling and rolling, handcuffed behind his back. Everything was so funny when he tripped!

"Where's Nate?" Nicole said. "Babo, where's Nate? I'm

going to get Nate." She stumbled away, leaving him alone with the police officer.

"Son," the policeman said in his concerned voice, "are you OK? Have you been drinking tonight?"

Babo smirked, eyeing Johnny Law unsteadily.

"If you've been drinking, that's a problem, but it's not our biggest problem right now. I can forget a little drinking. What's more important is that I need to know if you're Jeremy White, if your parents are James and Eileen White."

"I'm Jeremy White," Babo repeated dumbly, grinning, showing his bright teeth.

"Jeremy, there's been a car accident. Members of your family were involved—"

Now here came Nate, shouting something. "Don't!" he cried, reaching out, ever so slowly, in slow-mo, with a cartoon arm that burst into a thousand floating paper pieces—a piñata!—right before Babo's eyes. "Don't tell him!"

"Did you see that?" Babo said to no one in particular. "Did you? I'm fucked. I'm so fucked."

Lunar Synthesis

Deb crept toward the twins' house in her Town Car, drawn to the flaring Catherine wheels of police lights that were going off there. It looked like the twins had been having a party, and a dozen neighbors had come out to watch the roundup of staggering teens. The twins' parents were probably at the shore, like so many people were for the holiday weekend; the twins always had parties when their parents went away and inevitably the police turned up, arresting anyone they could grab for underage drinking—but kids were quick to scatter and hide. They had an instinct for it. Deb herself had run from the police more than once when she was a teenager and got drunk in cornfields (since razed for housing developments) with Don and their friends.

Babo was sure to be here, Deb thought, parking across the street. Everyone knew he and Nate were best friends.

A hundred or more partygoers had been corralled on the front lawn, kept in check by circling police officers—not that the kids seemed inclined to go anywhere. More than one teenager was doubled over being sick, and some were crying, clinging to each other, while the rest stared at a knot of policemen by the front door. A moment later, an

ambulance banked in the twins' driveway and two paramedics jumped out the back, carrying a stretcher between
them. The crowd began to murmur. An ambulance was
serious. The paramedics streaked for the door, the huddle
of policemen opening to let them through, and there,
restrained by four grown men, was Babo.

"Leave me alone!" he roared.

This was the moment everyone had been waiting for.
Deb joined her neighbors at the house next door. "What
happened?" she asked, but all eyes were on Babo and no
one answered. As they watched, he was wrestled onto the
stretcher and strapped down, bellowing all the while. The
noise he made raised the hairs on Deb's neck; it didn't look
right, what they were doing to him. Is this what her dream
meant? What was she supposed to do, if he was already in
the hands of the police and paramedics? She couldn't inter-
fere with *them*. Deb stood there helplessly.

Then he was in the ambulance, and the ambulance had
driven off. The police reacted immediately. "All right, break
it up. This party is over. Time for everyone to go home,"
they said, wagging their nightsticks. "Let's call it a night.
Go home to your folks. If you've been drinking, we're
giving out free rides, one night only, no questions asked.
One night only." Stunned, without protest, in trickling
streams, a few seeking out police officers who treated them
kindly, the kids were driven off in a herd down the street.

"What happened?" Deb asked her neighbors again, who
were also returning to their homes.

"Don't know," Mr. Jolly shrugged. "There was a party,

police came and broke it up. Babo White must have got sick or something, because they called an ambulance."

"He took drugs," Mrs. Diamond said knowingly. "That's what it looks like to me."

"All the kids today are on drugs," old Mr. West added. "My own grandson, bless his heart, is in rehab. His mother says he can't kick the white, whatever that means."

"Poor Babo," Deb said, still trying for information. "Do you think he'll be OK? I mean, he doesn't look OK to me."

"I feel sorry for his parents," Mrs. Diamond said.

"Poor? One thing they ain't is poor. They can afford to fix him. Looks to me like that kid needs a good lawyer, too, if the police been here," Mr. Jolly snorted.

Deb walked away and got back into her car. They didn't know anything, she thought impatiently. What a bunch of gossips! She didn't have time to waste on them. She followed the last of the partygoers down the street, until she found a police officer escorting two girls, both disoriented and drunk, holding onto each other for support. Deb rolled down her window. "What happened? I'm a neighbor," she added.

"There was an accident off 333, a one-car collision. Kid's family were in the car and someone got killed. He freaked when we told him."

"Who? What kid?" But Deb knew who; she just needed to hear him say it.

"Baby, I think they called him."

"Babo. It's Babo."

"Whatever," the officer said, sounding tired. He shuffled off, trailed by the girls.

"Who died?" Deb called after him, but he didn't reply. "What are you going to do with Babo? Is there something I can do?"

By then her neighbors had gone inside and turned on their televisions, haunting their windows with eerie light. She was left alone, full of fears, the night as it ever was, a depth of stars, the valley below punctuated with electricity. Back behind the wheel of her car, hungry to participate, to know what was happening, to be part of it, whatever it was, Deb pressed the gas and headed for the highway.

Hell Is Alone

There was blood on his hands when he woke, and an IV lead trailed from one arm. His nose was tender, itchy—when he went to scratch, he found it bandaged. Below the bandage, a mustache of dried blood flaked onto the white sheet. His head ached, and his jaw was stiff and dull, like with dentist's Novocain.

He tried to sit up in bed, but found he was exhausted. He could only sink back against the hard, rough pillow, so different from home. The IV dripped a wash through his veins that felt like cool Pennsylvania rain on a hot summer day. So nice, he thought, why not go to sleep?

But he was thirsty, and alone, and now he was afraid, even with a faded teddy-bear-print curtain draped around the bed. It was very quiet where he was, as if no one else was in the room. He wanted to call out, but his throat was sore, the sorest it had ever been. Glass, he thought. Pieces of glass were stuck in his throat.

Oh, he was sore all over.

The curtain whipped back on its rail, showing a brightly lit room. "You're awake," the nurse said, coming into focus. She was his mother's age, but big, with abundant breasts and hips over which her thin white trousers strained, showing the pucker of cellulite, the line of her massive underpants. She rested her hand briefly on his forehead and he smelled rosemary, lavender, and mint. "We gave you a couple hours of sleep to get through the shock. You hurt yourself pretty bad. Here's the doctor to see you."

The doctor's head was enormous, covered with clipped black hair that ran down his neck and disappeared into a white shirt collar, reappearing at the cuffs to curl thickly around his wrists. Great white teeth in even rows stretched far back into the cavity of his wide mouth. His voice was unnervingly deep. "We'll observe you tonight and see what we think, where you should go after that. For now you're upstairs, which means you've been a good boy." When he rubbed his hands together, they sang like grasshoppers' legs.

Then the doctor was fondling the IV's tubing, before running his fingers along the lead to its needle joint in the crook of Babo's arm. His hand was dead cold, his fingernails rimmed with black, his lab coat bloodstained around the buttonholes. Drawing the curtain wide, he strode into the brilliant light of the ward beyond, and Babo saw the bottoms of his scrubs were muddied, his black work boots caked with the stuff, footprints all around the room, leading from bed to bed—but as far as Babo could tell, all the other beds were empty. An icy draft rushed in and the teddy-bear curtain inflated like a sail.

"Mommy!" Babo cried as two nurses descended upon him.

The Broken Home

One week. That's all she had before the inclement natural event that left her stranded on the floor next to what remained of her marriage bed, scraps of eyelet canopy in both hands and a fringe of necktie silk clinging to her sweating lip, a ticklish polka-dot moustache. Cathy blew and it drifted off gracefully, landing like a parachute in the wreckage of the bedroom. What about the bright existence she had imagined for herself, the devils of her past replaced by Stairmaster, husband, and home, her clock reset to this new time zone? There was a sour taste in her mouth like she had been sick. Her tongue felt twice its size, dusty, coated with ash. She needed to use the toilet, but her left ankle, when she tried to stand, wobbled and gave way. Cathy grabbed at the broken-off edge of a bedpost, which tore her hand. The dam in her, stoppered long ago with sticks and stones, burst in a flood, and she heard her own voice, cruelly twisted at birth, withered like a damaged limb over the years, loudly swearing, "Bloody hell! Bollocks! Shite! Fuck! Bloody shite fucking bollocks! Fucky-fuck!" She hopped to the bathroom, where she found the floor inches deep in water and reflective with sharp angles of mirror glass, like a wishing well littered with silver. Both sink and bath taps poured mercilessly, flowing with the county's power behind them, and Cathy's bladder gave way at the sight, raining down her thighs.

"Bollocks! Balls!"

She wiped with a bath towel, then wrapped the towel around herself, for lack of anything else to wear. Hopping downstairs, hanging onto the stair rail for dear life, she found the carpeted floor running like a spring stream, its bottom spongy, littered with julienne carrots, broccoli heads, peas that mushed underfoot. She hopped—slosh—hop—slosh—down the hall to the kitchen, then hop—slap on the flooded linoleum. Cathy reached her hand under the already running kitchen tap and water bit the wound like a rat locks into a heel of moldy bread. Her scream seared the back of her throat.

"Please," she begged the operator when she managed to reach the phone. "Help me. I'm dying—I'm bleeding to death!"

"You're dying? Ma'am, you need to dial 911. I'm just the operator."

Overhead, the house creaked like a rusty bedspring and Cathy heard what sounded like a seam splitting. Then a great crash from the dining room, followed by the gentle, steady downpour of a newly sprung waterfall. She dialed 911. "Is this an emergency?" they asked.

"Yes!"

"Stay calm, ma'am."

"My ankle," Cathy sobbed. "It's broken. I'm bleeding,

and the house is falling down. It's not well built—it's not my fault!"

"How bad are you bleeding?"

Cathy looked at her hand; the puckered wound, drained of blood, gaped back at her. Her ankle simply throbbed now, comically swollen. "Not so bad," she admitted.

"Then you'll just have to wait. We're having a crazy night, all our drivers are tied up. Memorial Day weekend. There's always more accidents on Memorial Day weekend."

"I'll wait," Cathy bawled. "I don't want to be any trouble."

"Ma'am, sit tight and put some pressure on that bleeding. And get your foot up. We'll have an ambulance to you as soon as we can."

"Don't go! Stay on the line! I won't leave. I'll be good. Just talk to me. I'm alone."

"Is there someone you can call? A relative or friend?"

"Talk to me. I'm afraid," she pleaded.

A thunderclap sounded from the dining room, a terrible bang.

"What's going on there?"

"I have to go," Cathy whispered, putting down the phone. Dreading what she would find, knowing she had to look, she hopped to the dining room, where she found the bathtub docked in the table, and here came the toilet crashing down into the steaming pool at her toes. What a smash up! Tentacular pipes sprayed the room in hot and cold bursts. Tiles dropped like bombs. The sink, with its overflowing bowl, trembled on the edge of the hole in the ceiling as if it might, at any moment, be persuaded to jump.

Thinking only that she wanted to be safe (not really thinking, but acting instinctively), Cathy hopped back into the hall and through another door, which slammed shut behind her. It was dark and chilly where she found herself, the slightest breeze shifting the azalea that grew out front so that its heady fragrance bloomed around her.

"No!" Cathy frantically twisted the doorknob—locked, she knew. She could hear the racket of plumbing bedlam inside, and banged her head against the door like a knocker. "Please," she begged.

A voice rang out behind her. "Cathy?" She heard a car door close, then the woman's voice again: "Cathy? Is that you? Are you OK?"

Cathy scrambled to hide herself behind a flourishing, blush-pink branch. "Who is it?"

"It's Deb. Your neighbor. The Tupperware lady."

Cathy heard the slow scuff of Deb's shoes on her driveway. "Don't come any closer," she choked. "I mean it. I don't want your help."

"Did you and Dale have a fight?" The fat woman had reached the front walk. Cathy could hear her puffing.

"Dale's not here. Go away, I said. Leave me alone."

"That's right. I forgot Dale was away on business." Deb was just a few feet away from where Cathy hid herself. "What happened?"

"The house flooded," Cathy blurted out.

"Flooded?" Deb was within touching distance now; Cathy could feel her heat. "What do you mean, flooded?"

"I was running a bath. I fell asleep," Cathy lied. "The tub overflowed and I slipped. I hurt myself. I think I broke my ankle. Now I'm locked out. And Dale's gone."

"Come on out of there, Cathy," Deb said, reaching between the plant's branches.

But Cathy slapped at Deb's hands. "Why can't you just leave me alone? Don't you have anything better to do? Leave me alone!"

Deb stepped back and began to pull at her oversized barn coat. "You must be freezing. You're not wearing much. Here, take it."

"Leave me alone! Leave me alone," Cathy wept, but she reached for the coat and Deb pulled her out of the bush with it. "Just leave me alone," she whispered. "I'm no good. Let me die out here."

"Nonsense," Deb said briskly. She was trying to insert one of Cathy's frail arms into a voluminous sleeve when the towel dropped away. Now Deb saw Cathy's lank breasts and protuberant ribs, the right angles of her hipbones and, below them, the meager, scraped-up mound and her stick legs. She buttoned the coat right up to Cathy's hunger-sharpened chin. The coat drooped on her frame like it hung on a coat hanger. "Besides, no one ever died of a broken ankle, or not that I've heard of, at least. It's probably just a sprain. We'll go inside and get something hot to drink in you and see about this flood business."

"The door is locked."

"We'll go in by the garage," Deb reasoned.

"Locked. I locked it. They're all locked. I always keep the house locked. Dale said. He told me to lock the house when he left."

"We'll try the back door. I've never heard of anyone

locking every single door. There must be a key somewhere. Not under the mat? I keep my spare in a flowerpot."

"Locked! It's all locked! Didn't you hear me? Don't you listen?" Cathy screeched.

"We should at least try and see the damage—"

"We *can't*." From inside the house came a crescendo of splitting plaster peppered with what sounded like cannon shot.

Deb crushed Cathy against her in terror. "What was that?"

"We have to get away from here," Cathy sobbed.

Deb was ready to act—had, in fact, been ready all night. Here was her big chance. "My car is right there," she said, and all but carried Cathy to it.

Neither one said anything until they pulled into Deb's driveway. As they waited for the garage door, Deb asked, "Are you hungry? Because I sure am. I'm hungry for pancakes with plenty of butter and real maple syrup and a mug of hot chocolate."

"I'm starving," Cathy said. She looked at Deb gratefully and her gaunt, gray cheeks briefly creased to show her crumbling teeth. "Let's eat."

Morning Again in America

The *Post-Intelligencer* slapped down on the doormats of Atomic View, bearing news of a fatal car accident, a local politician's anti-abortion campaign, the high school marching band's success at a state competition, and the updated forecast for the holiday weekend. At Dale and Cathy Manley's door, the paper landed with a splash and was quickly soaked through; at Deb Foster's house, the paper lay until almost ten o'clock, while she and Cathy slept late after the long night before; at the Whites', the paper lay like a hurled brick, aimed with the precision of a knife-thrower.

Inside the big house on Quasar Lane, the coffee maker's pot was full and hot, its automatic timer having tripped, as usual, at 6:00. Upstairs, two bedside alarm clocks, both tuned to Warm 103, chattered in sync—today's news mixed with Golden Oldies—but the bed between them was tautly made and silent, the ironed pillow shams in place and bookmarks still in Thursday night's pages.

Down the hall, Mitch's room reeked of rotten food and dirty clothes; his bed smelled most strongly of his life, the mattress marked with the imprint of his sleeping body, DNA splattered carelessly across the sheets. Babo's room, too, was full of secret life: a thriving pot plant on the windowsill, a lava lamp busy dividing into twins and triplets (scientifically proven to enhance hallucinations), a humming aquarium, his pet piranhas whisking back and forth the length of the glass in search of feeder fish.

Shut the doors on the boys' rooms and the house was in perfect order, the windows and silver polished, white carpet spotless, the high-gloss paint of banister and trim further burnished with wax, furniture cushions just so, towels bountifully dryer-fluffed. To anyone looking from the street, 79 Quasar Lane must have seemed a paradise, at peace, full of everything a family might need.

Psycho Ward

Babo was drawing with Magic Markers the day Deb visited him. He didn't look up to see who had come into the room, but sensed her breathless bulk in navy sweats, very different to the slim, stiff figure of his mother or the twins' weedy teenage frames, and crouched over to guard his work with one arm, his forehead nearly touching the table.

"Hello, Babo," Deb said. She held a fresh paper bag that she offered to him. "I brought you some candy bars. The hospital said I could. I wasn't sure what you liked, so I made a selection: Twix, Milky Way, Snickers, and Three Musketeers."

He sniffed the tip of the green Magic Marker he was drawing with and wouldn't look up.

"I'm sorry about your brother. About Mitch," she said, but Babo snorted so aggressively that Deb stopped. She stared as he continued to noisily inhale the Magic Marker's artificial apple scent. "Why are you doing that?" she finally asked.

"These are my happy pens," he said, looking at Deb for the first time. His pupils were dilated, making his eyes appear almost entirely black. He blinked rapidly and twitched his nose—little sniffs, refreshing his nasal cavity.

"Maybe that's not good for you."

"I don't care what's good for me."

"Don't say that."

"Why not? It's true."

"You know, my husband died when he was Mitch's age. He was in a car accident, too."

"So? Like I should care. Why are you here, anyway?" Babo moved his arm so that she could see the black and green pattern of scales on a menacing serpent, the serpent's tail buried in a wildly curvaceous woman's private parts.

Deb quickly looked away. "Because I'm your neighbor and I care about my neighbors. I'm sorry about your brother. I think it's really sad what happened. I heard you were in the hospital—I always think anyone in the hospital could do with a cheery visit."

"I don't even know you."

"But I've known you your whole life, Babo," Deb protested. "I remember when you were born."

"No. Don't know you. Go away." He selected a yellow marker from the pack, pulled off its cap, and sniffed hard—lemon—daubing his nose with its tip.

Deb saw now that his nose was speckled with every color of the Magic Marker rainbow, and so were his lips streaked, like he had been sucking on the pens. He was obviously sick, suffering the effects of trauma. She continued to chat; she wouldn't give up just yet. "Don't you remember when you helped me paint my fence? Or when you won the Easter Egg Hunt? Remember that big chocolate bunny you won? It was as tall as you! And I'll always remember how Mitch loved my Cornflake Chicken and Broccoli Mayonnaise—he once ate half a casserole dish of Broccoli Mayonnaise at the Stewarts' Labor Day picnic. I thought I'd have to run home quick and make another one, he ate so much. It only takes a minute to put together, then fifteen in the oven. I gave Mitch the recipe way back when. I wonder what he did with it? Did he ever make Broccoli Mayonnaise that you can remember?" Deb asked hopefully.

"Look, a lot of people want to be my friend because my brother died. That's fucked up. It's like I'm famous or something, and I don't like it. You're just a poseur friend. Besides, I don't need any more friends. I have enough." Babo licked the tip of the yellow marker, then drew flames along the serpent's spine, rubbing in the color so hard the paper pilled like an acrylic sweater.

Deb tried again. "I want to help. I hear your dad's—" she paused, choosing her words carefully, "not feeling good, and I know your mom is busy looking after him. I thought that maybe you could use some company. I could tell you what's new in the neighborhood."

"Neighborhood news?" Babo hooted.

"Well, I have a roommate. Or a housemate, I guess, because I live in a house. She's from England and she's real quiet. I gave her the spare room upstairs where I kept my old sewing machine, and we carried that down to the basement. Someday I might take up sewing again. I used to make all my own clothes, but that was back in the Seventies when everyone did. And boy, can't you tell," Deb giggled.

But Babo wasn't listening; he was thinking about something Deb had said before. "My dad's fine. He's not crazy, and neither am I. Just so you know. So you have some *news* to tell everyone."

"I don't talk like that, Babo. I'm not a gossip. There's a difference between news and gossip."

Babo closed his eyes. "Whatever you say. I'm tired."

"Well, I guess I better go, then, if you're tired." But Deb stayed squarely planted, still clutching the paper bag, by now crumpled and damp. "Do you want this candy? I brought it for you. I'm not supposed to have candy, so I can't keep it. I'll just eat it if I do. I'm trying not to eat so much food."

Babo didn't answer. He didn't care. He was studying his drawing again, enlarging the woman's mouth with red stabs of the cherry-scented pen, making her bleed where the serpent entered her. He wanted to scare Deb away with his violent picture. She had no reason to be there in the first place; only his parents and Nate and Nicole were allowed to visit.

"Babo?" Deb said cautiously.

He didn't reply.

"I'm going to leave this bag on your bed. I'm real sorry for your trouble. That's all I wanted to say."

He heard the squeak of her sneakers as she walked to the door, the whoosh of the heavy door as it flew out and back, the shot of its lock clicking back into place. Babo reached for the blue pen with which to sign his name. He would add this picture to the gallery of patient artwork hanging in the psycho ward corridor. He had drawn something every day of his stay in the hospital, twenty-nine pictures in all, pictures his doctor noted as "disturbed," their scenes extravagantly savage or pornographic—but encouraged him to draw nonetheless. Babo would draw and draw, and maybe when he felt better he would stop. Maybe he would go home then. For now, he wanted to stay in what felt like the safest place, taking only the drugs the hospital prescribed him.

More than a month had passed since the funeral and Babo hadn't yet slept at home. Even at the lunch after Mitch's burial, he had stayed outside the house on the front step. Luisa brought him a plate of food, and Nate and Nicole sat with him, Nicole holding his hand. When everyone left, he asked his mother to drive him back to the hospital. She hadn't wanted him to go, wanted him to stay with them that night, within sight, within touching distance, so that she could reassure herself that he was still alive. But Babo needed his special calming, happy pills that only the doctor could give him, he said. He didn't say that he was afraid to stay. As he argued with his mother, a fuzz of light appeared in the corner of Babo's right eye and he was seized with hysterical fright: it was Mitch, he convinced himself, not a light trail, remnant of his last acid trip. His brother was still in the house, as Babo had suspected. He was a ghost, and he would torment Babo worse than he ever did.

His father had come to see him only once, pulling his son close so that Babo felt awkward and embarrassed, full of pity for his father, who was dressed in unfamiliar casual clothes, the shirtsleeve torn along one arm. There was a sour, unwashed smell hanging around him. He didn't stay long; back at home, his father mostly stayed in bed, and his mother was kept busy running between son and husband. She was too busy for work, from which she had been given an indefinite leave of absence, as had his father, although he wasn't badly hurt in the accident. Just some cuts and bruises, his right shoulder dislocated, and two ribs cracked. His bitten hands had healed, but he still wore thin white cotton gloves. There was a reason, his mother said, but she wouldn't tell Babo what it was. Babo knew: guilt. His father couldn't bear to look at the hands that had killed his son.

His mother said it was fine if Babo stayed in the hospital while his father got better, but he had to come home soon. He wasn't sure what it would be like to live with his parents when they were actually at home. It wasn't like when Mitch first went to college and nine-year-old Babo rejoiced to think he would have his parents' devoted attention—but if anything, his parents had worked *more,* citing the expense of Mitch's tuition. Babo, much to his surprise, had missed Mitch, despite the ongoing conflict between the two. Of course, then he knew that his brother would be back for holidays and summer vacation.

Babo lay down on his bed, a candy bar stuffed in his mouth to keep from crying. He was tired of crying, but every day he remembered something that made him sad, like the night Mitch woke him up to go swimming in the Millers' pool. He was ten, and Mitch had just arrived home from his first year at Conn College, when Babo woke to find him by his bed. "Shh," Mitch said, putting a finger to his lips. They crawled out Babo's window (when he learned how easy it was to do, creeping along until they reached the lower roof of the garage, where they could jump off), then cut through their own yard's privet hedge to the Wests' wildflower garden. They followed the Masons' sculpture trail, paused at the Jollys' Jacuzzi and considered it (but the cover was locked), before tramping through the Peters' vegetable patch to the Millers' pool, decorated with a beer can on its bottom. After they swam, Mitch stood at the pool's edge and relieved himself into the water, a satisfied look on his face, and Babo copied him. Back at home, they fixed peanut-butter sandwiches and Babo sipped from Mitch's beer until he fell over laughing on the floor. Mitch followed him down, the brothers wrestling playfully in their underwear. When Babo fell asleep in front of the television, Mitch carried him upstairs.

His mother arrived at five to eat supper with Babo—but she didn't really eat, just picked at her food and asked about his day, sometimes commenting on one of his drawings that she had passed in the corridor. Babo didn't tell her that Deb had visited him. Instead he said, "Do you remember when Mitch made Broccoli Mayonnaise?"

"No. Sounds disgusting," she replied, breaking a brownie into halves, then quarters, then eighths.

"It's delicious. Believe me, it's good. Really creamy and melty and hot, and the broccoli is soft. It doesn't even taste like broccoli."

"Must be something you two made when Dad and I were at work. Luisa helped you."

"No, we had it for dinner one night," Babo insisted. "Mitch made Broccoli Mayonnaise and everyone ate it. You and Dad, too."

"Eat, Babo. You don't get anything again until breakfast."

"I had four candy bars before dinner. I'm full."

"No wonder you like it here. No rules, no parents, candy bars instead of dinner. It must be kid heaven," his mother mused—but her voice was hard.

"There's more rules here than at home."

"Oh, Babo," his mother said, beginning to cry. Babo knew he should be more careful of what he said—but sometimes he didn't care, just like before Mitch died, when he wanted to say things to hurt his parents and he didn't know why, he just *felt* like it; he felt angry and mean inside. "That's not true. We were there for you."

"Sorry," he whispered.

"Someday you'll understand why I did what I did. What I do," she sobbed. "I didn't just do it for me, I did it for you. But I did it for me, too. I didn't think things would turn out this way."

"Someday I'll understand everything. Not for a long time, I hope." Because already Babo felt like he was growing up faster than he wanted to, like he had seen and felt more than he should.

My Family Begins with Me

They lay side by side in the backyard, lazily studying the patterns traced in the sky. From behind the clouds, the mellow fall sun showed itself sporadically, warming their skin. The September sun was fiery in color, yet its flames were gentle with their bodies—it was more a healing power than the burning force of the past summer. Still, Cathy spritzed her hair with a lemon-juice–peroxide concoction and hoped the sun would work its magic. She had even gone inside to change into shorts, shivering when the sun disappeared, while Deb covered herself from head to toe in a hat and her usual sweatsuit.

"Another glass of iced tea?" Deb said, turning to the tray by her side.

"You're a saint, Deb," Cathy murmured. She had her arms over her head, rolling her shoulders and kicking her legs. She looked like she was practicing the backstroke, which she was learning to swim at Ladies' Night, but Deb knew better than that: Cathy felt she had to keep some part of her body moving all the time, burning calories. She jiggled her knees, pedaled beneath the sheets, squeezed her thighs,

or drummed her fingers as she sat in front of the TV, sometimes the whole two hours of the Friday Night Movie.

"You're doing it again."

Cathy's face flushed and she halted, halfway down the
pool in her head.

It'll go, Deb thought. As she gets better, she'll relax
herself. When the divorce comes through, maybe that will
be the end of it.

Deb poured tall glasses of real iced tea. They drank
it sugarless, enjoying the astringent taste of the tea, and
fresh lemon gave it all the flavor they needed. Deb squeezed
the lemon halves energetically, wringing out every last drop,
then fished the seeds with her fingertip. Cathy wrinkled her
nose as she drank in tiny sips (there was something not
quite right about *iced* tea, she said) while Deb gulped hers
down, then lay back again as a pack of clouds ran past the
sun like something had startled them.

Sure enough, a sound pierced the quietness of the sheltered backyard, eating a hole bit by bit. At first the sound
was distant thunder in the hills, then a circling airplane,
then a snow plow scraping the road clean of pebbly slush—
and Babo leapt through the hole of sound to land in Deb's
driveway.

He was dark with summer, wearing his hair clipped close
to the scalp. A pair of large diamond earrings glittered
ostentatiously in his ears, at odds with the rest of him.
When he first started wearing the diamonds, Deb had asked
him where they came from.

"My brother," he'd shrugged.

"Lucky you," Cathy said. "They're proper rocks."

"I'd rather have my brother than these stupid earrings," Babo replied, then skated away in a hurry. Cathy was quiet all the rest of that afternoon—the first time in a long time her chatter had stopped.

"How could I say that?" she finally asked Deb at supper.

"He's probably forgotten by now."

Cathy shook her head, not believing her.

"Do you think people hang on your every word?" Deb joked. "Come on, honey, don't take yourself so seriously. It's not like you to be a mean person. Babo knows that. Besides, he has his little crush." She nudged Cathy and winked. "You could say anything and he'd still think you were God's gift."

Cathy blushed. Deb was always teasing her about Babo, the way he hung around their house on his skateboard, showing off. All summer long, Deb had sat outside and watched him work at his tricks, ready with applause and a plate of cookies—the only reason she kept cookies in the house anymore. Deb loved the show and loved the fact that the bereaved boy had chosen them to visit, despite his parents' continued unfriendliness to all neighbors. He visited every day, almost, ever since he returned home after his long hospital stay and called out "Hey!" when he skated past her house with Nate. Deb was out front with Cathy, swapping flags after their Fourth of July picnic, taking down the Stars and Stripes to put up a beaming yellow nylon sun circled with butterflies.

"Welcome back, Babo!" Deb called, waving wildly.

He and Nate looked back to stare at Cathy the way men always did. Deb was gratified that her new friend got so much attention—enough for two people, she said proudly. In restaurants and bars, she and Cathy were offered plates of dessert or sweet, fruity drinks they never paid for. Sometimes they refused and sometimes they didn't, but they could afford to be choosy these days. Men followed them through the aisles of the supermarket, drawing up alongside them to chat while they slyly inspected Deb and Cathy's cart's contents for some sign of synergy with their own— what caused Deb to giggle.

"They're so interested in you that they want to know what you eat," she exclaimed.

Cathy only looked confused and helpless—the kind of look that made men swoon and drop handkerchiefs and roses at a woman's feet. "I don't know what you're talking about."

"Keep it up and you'll have no trouble landing a rich husband."

"I don't want to get married again. Never, ever, *ever*," Cathy shuddered. Deb was secretly pleased to hear this. They were having too much fun for her to want it to end anytime soon. She loved the attention, and she was always thinking up new things for them to do or places to visit, "to stir things up," as she put it. One weekend they went down to the shore to swim in the ocean. Cathy had never been to the beach, and her excitement splashing in the waves, coupled with a startling tan and hot pink bikini, meant that men followed her like drones into the water or whizzed balls and Frisbees to get her attention. When she and Deb took a stroll along the beach, the lifeguards invited them to their parties.

"She's gorgeous," Deb told Maureen. "I wish you could see her for yourself. She says she wants to come and visit you, but it's me holding her back, to be honest. She was pretty sick when I found her. I had to fatten her up, you know—not too much, though! Now Cathy gives me willpower not to eat, and I make sure *she* eats. It's a pretty good double act, if you ask me."

"I want to meet her," Maureen persisted. "Especially if she's as pretty as you say she is."

"She is—and she lives with *me!*"

"I wish I lived with you."

"Me too. Maybe one day soon you will." Deb meant it; she was looking into ways to make her house wheelchair-accessible. Cathy thought it was a great idea.

"Tell everyone I said hi, Deb. Tell Babo I added him to my God Bless list at night, and Cathy, too."

"I will, honey. And they all say hi to you, too."

Back on Deb's driveway, Babo was trying to master a 360 flip. He had been practicing the trick for weeks. "It's really easy. I don't know why I can't do it," he complained, studying the magazine picture he carried in his wallet, a how-to in numbered frames.

"I hope he gets it right," Deb whispered to Cathy. "I can hardly stand to watch. It breaks my heart to see him fall."

Babo cursed as the skateboard slid out from under his feet and bucked into the forsythia. He tried again, and again, with each attempt releasing the board before he landed the trick successfully. Once he skidded on his bare knees on the macadam with a surprised look on his face.

"Babo," Deb called, "are you OK? Let me look at those knees. How about a glass of iced tea?"

"I can *do* this," he said through clenched teeth. "Do you think I can't do this?" But he wasn't looking at Deb, and she got the feeling he wasn't talking to her, either. Babo stared at a grease spot on the driveway, what had become the trick's leaping-off point over the weeks. He circled the spot on his skateboard, his bloody knees leaking down his shins, soaking the tops of his white socks, then he doubled back to the garage. The garage door was up and he disappeared inside the cool, fume-rich stable of the Town Car. A minute passed before he shot out like a fireball, diamond earrings flashing in the sun like two bright headlights to guide him on his way. With a sudden, pungent gust of September wind, Babo lifted off and kicked the board into its spin cycle.

He was doing it.

He was doing it!

Babo hung as if suspended from a light-infused tensile line connected directly to the heavens above, where the choir of angels washed down hotdogs with beer and soda pop, cheering him on.

Acknowledgments

Lyrics on page 32, "Stand Up" by Minor Threat from the CD "Complete Discography," used with permission of Dischord Records and Minor Threat. Lyrics on page 85, "In My Eyes," written by Andy Breslin (1971–1993) and performed by The Passed. Lyrics on page 93, "Sit On My Face, Stevie Nicks," written by Phester Swollen and performed by The Rotters, used with permission.

KENT HARUF

Plainsong

PICADOR

This is the story of teenager Victoria Roubideaux, pregnant and homeless, and of Raymond and Harold McPheron, the rustily uncommunicative cattle-farming brothers who take her in. It is also about Tom Guthrie, a high-school teacher, left to bring up his two young sons alone after his wife's total retreat from life, and it's their story too, the boys Ike and Bobby, who grace the pages with their wise and gentle thoughtfulness.

'Kent Haruf's novel is a literary soap opera of the highest calibre . . .
Haruf is a fine writer'
The Times

'*Plainsong* is beautifully crafted, alive and quietly magnificent.
I read it in one mesmerising sitting. I had no choice;
it wouldn't let me go'
Roddy Doyle

'A perfectly formed, beautifully executed piece of writing that will
stay with you long after you reluctantly put it down'
Mariella Frostrup, *Mail on Sunday*

'Here is a poetry of landscape, a tender and passionate evocation
of ordinary people in majestic country . . . written with a kind of
compassion that makes it ultimately powerfully uplifting'
Niall Williams, author of *Four Letters of Love*

BRET EASTON ELLIS

American Psycho

PICADOR

Not for the faint-hearted, Bret Easton Ellis's *American Psycho* is a notorious indictment of the modern world's obsession with money and status. First published in 1991, this black-hearted satire has provoked admiration and controversy ever since.

Patrick Bateman is twenty-six and works on Wall Street; he is handsome, charming and intelligent. He is also a psychopath. This bitter, black comedy takes a hilarious and spine-chilling look at the preoccupations of modern American society, and in so doing exposes the darkness that lurks behind the mask.

'A serious, clever and shatteringly effective piece of writing. For its savagely coherent picture of a society lethally addicted to blandness, it should be judged by the highest standards'
Sunday Times

BRET EASTON ELLIS

Less Than Zero

PICADOR

Set in affluent Los Angeles, *Less Than Zero* is a raw and powerful portrayal of a young generation that has experienced sex, drugs and disaffection at too early an age. The narrator, Clay, returns home to Los Angeles for Christmas, but his holiday turns into a dizzying spiral of desperation that takes him through the rich suburban homes, the relentless parties, the seedy bars and the glitzy rock clubs. Morally barren, ethically bereft and tinged with implicit violence, *Less Than Zero* is the shocking coming-of-age novel about the casual nihilism that comes with youth and money.

'Bret Easton Ellis is a master stylist with hideously interesting new-fangled manners and the heart of an old-fashioned moralist'
Andrew Motion, *Observer*

OTHER BOOKS

AVAILABLE FROM PAN MACMILLAN

COLM TÓIBÍN
THE MASTER   0 330 48566 0   £7.99

ALAN HOLLINGHURST
THE LINE OF BEAUTY   0 330 48321 8   £7.99

KENT HARUF
PLAINSONG   0 330 39314 6   £7.99
EVENTIDE   0 330 43371 7   £16.99

BRET EASTON ELLIS
AMERICAN PSYCHO   0 330 31992 2   £7.99
LESS THAN ZERO   0 330 29400 8   £6.99

All Pan Macmillan titles can be ordered from our website,
www.panmacmillan.com, or from your local bookshop
and are also available by post from:

Bookpost, PO Box 29, Douglas, Isle of Man IM99 1BQ
Credit cards accepted. For details:
Telephone: +44 (0) 01624 677237
Fax: +44 (0) 01624 670923
E-mail: bookshop@enterprise.net
www.bookpost.co.uk

Free postage and packing in the United Kingdom

Prices shown above were correct at the time of going to press.
Pan Macmillan reserve the right to show new retail prices on covers
which may differ from those previously advertised in the text
or elsewhere.

REDBACK QUARTERLY BACK ISSUES

☐ **REDBACK QUARTERLY 1** ($19.99)
Battlers & *Billionaires: The Story
of Inequality in Australia*
by Andrew Leigh

☐ **REDBACK QUARTERLY 5** ($19.99)
Crime & *Punishment: Offenders and
Victims in a Broken Justice System*
by Russell Marks

☐ **REDBACK QUARTERLY 3** ($19.99)
Dog Days: Australia After the Boom
by Ross Garnaut

☐ **REDBACK QUARTERLY 6** ($19.99)
*Supermarket Monsters: The Price of
Coles and Woolworths' Dominance*
by Malcolm Knox

☐ **REDBACK QUARTERLY 4** ($19.99)
*Anzac's Long Shadow: The Cost
of Our National Obsession*
by James Brown

☐ **REDBACK QUARTERLY 7** ($19.99)
*An Economy Is Not a Society:
Winners and Losers in the New
Australia* by Dennis Glover

Payment Details. I enclose a cheque/money order made out to Schwartz
Publishing Pty Ltd. Please debit my credit card (Mastercard or Visa accepted).

CARD NO.

EXPIRY DATE / **CCV** **AMOUNT $**

CARDHOLDER'S NAME

NAME

ADDRESS

EMAIL

PHONE

RECIPIENT'S NAME

RECIPIENT'S ADDRESS

Post or fax this form to: Redback Quarterly, Reply Paid 90094, Carlton VIC 3053
Freecall: 1800 077 514 • Tel: (03) 9486 0288 • Fax: (03) 9011 6106
Email: subscribe@blackincbooks.com • Subscribe online at **REDBACKQUARTERLY.COM.AU**

SUBSCRIBE TO REDBACK QUARTERLY
AND SAVE UP TO 25% ON THE COVER PRICE

Enjoy free home delivery of the print edition and full digital access on the Redback Quarterly website, iPad, iPhone and Android apps.

FORTHCOMING ISSUES OF REDBACK QUARTERLY

MAY 2016
GENERATION LESS: HOW AUSTRALIA IS CHEATING THE YOUNG BY JENNIFER RAYNER

JULY 2016
GUY RUNDLE ON AUSTRALIA AND AMERICA

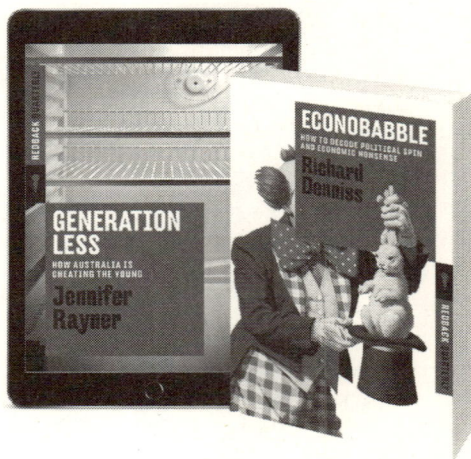

SUBSCRIPTIONS All prices include GST, postage and handling.
Receive a discount and never miss an issue. Mailed direct to your door.

☐ 1 year print and digital subscription (4 issues): $79.95 within Australia. Outside Australia $119.95.

☐ 1 year print and digital gift subscription (4 issues): $79.95 within Australia. Outside Australia $119.95.

☐ 2 year print and digital subscription (8 issues): $129.95 within Australia.

☐ 2 year print and digital gift subscription (8 issues): $129.95 within Australia.

☐ 1 year digital only subscription (4 issues): $39.95.

☐ 1 year digital only gift subscription (4 issues): $39.95.